Don Hunter grew up in Distington, Cumbria, attended Workington Grammar School and did his national service with 23 Parachute Field Ambulance, Royal Army Medical Corps, before training as a teacher at Chester. He taught secondary school in England and BC. He gained his B.Ed. at the University of BC before joining the *Vancouver Province* daily newspaper as a reporter and feature writer and, eventually, senior columnist. He is the author of four other books and a credited screen writer. He and his wife, June, have two daughters and three grandchildren, they live in the village of Fort Langley, BC.

To the memory of my great-grandmother Eliza Jane Williamson, who, at age 15, worked as a screen lass in the Whitehaven pits in the 1880s.

Don Hunter

MEG TYSON — SCREEN LASS

AUSTIN MACAULEY PUBLISHERS™

LONDON • CAMBRIDGE • NEW YORK • SHARJAH

A CIP catalogue record for this title is available from the British Library.

ISBN 9781788481236 (Paperback)
ISBN 9781788481243 (Hardback)
ISBN 9781788481250 (E-Book)

www.austinmacauley.com

First Published (2018)
Austin Macauley Publishers Ltd
25 Canada Square
Canary Wharf
London
E14 5LQ

I wish to thank the following for their invaluable assistance:

My wife, June Lloyd Hunter, whose family history research discovered our Eliza Jane.

My cousin Edna Branthwaite, writer and coal miner's daughter.

The Illustrated Mayhew's London.

London: The Biography, Peter Ackroyd.

Voyages of Hope, Peter Johnson.

Above Stairs: Social Life in Upper-Class Victoria, 1843–1918, Valerie Green.

A History of Victoria, 1842–1970, Harry Gregson.

Three Dollar Dreams, Lynne Bowen.

Boss Whistle (memoirs of Nanaimo miners), Lynne Bowen.

When Coal Was King, John Roderick Hinde.

The Coal Coast, Eric Newsome.

British Colonist, courtesy of BC Archives.

Marion Turstanoff Royal British Columbia Museum.

Colonization and Community: The Vancouver Island Coalfields and Making of the British Columbia Working Class. John Douglas Belshaw.

Amor de Cosmos, George Woodcock

Amor de Cosmos, Roland Wild.

The Judge and the Lady, Marlyn Horsdal.

Victoria: A History in Photographs, Peter Grant.

Black Diamond City. Nanaimo – The Victorian Era, Jan Peterson.

Kilts on the Coast. The Scots Who Built B.C., Jan Peterson.

The Coal Mines of Nanaimo, Arthur Leyland, P. Eng.

Courthouse Libraries BC.

Amanda Ginther, supervisor, Fort Langley community library.

Fellow author Ian Weir for the generous loan of his novel's eponymous *Daniel O'Thunder*.

Cameron's Crossing, B.J. Pettit.

Vancouver Maritime Museum (Lea Edgar, archivist)…

The West Beyond the West, Jean Barman.

British Columbia Chronicle, 1841–1871: Gold and Colonists, G.P.V. Akrigg.

Chapter 1

The sleet and hail blowing in from the high ground blunted the clatter of iron-shod pit clogs on the cobbles as Meg Tyson and the rest of the morning shift from Coater Pit hurried to get home and out of the storm, which was a harsh one for late March in the village of Morthwaite.

The village sat atop bracken-clad moorland that rose gradually from farms and woodlands, and looked west to the slate-grey Solway Firth. To the east, sat the first low fells and deep waters of the English Lake District, a region celebrated for its natural beauty and its renowned poets.

Morthwaite claimed neither great beauty nor anything in the way of poets in this year of 1862.

The village was a place of ninety small identical brick-built houses laid out in three rows of thirty. The houses had been built by the Benson family, who owned Coater Pit, and were rented out to the colliers and their families. Each house had two rooms downstairs and two up. Three stone steps led down from the back door of the houses into the yard which was separated from its neighbor by a low brick wall. In each yard was a lavatory-closet, whose contents were collected every fortnight by a team of two men with a horse and cart. Next to the closet was a wash house that held a large copper boiler set over a brick-walled fire place. This set pot was for washing of bedding and clothes on Mondays, and cooking of broths at other times. In the lane that ran behind each row of houses were three taps connected to a single water line, one in the middle and one at each end. Families used buckets and bowls to collect the water for washing and cooking. On the side of the lane, nearest to the houses, a gutter lined with slate ran the length of the row. It carried the village's waste water and drained it into the moorland. Half a mile from the last house stood the headframe and smokestack of the pit, the source of income for Morthwait's population and a reminder of who controlled their lives.

***

Lizzie Tyson poked the fire and added a shovelful of coal. She pushed back a few strands of her tied-back hair, just a few grey threads among the black in her thirty-ninth year. She was a woman with a self-possession born of a life of challenges as a child and then a wife and mother of coal miners, challenges which, if she had not always defeated, had faced and come to terms with.

Meg should be home soon, after another long shift on the screens. She would have spent the day sorting stone and slate from the coal that was raised in tubs from the seams half a mile and more underground and dumped onto the screening tables. Large pieces would have required her to wield a hammer, which weighed eight pounds, to break them up. The discarded pieces would have piled up around her and her screen-lass mates, until one or two of them would stop sorting to shovel the rubbish down chutes and into carts which would be taken and emptied onto the hills of waste that grew around the mine and the village.

The lass would be frozen. Lizzie had the tea mashing, a pan of fresh-baked teacakes warming in front of the hearth, and a tatie pot in the oven. She wished she had more than that to offer Meg. She wished her eighteen-year-old daughter did not have to spend ten hours a day slaving on an endlessly filling screen table. She wished…aye, and if wishes were horses…

Lizzie pulled the front door open just as Meg was reaching for the sneck outside. The girl laughed as she stepped inside. Her top coat and her old cap glistened with a coating of sleet. The thick trousers she wore under the long skirt, which she rolled up while at work, would be soaked as well, and would need drying in front of the fire.

"Teacakes, that's grand, Mam. I could smell them from the corner," she laughed. She struggled out of the heavy coat, shook moisture from it and hung it on one of the row of hooks on the back of the plank door.

"It was bitter cold today. There was talk of shutting down the screens. We could hardly see what we were picking."

"Just talk though," Lizzie Tyson said. "That'll be the day when any a' the Bensons let it shut down to please any ev us, or mek life a bit easier."

"You're right, Mam. And if they did, it would be that much less in the pay packet."

She said, "I passed Dad on t' road. And our Matthew and Thomas. They didn't look that pleased. They turned off at t' Welfare."

Matthew and Thomas were Meg's brothers, aged 20 and 16, and both experienced underground workers, as was their father, Tommy. The Welfare was a simple hut with a wooden floor where sometimes on weekends dances were held, donations were taken for families worse off than most; due to injuries or illnesses, and where the colliers gathered to play cards and talk about their work. This week, there was concern over rumours of a reduction in wages, supposedly a result of a forecast of slackening of orders for coal.

Lizzie said, "Aye. They've ca'd a meeting about these wage cuts that Bensons are threatenin'. Say they're not ganna stand for it. And they're bothered aboot firedamp. There's been some flare-ups in that new level they've started. Say they need bigger fans t' move it aboot. Then efter t' meetin' they'll gaa on to t' Dog. That'll sort things oot, fer sure!"

Meg laughed at her mother's irony. 'T' Dog' was properly The Hound Trail Inn, a public house half a mile north of the village, where the colliers drank and set the world right.

Meg said, "There was talk about it on t' line. Some of the lasses said we might walk off an' all. Said it's time we had a proper union, like those in Yorkshire."

"Like them in Yorkshire where they shut the pits y' mean, and families starved afore they took them back – at hafe pay. Aye, we need a union aw'reet, but a' think it'll be a lang time cummen." She sighed. "You would think that their kind, Bensons, would have mair sense. Our lads know what they're dyern underground, and they're good and willin' workers. If they got a fair wage there'd be nae problems. Pay them what they're worth and sell y' coal and still mek a fortune – there'll allus be a need for coal and lots ev it. They're just bloody greedy. The mair they git the mair they want. It meks nae sense."

Lizzie spoke in the West Cumbrian way which was unusual, not so much because of its broad-vowelled accent – 'a's' were short and flat, aitches were dropped, 'the' became economically 't', and 'thoo', 'thee', 'thy' and 'thine' were the common pronouns and possessives as they had been for centuries – but in that it accompanied a dialect that rendered the whole virtually impenetrable to outsiders. One village lad had married a Welsh girl he'd met when he'd tried sea-going for a couple of years, and

11

brought her back with him. On meeting this Olwyn, Meg's father, Tommy, had greeted the young woman with, "Hoo do lass, hoos tha gaan on?" Her face had gained a lost look, until her young husband explained, "He just said 'Hello, how are you doing – how are you going on?' You'll get used to it."

"A' wish you didn't have to be theer, lass," Lizzie said. "It's nae life for a young lass. There should be summat better."

"Aye, well, it's still a lot better than you had, Mam, isn't it?"

Lizzie nodded. "It is, but still…"

Lizzie had told Meg of her own time in the pits, before the 1842 act of parliament that banned the employment of women and children underground.

"I went down Saltom pit when I was eight. My dad hadn't worked for ages frae an accident and your Nana was scared we were bound for t' workhouse. She was terrified of t' notion. So I went down. Saltom was right on t' sea-shore, at Whitehaven, and it was t' first pit where when you went in-by, you were reet under t' sea. Maybe hafe a mile or mair. That was summat to think aboot – or mebbe better not to!" She laughed at that. "Me mam would fill me billy-can wid cold tea and give me some bread and cheese or mebbe bacon for me bait, and that would be me off doon into t' dark. Oh, I didn't like that, I can tell you. That an' thinkin aboot a' that watter on top o' you. Start at fower o'clock in t'mornin' and sit theer 'fower or five in t' efternoon. Oppenin' and shuttin' trap doors to keep t' air moving. A shillin' a day they paid me. Many a week I nivver saw daylight frae Monday mornin' to Seturday neet. But we managed to keep a roof ower us and oota t' workhouse. And I wasn't as bad off as some of the older lasses. It was that hot underground that you could hardly wear a thing, just a shift. Some a' them lasses worked like that reet next to the hewers and their marras, and they didn't have much on eether, just under-things. So a lot went on, a' can tell you."

"I can imagine," Meg said.

Lizzie continued, "They stopped drawing coal at Saltom in forty-eight, when you were three. A' course, I was well out of it by then."

"Did they run out of coal?" Meg had asked.

Lizzie laughed. "They said it had become 'inefficient'. What they meant was that because that Royal Commission they had in 'forty-two stopped kiddies working underground, they had nae mair cheap labour. That's what they ran out of, lass – kiddies! Before that they'd put laal'uns wherever they could, and pay them next to nowt and wuk them sometimes to death – A've seen that happen. Didn't matter if you were a lass or a lad, that was your destiny."

Meg smiled at one of her mother's unlikely words. Lizzie had made sure that Meg and her brothers had some schooling, as Lizzie's parents had done with her when they could afford it. Lizzie had kept enough money back to let Meg attend Sarah Teasdale's back-room school of an afternoon from when Meg was about six until she was fourteen, when she had gone to work on the screens. In that, she was one of the fortunate ones. Most families could not afford to send their children to places like Sarah's. Most of the other lasses on the screens had started work as soon as their families had been able to persuade the Benson's to let them, something that was never a problem for the mine owners, for whom the younger, and thus cheaper workforce, was always welcome.

All that Morthwaite knew of the teacher, Sarah Teasdale, was that she appeared in the village some eleven years previously, a tall, slim, red-haired and vividly scarred woman, seemingly then in her mid-twenties, a one-time screen lass who had worked until she had scraped up sufficient savings to allow her to rent a ruin of a house at the end of the row closest to the mine, a house then unfit for any collier's family, where she established her school.

The facts were that Sarah's early life had been as the eldest of five children – three other daughters and a son all much younger than Sarah – of an Anglican vicar with a modest living in the Lakeland village of Ambleside. And that as a girl of seventeen, Sarah had witnessed that living reach an ignominious end as she sat in the front pew – the Teasdale family pew – in the village church. The ornately carved pulpit with the figure of Jesus on the Cross was slightly to the left of the pew, with its five steps that took the vicar – as Sarah had always surmised – closer to Heaven and thus the authority to denounce the sinners seated before him, at which he was adept.

Her father's basso profundo from the pulpit had just thundered the final, triumphant, syllables of the fine old hymn 'Rock of Ages' – "...*hide myself in Theeeeeee.*"

This should have signaled the end of that Sunday morning's service, but instead of offering the congregation his usual concluding smile and gesture of universal beneficence, the vicar boomed out, "Oh, God!" at a volume that sent into clattering flight a pair of pigeons that had found sanctuary among the roof arches, and suggested to Sarah that her father suddenly had decided on one more hymn. She prepared to join in on "*...our help in ages past,*" but the vicar was done – struck-silent it seemed, as a young Irish woman of gypsy extraction, who had just then lurched drunk through the church doors, one of her immense rose-tipped bosoms freeing itself from a skimpy blue satin shirt which seemed to Sarah, by needs a dressmaker herself, to have been designed to facilitate, if not indeed encourage, that very escape; it commanded every attention as she rampaged down the aisle shouting, "Where's yer fecken man, then?"

A lad's sniggered, "...her paps!" from two rows behind Sarah was followed by the smack of a flat hand to the side of his head.

It would transpire that the Rev. Samuel Teasdale had been diverting the church's slender funds to support both the gypsy as a mistress and their mutual thirst for more than just communion wines, and had – unwisely, it now appeared – decided to end the relationship and advised her so by way of the Royal Mail service and a penny stamp. In one startling move, Rev. Samuel Teasdale abandoned his pulpit, his congregation and, apparently, all hope, as he fled past the Sunday-best dressed occupants of the front pews and on into the vestry through which he clattered and exited by its ancient rear oak door. With his black cassock flapping at his ankles he galloped across the graveyard, deftly side-stepping or hurdling moss-covered headstones, and on through a field of dancing daffodils and alarmed white-faced Herdwick sheep to where a row-boat lay moored at a frail jetty. With the gypsy woman staggering and roaring after him, though failing to get hands on, he climbed into the boat and rowed out into Lake Windermere, where he stepped over the side and sank from sight.

The gypsy stood a while on the bank until it was certain that the vicar was not about to rise, whereupon she marched unevenly while shouting "fecken prod shite!" back through the church and the stunned congregation, and started north on the road toward Grasmere, stopping just long enough to continue her ranting, and detail the vicar's deficiencies, to a passing few.

The community remained charitably silent on the coroner's generous ruling of 'accidental death by drowning' after the body was recovered, but their stock of Christian clemency ended there. The vicar's shamed family were bereft of home and income.

Though in shock, with illusions in tatters and faith sorely strained, when her mother wilted, Sarah took charge. Her first action was to deal with an item that had languished in a cupboard under the stairs since the Rev. Teasdale had had it delivered the previous year. The vicar had, like many a person, become alarmed by reports in various newspapers and magazines of people who had been thought dead but were buried while still alive – shocking stories of underground noises, coffins dug up, shredded shrouds and bloodied hands. With a growing dread of this possibly happening to him – the increasingly popular condition was known as taphophobia – he had purchased a Bateson Life Revival Device, advertisements for which co-incidentally often appeared alongside the blood-chilling reports. The device amounted to an iron bell mounted on the coffin and a rope from the bell attached to the body's hands through a hole in the coffin lid. While preparing for the funeral, Sarah pointed it out to her mother, who said, "Not as long as I live and breathe." Sarah smothered a laugh, and presented it to the ladies who organized the church-improvement committee's annual jumble sale.

Sarah also dealt with her widowed grandmother, Annie Teasdale, who travelled for the funeral from her home in the town of Beverley; on the outskirts of Hull in Yorkshire, the birthplace of her son. She had visited the Teasdale home in Ambleside only once before her son's death, and that was two years earlier, just after the late-arrival birth of Francis, Sarah's infant brother. Then, she had dandled the child on her knee and sung old North Country airs. At the time she seemed frail and she had with her a companion, a woman several years her junior and whom she clearly needed alongside. When she returned with the same companion for her son's funeral, she held long and often incoherent conversations with the little boy that seemed to concern what she called 'his proper place in life'. Whatever she thought that to be was never defined. Sarah stood watch over her grandmother until the old lady returned to her Yorkshire home unencumbered by the facts about the Vicar's leaving his mortal coil. Within two months of returning to Yorkshire, Annie suffered a seizure and died.

Sarah's mother, Hilda, had been too concerned about her own and her family's future to worry about her rarely seen mother in law's ramblings, or indeed her death when they learned of it. Hilda's sister lived in comfort as the wife of a wealthy banker in the southern county of Suffolk, and it was to them that she and Sarah's three sisters and baby brother departed. The couple had no children of their own, and they had welcomed the family from Cumberland with graciousness and great affection and, Sarah was sure, ignorant of the truth of the Vicar's demise. Sarah had visited them once since their move and was relieved that they had found a home. She maintained communication with them by post twice a year. The letters from them were always included in bundles of copies of *The Times, The Telegraph,* and other London newspapers, with the penny-red stamps of the post office on the package. Occasionally, there would be a gift in the form of a bank note, which Sarah was able to exchange for cash at a bank in Workington or Whitehaven.

Sarah had chosen independence when the rest of her family went south. With a decent schooling behind her, and then aged seventeen, she had been retained as a governess and tutor to a titled family, the McAdams, near Penrith. After a year, when the fifteen-year-old son in a quiet corner of the house posed in front of her with his erect penis in his hand and suggested what she might perform for him, and that she could earn a half-crown for this and another for any encore, she went to the boy's mother. Sarah was dismissed as a liar and troublemaker, without a reference and with a warning to move well away. As an able woman, she felt she could not impose herself on her mother's family in the south. She moved nearer the coast, to Cockermouth, the birthplace of the poet Wordsworth, where she did maid's work in a wool merchant's house for a year until a fire destroyed the man's business and left Sarah to her own devices. It left her also with a lurid ridge of shining purple scarring down the left side of her face, a consequence of her staying inside the burning house long enough to bring out the merchant's three-year-old daughter who otherwise certainly would have perished.

The ruined merchant's sincere thanks were not sufficient to provide further for Sarah, and her marred features disqualified her, as she would soon discover, from any employment that involved being seen 'by decent people'.

The one constant in West Cumberland was coal mining, where injury and disfigurement among colliers and women mine workers were more common than rare, and Sarah had been accepted. For four years she worked on the screens of various pits along the coast and saved her shillings until she was able to negotiate the tenancy on the broken down house in Morthwaite. Along the way she had rejected proposals and propositions from a number of men, all of whom indicated that her disfigurement would be no hindrance to a place in their beds and kitchens. Most of them were older men who had lost their wives and had a houseful of children in need of mothering. She had easily decided against such a future, had declined the offers, and was confirmed in her decisions by the 'ungrateful ugly cunt' insults that ensued.

At Morthwaite, Sarah had turned her house into a warm and welcoming school room, where she taught Meg and a handful of others the three R's and a smattering of history and geography. For the latter, she employed a large map of the world which had the British Empire areas coloured in various shades of red: Australia, India, parts of North America, and what seemed to be a great portion of the rest of the known world.

Also, Sarah insisted on 'elocution' lessons:

"So that you can speak to people in the real world – if you ever venture into it – without them thinking you're some kind of sub-human." When she talked like that, she always added that the real world included more than the annual three-mile trip to Egremont Crab Fair and its gurning competition – who could pull the funniest or ugliest face – or the odd walking visit to Whitehaven or Workington markets.

Sarah stressed the importance of 'being your own person'. She said, "Just because you were born into a pit village does not mean you have to live a life already mapped out for you.

"There's a reason why pit villages like this sit apart from the rest of society: Coal miners have to marry within their own kind because marrying a miner means also working in the mines – and only a collier's daughter is willing to do that. It's an inescapable circle. But because you are born into it does not mean that you have to become a victim of it. There are more things in life, Meg."

She said, "You love Charles Dickens' books. As a little boy, he worked in a blacking factory, pasting labels onto bottles of boot blacking, while his bankrupt father was in a debtor's prison. And look at him now – the most famous writer in England, maybe in the world! You can control your own destiny, Meg." (That word again!)

She quoted: "A man's reach should exceed his grasp..." and showed Meg the line in the long Browning poem, and added, "and so should a woman's, by God! So keep that in mind."

She cited young women who had accomplished great things: Boudicca/Boadicea, the legendary Queen who became the leader of a violent uprising against Roman rule and whose rebels destroyed London and slaughtered thousands; Joan of Arc – "Just a lass like yourself Meg, a 'peasant lass', it says here. She led the whole French army..."

Sarah read this from one of the well-used *Encyclopædia Britannica* volumes which sat on plank shelves in her front room, alongside a collection of the plays of William Shakespeare as well as several volumes of poetry and a collection of novels. The books were Sarah's treasure. She had bought the twenty-one volumes of the 1842 Britannica's Seventh Edition one or two books at a time, whenever one turned up in the book shops at Workington or Whitehaven. She joked that she prayed she might never be required to move house.

She added, "Boadicea's name means 'victorious,' or 'Victoria', and look at who rules our empire today!"

Meg chuckled and said, "Aye, but she had a bit of a start, didn't she?"

*****

Lizzie had heated water and Meg washed up in the back kitchen, just a quick clean of her hands and face where the grime and coal dust had left their usual black scum. She examined her hands, cut and bruised from the endless sorting of slate and coal, the badge and heritage of all screen lasses. No amount of scrubbing would remove the signs; in fact, it would simply make the skin raw and more vulnerable for the next shift on the screens. The cuts, eventually, would turn into blue-black marks as the coal dust entered the cuts, the same marks that covered the bodies of the hewers and their marras who worked down the pit. The hands of the older women who had been on the screens much longer than Meg were hard to look at. *Hers were not that bad,* she thought, *not yet*.

She worked up a thin lather with the block of hard carbolic soap and got the worst of the coal dust off. She would get her weekly bath on Saturday, when the tin tub hanging on the back kitchen door would be taken down and filled and emptied repeatedly as all members of the family took their turns. She studied her reflection in the tiny mirror fastened to the wall. Without her work cap, her hair, straight and, as her dad described it: "Blacker than midneet doon t' pit," but with a shine to it, fell to just above her shoulders, where she chose to keep it, unlike her friends, many of whom cultivated 'fashionable' curls, ringlets and braided buns, which they saw in magazines and newspapers and strove to emulate in their spare hours. A small, slightly sharp nose with a tiny white mark on the bridge, result of a ricocheting ball while playing cricket with her brothers, who laughed and said, "Go on, cry!" which she refused to do. Green eyes with gold flecks stared back. "Emerald. They're emerald-green," Tommy Tyson had told her when she was a child. She had thought of asking her coal-hewer dad when he had ever seen an emerald. Dug one out of the seam once, maybe? She smiled at the thought now.

Meg ate buttered teacakes along with the tatie pot, the essential Cumbrian dish that served the gentry at their hunt balls as well as the families of the farm worker and collier. It consisted of browned mutton or lamb chops combined with potatoes and onions, and topped with pieces of black pudding which cooked to a crisp in the oven

Lizzie said, "Ah'm off doon to Kitty Messenger's for t'crack and a cup a' tea, did you want to come?"

"No, it's all right, Mam. I'll just have a read. I have another of Mr. Dickens' books, from Sarah."

Lizzie smiled at her daughter's way of speaking, which was far removed from Lizzie's own rough manner, and which was a legacy of her hours with Sarah Teasdale. She'd heard some of the other lasses gently mocking Meg's 'toff' voice.

"Ah'll be back in a bit, then."

"Right, Mam. See you later."

Meg took her usual stool by the fire and turned up the wick on the oil lamp on the mantelpiece. She picked up the copy of *David Copperfield* and opened it to the first page. She had earlier read *A Christmas Carol*, and *The Adventures of Oliver Twist*. Such stories! She had been enraged at Ebenezer Scrooge's contempt for Bob Cratchit, and him with a son like Tiny Tim! She had been enchanted at the changes wrought by Dickens in the mean old businessman. Humbug, indeed!

She read the first sentence in *David Copperfield*: "Whether I shall turn out to be the hero of my own life, or whether that station will be held by anybody else, these pages must show."

She sighed. What was her own life going to be, her destiny? Working on the screens until one of the village lads finally talked her into getting married – lads the like of Geordie Hodgson or Patrick Kelly, of whom she knew she could have her pick? And after that, pregnant and kiddies underfoot, and later back to the screens, because there was never enough money? Was that to be it?

The thought returned after she finished the novel's first chapter and stayed with her until she slipped into bed and fell into an uneasy sleep, the word 'destiny' turning and tumbling in her head.

She could not have envisioned what the following day would bring.

Chapter 2

The previous day's storm had passed and an unusually warm day followed. For Meg it was a day off work under a new rotational system. In the morning, she helped Lizzie around the small house, emptying the fireplace of yesterday's ashes, then blacking the grate. As a special treat, and at Lizzie's urgings, they took the bath down from the back kitchen door and Meg soaked while Lizzie kept the front door shut.

After dinner, Meg put on a frock and coat, and walked up the rising road to the south end of the village. Off to the west, the Solway Firth glittered in the afternoon sun, and whitecaps frothed and raced in disorderly ranks to the shore. On a hedge, hawthorn petals imitated a fresh snowfall. Soon, the red haws would appear and youngsters would chew the tiny berries and spit out the pips. The hawthorns themselves crouched, stunted by an unremitting wind from the Solway. On the low bank under the hedge, a cluster of pale-yellow daffodils had already bloomed.

'I wandered lonely as a cloud...' Sarah had made Meg and all the others learn Wordsworth's poem by heart and told them that they should be proud of a fellow West Cumbrian.

The air was clear, and to the north-west across the Solway, Meg could easily make out the Galloway shore of southern Scotland. To the south and west, in the main Irish Sea, she could even discern the faint outline of the Isle of Man. Sarah Teasdale had been to the Isle of Man, on a steamer trip. She had told them of the island's Manx cats that had no tails. It sounded to Meg like a far and foreign land.

Meg had never been anywhere near that far. To Whitehaven or Workington for the fairs once or twice a year was the furthest. Sometimes in the summer, the whole family walked the three miles or so west to Micklam Beach, passing the hamlet of Gilgarran and the village of Distington, and finally Micklam Brickworks before scrambling down the prickly gorse-fringed steep bank on trails worn by generations of families to whom the beach was a brief escape from a life dominated by the pits and their owners. On the pebbled and rocky shore, they collected the tiny sea snails they called cuvvins from the underside of rocks, and boiled them in a tin can over a fire of driftwood kindling and sea coal that washed up from seams under the Solway. They picked the boiled cuvvins out of their shells with a pin to eat them, and washed them down with bottles of Spanish water. If it were low tide, they searched for crabs under the sandstone ledges, using a hooked stiff wire to snag them and pull them out. These were destined for home and a pan of boiling water. Meg's young brother, Thomas, tipped rocks over and grabbed the immature green-backed ones. He would try to get two of them to race each other to a line scratched in the sparse patches of sand, but they were of independent nature and would scuttle away back under the next nearest rock. Some of the stretches of sandstone had deep hollows in them that were left filled with water when the tide ebbed. The sun turned them into big warm baths. Meg would change into an old set of underwear and sit in these rock baths for ages, getting cleaner than she ever could in the tin bath off the back door at home.

She looked up now at several squawking seagulls that had just appeared from the west. Gulls flying inland usually meant a storm on its way. Overhead a pair of buzzards spiralled upward, mewing like lost kittens. A pee-wit voiced its drawn-out call. She caught a glimpse of its white belly and sides, along with its upright head plume before it sank to the ground. No doubt the bird had started its nest, no more than a shallow depression in the short grass. The village lads would be out hunting for the earth-coloured eggs as soon as they were laid. She looked over to the Greggains' farm fields and saw the small herd of black and white Friesian milk cows lumbering towards the hawthorn hedge, anticipating the need for shelter.

Meg began retracing her walk. The storm was some way off. Time enough to get home before it broke. With the afternoon sun still warm on her back, she removed her top coat and slung it over her shoulder. She had foregone wearing any head-cover, letting her hair swing free.

As she neared the houses, off to her left and below, she heard children laughing. They had left the confines of their cramped homes and were playing on the banks of Drigg Beck, throwing scraps of wood in as ships and cheering them on until they disappeared in a stretch where the beck ran under a steep overhang. The beck, at one time, had run clear and been a home to brown trout and myriad other water-life. Now, it flowed black with run-off sludge from the waste piles of Coater pit. Despite its colour, in the summer time the village youngsters still damned sections of the beck, building sod and stone walls, and splashed and swam in the pools they created.

Two of the young ones she saw were her niece and nephew, eight-year-old twins Roseanna and Johnny Rourke, her older sister Isabella's children. Isabella had served her time on the screens. Meg walked down the bank to the beck's edge and beckoned to the twins.

"Hiya Meg," Roseanna said. Her brother grinned at his aunt. "My ship won," he said.

"That's grand," Meg said. "But I want you two – and the rest of you," she added, indicating the two other boys and one girl comprising the group of adventurers – "to stop well back from the edge, I wouldn't want to see you getting drowned."

The children giggled at the thought and one of the boys, a Kelly, Meg knew, flopped down onto the grass, cried "A's droont! A's deed!" He became a convincing corpse. The others hooted, and Meg couldn't help but laugh.

"Just think on," she said. "Anyway, it's coming on rain and getting on for tea time, your mams will be looking for you."

"Aye, we're gaan yam," the drowned one said as he jumped to his feet. "Let's away," he said, and the five of them trooped off, pushing and shoving and giggling.

Little Roseanna Rourke stopped and pointed. "Kingfisher!" A blur of deep blue and orange as the bird swept down to the beck and impaled one of the few remaining sticklebacks in the blackened water, found a perch in a small birch tree on the bank just steps from them, beat the tiddler against the branch, and swallowed it in several gulps. The girl breathed, "Whoosh! Fly away!" and laughed as the bird took flight again. She waved a hand. "Ta–ra Meg," and was gone.

Meg watched the Kingfisher swoop on its way and disappear from sight. She stood looking at the rushing beck for a few moments, thinking. Five little kids just starting out in life. A future down or on top of Coater Pit, no doubt. And she thought, *Christ Almighty!* echoing the cry of Sarah Teasdale whenever other words failed to serve the moment, and who then would glance beyond the ceiling, delivering a quick, and unconvincing, *'Sorry.'*

There was a sudden flurry of raindrops, pushed by a now chilly breeze, and then from above and behind her, a voice.

"Miss Tyson, I believe."

Meg turned.

Alexander Benson stood on the bank above her. Alexander, or 'Sandy' as he liked to be called, stared down at her. He was in riding dress, breeches and high polished leather boots, a tweed jacket over a black buttoned waistcoat, a white shirt with a scarlet silk neck piece. His mount, a stocky chestnut cob, nibbled on the grass nearby, its reins trailing.

Meg knew that Sandy Benson, the youngest of three sons, following schooling at a famous place for toffs – Eton – had been sent on to Cambridge university for an education, one that in all likelihood would propel him into a life in either the army or the church: apart from the fact that his two older brothers – under the law and custom of primogeniture – would, in order of seniority, inherit title and property; his father, Lord Richard Benson, had long determined that Sandy should never be entrusted with any part of the family business operations or accounts. Far better that his energies and his questionable character be visited on an unwary regiment, one in which Richard could purchase a commission – at a reasonable price – or a gullible Anglican congregation.

Meg acknowledged his presence with a slight nod, but said nothing. She looked about her. The children had gone. There was no sign of anyone on the road to or from the pit. There was just her, and Sandy Benson.

She knew of Sandy Benson.

Sarah Teasdale had described him to Meg.

"He's a rotten bastard. He's deluded into thinking he possesses 'Droit du seigneur'. That's where the lord of the manor felt he had the right to take the village girls for sex. It's a behavior that the Benson men developed while they were in the slave trade, and *he* thinks he still owns it."

She continued, as Meg's eyes widened, "That's where they made their money. The Bensons were small merchants, little more than peddlers, when one of them, more than a hundred years ago, bought a share in a cargo, in the triangle trade on a ship sailing from Whitehaven. Those ships took cargoes such as weapons and cloth to Africa, where they traded them for slaves, which they bought from other Africans. They took the slaves for sale to America and the Caribbean countries where they sold them at auction and bought more goods such as rum, sugar and tobacco, which they brought back and sold here. The Bensons took their profits, invested in more cargoes, more slaves, and became very wealthy. Their story has been recorded in many journals and newspapers. They bought their place into the so-called nobility." She went on, "Then when the slave trade was finally abolished back in the thirties, they invested their money in coal mines. That's where we stand today, with the likes of Sandy Benson strutting around the countryside, behaving as if he is still a slave owner able to have whomever and whatever he wants. I think it must always have been in their bloodlines. He seems to believe that the family motto is, 'We are entitled.'"

Sandy Benson had not lasted at university, having been expelled after a year of drunkenness and whoring, which had further confirmed his father's doubts about his son's fitness for anything other than military or religious activities.

The *Whitehaven News*, a journal that had started up two years previously in the seaside shipping and mining town, had boldly printed a report that claimed an Alexander Benson of the prominent Cumberland family of coal mine owners had been charged with an offence at Cambridge involving a beating of and theft from a girl of that town. The Benson family responded to the report by saying the woman in question was a notorious prostitute, drunkard, and liar, that indeed she had subsequently recanted her story and the charges had been withdrawn.

"And undoubtedly, she now enjoys a pension," Sarah had said, adding darkly, "If indeed she is still alive."

The correspondent whose name had appeared on the report in the *Whitehaven News* moved on to other employment.

That had been the previous year, in early summer. Women of Morthwaite had felt Sandy Benson's presence since he returned. His targets were mainly the daughters of pit widows and the widows themselves, women who needed work on the screens to keep themselves in food and shelter and out of the workhouse at Whitehaven. His demands were simple: he enjoyed their bodies, they were permitted to keep their jobs and the poor houses they rented.

Sandy Benson smiled down at her. A smile that held no warmth and promised no good. Whenever Meg had seen him, somehow she was reminded of a breed of dangerous pit-bull terriers that some of the miners kept. Benson's premature jowls beneath skimpy whiskers, and cold flat eyes, completed the image.

"Meg, isn't it?"

Meg said nothing. She turned, began walking up the bank toward the road.

In a moment he was at her side, gripping her arm.

"I spoke to you, girl," he snapped.

Meg pulled her arm free.

"I heard you," she said. "Yes, that is my name."

"You know who I am." Not a question.

"Everybody knows who you are," Meg replied.

His mouth tightened at the inference.

She swung her coat off her shoulder, went to put it on as the rain increased. She stepped further away. Benson took in her slight but full-bosomed figure.

He indicated her coat. "That's a very good thought."

"What?" She was puzzled, but not for long.

"Lay it on the ground," he said. "It will be fine for us."

Meg shook her head. "No," she said, "There will be no 'us', Mr. Benson."

He scowled. "There will be whatever I say there will be." He reached a hand towards her, just managing to brush her breasts before Meg responded.

Meg's older brother was known to be 'handy with his fists.' Indeed, Matthew Tyson enjoyed wide respect as a clever and tough fighter from his appearances at the boxing booths which appeared at nearby town fairs twice a year. The booths had their resident 'former champions'– men with bent noses and buckled ears – who offered to take on all-comers, with a money prize for any who could last three rounds under the London Prize Ring Rules. Despite the often whimsical interpretation of those rules by the travelling booths' 'house' referees, Matthew had not once failed to collect the money. Indeed the 'champions' – who had been heard suggesting that Mathew reminded them of the great middleweight Tom Sayers – were invariably happy to see the back of him. Mathew had declined offers from several booth owners to join their travelling company of boxers.

Matthew enjoyed demonstrating his boxing skills for his brother and his younger sister: "This is a left jab. It keeps your opponent away and sets him up for this, a right cross. And all the time you are moving. Don't stand still. Side-step, duck, keep moving. As if you're dancing."

He would have them repeat the moves and punches until they performed to his satisfaction.

Meg Tyson was slight of build, but physically strong from her job on the screens and her hands were hardened from her work. Her left jab landed squarely on Sandy Benson's fleshy nose. She blocked his wild right hand swing with her still-raised left forearm, turned her right hip forward and put all her momentum into a right cross to his left lower jaw. *Get your shoulder into it, punch through the target.*

Benson's head shot back from the first blow, and ducked sideways after the second. He staggered away from Meg, his legs astride in a bid to regain balance. This posture put him in place for Meg's next response, one in which she had been schooled by Sarah Teasdale: "In case you need to discourage any of them."

Meg's right shoe made contact with Benson's crotch. It was not a full contact, but it served to slow him – and to enrage.

"Fucking bitch!" he gasped, his hands falling to the painful parts. "Fucking bitch!"

He straightened up and lunged at Meg. Meg darted away to avoid his rush, but tripped on a loose shard of slate and went to her knees. Benson flung out a hand, grabbed a shank of her hair and snapped her head back. Meg cried out as she fell and landed heavily on her side. With lust and rage overcoming the dull pain in his testicles, Benson forced her onto her back and straddled her. His hands went to the top of her frock, opening the garment until her breasts were exposed to the nipples. His weight was crushing the breath out of her.

"Now we'll see." He pulled away more of the frock. He began to undo the lacing on the front of his riding breeches with one hand while with the other started groping at the long skirt of Meg's frock. "Now we will fucking-well see what you have down there for me!"

Meg tried to wriggle from under him, but could not shift his bulk. She aimed a fist at his flushed face, but it bounced weakly off him, and she was tiring.

Benson reached a hand into the top of her underpants, slid the hand down over her stomach and onto her mound. He reached the first line of her patch of pubic hair with his fingertips.

Meg turned her head, reached out with her right hand and felt the piece of broken slate that had tripped her earlier. The end of the slate where she touched was narrower than the rest, creating a handle, not unlike that of a knife. She made contact with the tip, tried to draw it closer, but it was wet with the harder rain now falling, and it slipped from her fingers.

Come back! She strained to reach it, crabbing her fingers, begging for them to stretch.

Benson forced his hand down lower, grunted with satisfaction as he felt her cleft.

Meg stretched her right arm fully out, reaching for the slate. She felt it, curled her forefinger around it, and groaned as it slid away again in the mud.

She screamed, "Help me!" The wind and the now slashing rain swallowed her plea.

Benson laughed. He grunted as his finger searched deeper, began a rough, repeated stroking and prepared to enter her.

Get a grip on that slate! Her thumb touched the broken edge, nudged it back towards her palm. She grabbed at it, lost it again to the mud.

Christ!

Benson's finger had almost entered her. With his free hand he was releasing the lacing on his breeches.

Meg forced a breath in. "Wait! All *right*!"

Benson stopped. He stared down at her.

A hoarse grunt, breathing hard. "What?"

Meg worked to control her shaking voice. "All right. I'll do it, but not with my underpants on. You're going to tear them. I can't...can't go home like that."

Benson grinned. The pit bull. "That's better. Get them off, then. Hurry!" He rolled her onto her side, lifted her dress and began to remove her underpants, grunting and panting like some beast in rut. His breeches were now open, freeing a stubby, engorged cock.

"Just a minute!" Meg moved her hips as if to help him, and slid sideways. She reached out and closed her right fist on the thinner end of the slate, which was still slippery with mud. Benson had dragged her underpants down to her ankles and she was fully exposed. Meg felt the slate slipping from her grip again.

Benson grunted, "Oh, yes!" He parted her vagina, took his cock in his right hand, and bent towards her. Meg summoned all her remaining strength and closed her grip on the slate. "Like this," he grunted. "Just like this."

Meg swung the slate-knife up and across, and in.

Benson's hands stopped moving.

For a brief moment there was no sound. Then came a long, low moan. The slate seemed to hang from Benson's left eye. The shard fell away as he raised a hand to his face. He screamed, an unintelligible sound, as he felt warm blood running through his fingers, and he slumped sideways, his erection now just a memory.

Meg pushed him off her and scrambled to her feet. She was shaking. She took several deep breaths as she fixed her clothing. Benson was crouched on his knees, his hands covering the left side of his face and his eye where blood continued spilling. It ran down to soak his sleeve and cuffs.

Meg looked about her. They were still the only two on the bank of Drigg Beck and still the road from Morthwaite to Coater Pit was empty. She had a mad thought of pushing Benson into the swirling beck, but as quickly dismissed it. Mainly she knew she had to get away from there. She looked up as Benson's cob whinnied and stamped a hoof. He would soon be up and, no matter his condition, the horse would carry him home, to the start of what would be the consequences of the work of the last few minutes.

Had it only been that long? It seemed somehow as though a lifetime had passed.

Alex Benson groaned, started to rise to his feet. He staggered, slumped back to his knees. "Bitch," he mouthed. He reached for his silk neck piece, tore it away and began dabbing at the blood still oozing from his face and eye. The pain of the movement tore a sob from him. He turned his head towards Meg. "You fucking little cunt. You...I'll kill..." it ended with a moan as he rocked on his knees.

Meg looked about her. She picked up a broken birch branch that lay on the bank. She scrambled up the bank to the horse, turned the animal using its reins, and she let the reins fall. With the stick she delivered a hard slap on its rump while yelling, "Get away! Go!" The horse bucked and she lashed it again and again. The horse whinnied, reared up, spun towards her. Meg swung the stick, lashed the cob across the neck. The horse swung away from her. She lashed it again, twice on the rump. This time it shied away. It stood, legs splayed, its eyes wide. One more smack with the switch and the animal backed away uncertainly. Meg raised the switch. The horse shied again, turned sharply then started into a trot, which quickly became a canter and then a gallop. Soon it was out of sight around a bend in the beck, headed in the direction of the Benson estate, two miles away.

Meg gave a last look at Benson, who remained on his knees, moaning, with his head cradled in his hands. She donned her coat and began walking towards the village. She was muddied, soaked, and shivering. Her steps quickened into a run.

Chapter 3

Meg slowed her pace as she neared the first row of houses. Her first, instinctive thought was to get home. Her mother would be there, possibly one or more of the men.

It was the thought of her brothers and her father that slowed her down, made her reconsider. She knew exactly what would happen if any of the men were home when she described what had happened.

The Tyson men, the boys taking after their father, had neither fear of nor undue respect for their titled employer. At a village fête in the summer, when the crowd were advised that any minute Lord Benson himself would be putting in an appearance, Tommy was heard by the mine manager Stanley Carrick saying, "I wouldn't gah oot to see the bugger if he wuz in oor back yard."

"You need to learn manners, Tyson," Carrick said.

Tommy laughed. "You mean arse-lickin', Carrick. That's for your kind. I work and he pays me, and that's it. Fuck off."

When Sarah Teasdale learned of that, she laughed and told Meg, "Your father could have been the model for the original poacher and aristocrat tale."

That story had passed through generations of colliers in the county of Cumberland, and likely in other pit villages throughout England. No one knew if the story was true, nor did they care.

This is how it was told:

The land-owner, usually the earl of something or other, accosts a collier carrying a fine salmon from the titled man's river and threatens him with imprisonment or deportation. The collier asks how it was that the earl's family had come to own all the land and rights to it that they now claimed.

"Centuries ago, my ancestors fought for it and won it," is the haughty reply.

"Well, Ah'll tell thou watt," the collier says. "Thee tek thy jacket off and A'll tek mine off and we'll have a feight, and t' yan that wins gits ivrything. Just like thy lot did."

"And my dad would have won," Meg laughed. "Imagine us now!"

Tommy and his sons were also fiercely protective of their women. There would be no mercy for Alexander Benson, injured or otherwise, if the men learned of his attack on Meg. They would worry about the consequences later.

Which is what Meg had realized as she slowed her walk. The Tyson men no doubt would exact a vengeance on Sandy Benson, but they would reap a whirlwind afterwards, one way or another. With all the Benson influence at work, at best they would be without jobs and a home. At worst, rotting in a jail, or transported, which still sometimes happened; and her mother would suffer more than any.

She turned off at the first of the houses, was relieved when Sarah Teasdale opened the door to her knocking.

Sarah studied her for a second. "Meg – what has happened?" She took Meg by the arm, ushering her into the house. She gestured to a wooden rail-back chair set near the fireplace, where coals burned and flickered and fed the room warmth.

"Sit down. There is tea." She lifted the knitted cosy off the teapot, poured into two cups, added sugar and placed the cups on saucers. She sat across from Meg on a twin of the chair that Meg occupied.

"Now then."

Meg told her, recounting every detail, catching her breath often as she re-lived the struggle.

"He was a brute, Sarah. He went mad. I had to fight back, otherwise…"

"So you injured him – apart from the kick in the cods, I mean – and well done on that!"

This forced a laugh from Meg.

"There was a great deal of blood. He was in pain. I sent his horse off," Meg said. "He would have had to walk home. Or to the mine!" she said, sitting up quickly, alarm on her face.

"I think not," Sarah said. "Even though it is much closer than his home. He would have to explain how he came by his condition. He is not about to admit that he had been bested by a girl, and a screen-lass at that!"

Meg nodded. Her whirling thoughts were beginning to settle as she listened to Sarah's logic. She explained her concerns about going straight home to Number 13, what might – no, what *would* ensue.

"That is good thinking," Sarah said. "Now, we need to consider. I believe we have time to do that. A certain amount anyway."

Sarah paced before the fireplace as she spoke her thoughts.

"Benson is going to have to concoct a believable event to account for his injuries. He is not going to say the truth."

Meg sipped on the hot sweet tea. Her breathing had slowed by now. She listened as Sarah talked.

"He may say he was waylaid by some tramp or stranger attempting a robbery." Then she shook her head, rejecting that notion. "No, if he said that, then he would have had to explain first why he, an example of England's finest, had been unable to deal with a common ruffian, and beyond that, then why he did not immediately hurry to the mine and ask that a search for the attacker be started. So, given the circumstances – he was out riding, after all – I believe that when he arrives home he will attribute blame to his horse. He will invent a fiction saying that the animal was startled, and threw him from the saddle, whereupon he landed on a rock or some such and so received his injury. Also, that version would suit his need to be seen as manly, and a legitimate victim."

Meg said, "That sounds very likely, but—"

Sarah held a hand up, as she typically did in her classroom. Meg waited.

"If the injury is serious – I have to think it may well be from what you say – and I truly hope that it is because that man deserves no half measures where punishment is involved, a doctor will be called for. That will take time. Time is our greatest ally, Meg."

She took Meg's hand. "Possibly our only one."

***

Sarah's conjecture concerning Alexander Benson's account of his condition was remarkably accurate.

The Bensons had been alerted by the arrival of the cob, darkened with sweat and foaming as it galloped through the estate's western set of massive wrought iron gates, with their family crest atop adorned with an extravagant menagerie of lions, hounds, and stags above the word 'Fell View,' the name chosen for his property by Richard, Lord Benson, Earl of Long Fell. The name was somewhat ambitious, as the only thing in sight resembling a fell, or Cumbrian mountain, was an upward-sloping stretch of moor headed east in the direction of two adjoining bodies of water named Big Tarn and Laal Tarn respectively.

An hour later, of the gang of servants of various ranks sent to search in every direction the horse may have come from, it was a gardener who found Alex staggering, ragged and bloodied, reaching out a hand as if trying to find his way. This was explained later when the doctor who had been sent for, while attempting to repair torn flesh on Benson's face, explained, "I have used laudanum to disguise the pain for now, have cleaned it and done what repairs I could, but the injury to the eye is in the hands of God. I can do no more than dress it and hope it may heal."

With his pain dulled by the laudanum, Alexander Benson offered a rambling, self-serving account of his betrayal by "that useless beast" which he said had been alarmed by a badger and unseated him. He ordered a groom to take the cob to the stables and shoot it; but his father, knowing well his youngest son and thus suspicious that his account of events may lack some veracity – even the mention of a badger, a nocturnal creature, being on patrol in the light of late afternoon, was suspect – and sensitive to the cost of replacing what he knew to be an excellent hunter, interceded, "Perhaps not so hasty, Sandy. You are not at your best at this moment. Let us think on it. The horse has always been a sound animal, any one of our mounts could have fallen to the same situation."

The son embraced the chance to keep the horse, provided the animal still seemingly bore the blame for his condition, thus allowing him to appear to be gracious even in his distress. While the laudanum eased the throbbing in his damaged eye, and hallucinations from the drug danced in his brain, he seethed.

Sarah said, "We have to use that time to get you away from Morthwaite."

Meg's eyes widened. "Away? Where to? For how long?"

"I have a thought on the first, Meg. We will talk of that with your mother shortly. For how long?" She shook her head. "You will never be safe here as long as Alexander Benson or his influence is here, and that could be for a very long time."

"But you say you believe he would never tell—"

"That he was bested by a screen lass – or any lass, in fact? No, of course he would never admit to that, but at the same time he will never forget it. Not until the day he dies. His mind will be poisoned with it. You will be his obsession. You will be in danger, if not from Benson himself then from whatever thug of a hireling or retainer he engages to do you harm, for he will do so. It will happen in a moment. Your father and brothers cannot be there to protect you at all times. It will come in the dark, it will come even while you work. You will never be safe in this village, or anywhere that Benson can reach you."

Meg shook her head, "But—"

Sarah waved her down. "We must get you away, Meg. A long way from here." She took Meg's cup and saucer and placed them on the table. She crossed the room to a tiny, aged writing desk that sat under her books shelves. She took a small key from a hook on the end of the shelf, opened the desk's centre drawer and removed a few items from it. As she did these things she talked to Meg, telling her of her own experience as a tutor, with the McAdams family. "It seems to go along with positions in high society, Meg, the whole entitlement business." Next she took down several folded copies of newspapers from her bookshelf and busied herself with scissors, clipping the pages. With that finished, she shepherded Meg to the door. "Now, to your house."

***

At No. 13, all the Tyson men were out, starting a late shift at the pit, for which Sarah offered a silent thanks as she and Meg described the situation to Meg's mother.

Lizzie Tyson listened until they were done and Sarah had explained her reasoning, her fears.

"I'll kill the fucker myself," Lizzie said.

Meg had never heard her mother use the word.

"You would have to join the queue," Sarah said. Despite the situation, both the Tyson women laughed.

Then Sarah told them what she had in mind.

Lizzie said, "Good Christ!"

Meg stared in disbelief.

Chapter 4

Sarah Teasdale took charge at No. 13.

Lizzie Tyson concentrated on every word as Sarah expressed the urgent need for Meg to get away from Morthwaite, from any chance of Sandy Benson or of anyone connected to him ever finding her.

"We cannot allow that to happen," Sarah said. "This way guarantees she will be safe. But also, it is an opportunity for Meg to build a new life, an opportunity that she would never find here in Morthwaite."

She let the thought register, then, "It is not going to be easy. Meg will be leaving the only life she has ever known, but she can do it. I know that."

Lizzie Tyson was a woman practiced in life's realities. She nodded, a reluctant, fearful understanding, while holding back tears.

They would set out immediately to walk the four miles to Whitehaven, where Meg would board a train that would begin her long journey, the first stage of which was to London.

At Sarah's direction, Lizzie put together a food packet containing a meat pasty, some sweet biscuits, and a bottle of barley water. "You will be able to buy more along the way," Sarah had said. She handed Meg three gold sovereigns along with a few florins, shillings and pennies in a small leather purse, the items she had taken from her desk drawer.

The sovereigns drew gasps from the two women, and a protest especially from Meg. "But Sarah, you cannot—"

A familiar, imperious hand from Sarah. "I can do what I choose to. I have no need for the money, and you have every need." She smiled. "Someday you can repay me, Meg."

An event that seemed far from likely, in all three minds.

She instructed Meg to keep the sovereigns separate from the smaller change. Lizzie quickly sewed an extra fold that would serve as a pocket on the inside of Meg's frock. Meg tucked the gold coins into it.

"And these, most important," Sarah said. She gave Meg a package of papers, the pages she had clipped from the *Times* of recent weeks, which she had gathered before she and Meg had left her house. "Read these reports, find these people. Particularly, find this woman." She placed a finger on a name – Baroness Angela Burdett-Coutts – in the report on one of the pages. The full report, which Meg would read as the train made its way down the coast towards Barrow and further into Lancashire then on to the nation's capital, concerned two groups being organized in London to help women emigrate to the colonies of British Columbia and Vancouver's Island on the Pacific coast of North America. They were the London Female Middle Class Emigration Society, and the Columbia Emigration Society – two groups with similar goals, but for distinctly different clients, as Meg would soon learn.

Meg had barely been able to take in everything Sarah had said, her thoughts spinning with the significance and consequences of what she was about to undertake, and the speed of events as Sarah pressed her message that time was critical and they must leave immediately.

Lizzie quickly gathered Meg's spare clothing, her one 'good' dress, underclothing, and stockings, and her pair of black leather Sunday shoes. She folded them into a small cloth carrying case, to which Meg had added her copy of *David Copperfield*.

"What will you tell my dad, and our Matthew and Thomas?"

Lizzie looked away and gazed into the fireplace for a long moment, then, "They'll be hours yet. When they get in Ah'll tell them exactly what happened at Drigg Beck. Ah'll tell them that they're ganna dyer nowt aboot it, that that's what you want, Meg. Ah'll tell them that you took nae harm, that you handled Mr. bloody Sandy Benson an' that he might not be sae free an' easy wid lasses in t' future. An' Ah'll tell them that when this a' settles doon, you'll be able to come back – an' until that happens, they can keep their mouths shut an' their fists t' their sels. An' that'll be it."

Meg knew her mother's words would be final for the Tyson men. Like most colliers' wives, Lizzie commanded house and family. The men's wages were handed to her each Friday payday and she doled out what she thought enough for ale, tobacco and any other sundries she deemed fit.

Meg looked around the small front room where the family did most of their living. The stool by the fireplace, where she sat to read, the marks on the wall that indicated her and her brothers' growing height, and the years. The scarred pine table that had belonged to her grandparents, and the four rail-back chairs tucked under it. The ancient sideboard with two cupboards and a single shelf that held the family's meager supply of cups and plates. All the things she had taken for granted all her life. She fixed them all in her mind, then turned to her mother.

Lizzie took Meg in her arms. "It's for t' best, lass. It really is." After a moment, she added, "It has to be, lass." She kissed Meg's face, on one cheek, then the other, her tears now mixing with those of her daughter.

Despite Lizzie's brave stance, none of the three felt any certainty that Meg Tyson would see the village of Morthwaite again.

Chapter 5

Meg read the reports from the *Times* pages on her long journey to London which involved changing trains once at night and once in the early morning at two different railway stations, before arriving in the early afternoon at London's massive Euston station, with its crowds of travellers thronging on the arrivals and departures platforms. She stared up at the towering wrought iron roof, wondered how on earth such a structure might have been erected. She made her way through the imposing Euston Arch on to Drummond Street.

On the trains and on immediate arrival at Euston her senses had been assailed by smoke, soot, steam, the ceaseless thundering and clanking of steel wheels on steel rails. Now on London's streets it was the sights, sounds and powerful smells of masses of people and animals – dozens of horse-drawn conveyances the like of which Meg had never seen, roaming dogs, and at one spot on the street two cows being driven by a herder to some purpose or other and splattering the road with their shit as they went – that were overwhelming to a girl from a northern pit village. A dirty-yellow fog swirled about the whole, carrying acrid fumes from the countless industries that the city had acquired over the last several decades, and which had attracted the thousands who now populated the cheap, festering housing and the city's streets. Meg took out a handkerchief. She held it over her nose, though to little effect.

Sarah had written the address for the Columbia Emigration Society, which she had copied from a letter in the *Times*. The office was at 54 Charing Cross Road.

Sarah had been to London while visiting her mother and siblings in the south. "You will be able to take an omnibus there, I should think. They run frequently and are reasonably priced."

Meg wondered if there was anything that Sarah *didn't* know.

She saw across the street a sign for Kings Cross Omnibuses. Two of the horse-drawn vehicles were loading and unloading passengers. She had taken two steps into the throng of pedestrians between her and the omnibuses when a burly man, a blur in the fog, smashed into her on her left while in the same moment another, smaller person, grabbed her right arm and twisted and pulled until their combined attack forced her down on her knees into the horse droppings and other mess and slime that covered the road. The first attacker grabbed for the bag that held her copy of *David Copperfield*, her few extra clothes, and some of her money. The second attacker, a thin faced wiry boy of nine or ten she saw now, forced her further down into the mess. At that moment another woman appeared out of the fog. She screamed as she tripped over the boy and sprawled face-down alongside Meg.

Meg yelled. "Stop it! Let go of me!" The fog shifted and swirled around them. People passed by, stepping around the struggling bodies as Meg used her strength to regain some control. She was able to throw the smaller of her assailants to the side. The boy shouted his surprise, came back aiming a kick which caught Meg on the side of her face and had her senses reeling. An image of Sandy Benson flashed into her mind and with it a rush of anger, a surge of strength, which brought her back to her feet. She still had her grip on the straps of her bag, but sensed she was losing that part of the fight against a man older and much bigger. She smelled a foul breath as he suddenly leaned in, snarling, and crashed his forehead into her nose and mouth. She tasted blood from her damaged lips. She aimed a punch at his rough-whiskered face and connected, but the blow had little effect and the brute yanked harder on her bag of belongings. The bag tore. Her extra pair of shoes fell to the road, as did the Dickens novel and the small purse with part of the cash Sarah had given her. The boy, who had been busy at the woman who had fallen and now clasped something in his folded hand, pounced on the purse, took a quick look inside. He said "readies" to the man. The man bent down, grabbed the shoes, dropped the ruined bag. "Let's hook it," he said, and in a second they were gone, swallowed by the fog amid the surging crowd.

The woman who had fallen beside Meg struggled to her feet. She was tall and well dressed, though now her jacket and skirts were fouled and reeking. She glared at Meg, who had just picked up the remains of her bag and its contents. Meg checked the fold in her frock where the sovereigns remained safe. The thieves had got away with about ten shillings, for them no doubt a satisfying few minutes work.

The woman said, "Don't you move."

"What? What do you mean?"

"I mean that I'm not fooled by you and your gang!" She grabbed Meg's arm and she turned into the crowd and called, "A thief! I have a thief! Get a policeman!"

Meg wondered if the woman might be mad. Her blood rose. "I'm not a thief! I was attacked. They hit me and took my money, ten shillings. And my shoes!"

"Shillings, indeed! A fine story. And what will you get for the necklace and rings that boy ripped from me. I know your style – pretend to be hurt while your others do the thieving. Who are they? Your husband? More likely your pimp, I should think. The young one your brother? You are an evil lot."

A dark-blue uniformed London policeman wearing the Bobbie's pointed hat pushed through the small crowd that the woman's shouting had drawn. Here was some sport for them.

"That's her." A man in the crowd who could not have seen any of the preceding events pointed at Meg, "We seen it." Others noised their assent. If he said so, then it must be, and they were always ready for a show.

"What's happened here?" the policeman said. He nodded to the woman. "You're Mrs. Gold, from the Ladies Clothing Emporium, aren't you?"

"I am." She aimed a finger at Meg. "I was attacked by this trollop and her helpers – her man, and a boy. They stole my necklace and two of my rings." She placed a finger at her throat where a shallow, bloody scratch was visible.

"We seen it!" the man in the crowd called.

Meg could not credit what was happening.

"*I* was attacked and robbed," she said. She indicated her torn and now filthy frock. "I'm covered in horse shit!"

Mrs. Gold's lips tightened at the word, confirming Meg's station in life. The reaction escaped Meg. For her it was an everyday word: cow shit in the fields, bird shit on the washing line, horse shit everywhere, and her father – along with most everyone else in the village – invariably referred to the outside closet as their shit-'oose.

Meg said, "She's right about her being two of them, a man and a boy, but not anyone that I've ever seen before. I've never even been in London before today."

"Nonsense," Mrs. Gold snapped. "Look, she's wearing a stook, just as they were." She pointed to the white silk scarf that Meg wore at her throat, another gift from Sarah. Meg recalled now a glimpse of white scarves that both her attackers had worn around their necks.

"You know that's their sign, these gangs."

The policeman said, "Some of them, yes."

"Also she has something hidden in her dress." She pointed to where Meg had checked for her sovereigns. "A secret pocket. It's how they do it."

The policeman looked at Meg, and at where the woman had pointed.

"Well, Miss?"

"It's my money. It's where I keep it safe. If I had had it in my purse with the rest—"

"And maybe two rings," Mrs. Gold said.

The policeman held out his open hand.

"Would you care to show me, Miss?"

Meg had no choice. She opened the fold in her frock and took the three sovereigns from the pocket. She showed the coins to the policeman.

"Ah!" from Mrs. Gold. "I knew as much. Where would she get that, if not from a robbery? She's nothing but—"

The policeman raised a hand. "We're not sure of anything yet, Mrs. Gold. There's no rings here."

And to Meg, "That's a lot of money to be carrying, Miss."

"It was a gift," Meg said. "To keep me going until—"

"Until she could steal more!" Mrs. Gold.

"She's a thief!" shouted the man in the crowd, which was growing in number and pushing closer to the unexpected and most welcome entertainment.

The constable waved them to go back, but they stood fast, and more cries of "Thief!" went up, voiced loudest by the man whom the increased number appeared to have accepted as their leader.

A hand reached out and grabbed at Meg's shoulder. She shrugged it off. Another man, reeking of liquor, stumbled from the crowd, laughing at the game, and tried to put his arms around Meg. "I'll take her in myself!" he roared, and was rewarded with loud applause from the herd.

Meg punched him with a hard right fist and pushed him away. He stumbled and toppled to the ground, but was up quickly, hurling himself at her again. He groped, and missed, then he stopped. He swayed, his face took on a pained, surprised look, and suddenly he vomited a brownish-green stream of his stomach's contents which landed at the feet and partly on the boots and lower

41

trousers of the constable, which was all the officer needed to bring down the curtain on this particular performance. He reached to his belt and removed a wooden rattle. Its loud ratcheting noise was echoed almost immediately by another one close by, and then by a third. It was just seconds before two more policemen pushed their way through the crowd, which now dispersed as quickly as it had gathered, its leader gone like a magic trick.

"These two ladies will accompany me back to the station," the first policeman told the others. "You keep a watch for any more trouble makers. Does that suit you, Mrs. Gold? We will need you to make a statement." While he had politely put the question, it was clearly not intended as an option.

Mrs. Gold nodded a stiff assent.

The policeman did not ask Meg if she was suited, just nudged her in the back and said, "This way, young lady."

They walked no more than a hundred yards before arriving at an imposing two story building with large double doors and a sign above reading "Metropolitan Police." From an arched opening at the side of the building, a single horse-drawn enclosed black wagon clattered. It also bore the police insignia. Meg guessed that the vehicle would be used for moving malefactors to and from the building. Her guess was confirmed when the constable said, "It's called the Black Maria. It's a new thing for us. If your trouble had been a bit further away you might have had a ride in it." With a smile, which gave Meg some small relief.

Inside, the constable instructed them to take a seat on a bench against the dirty-green painted wall to their left. He went to a long, broad desk on the opposite side of the room behind which another officer – a sergeant with close cropped black hair, wearing a frown he might have been born with, and below it a luxuriant mustache with waxed tips – picked up and flourished a steel-nibbed pen before dipping it into an inkwell sunk into the desk.

"Constable Pepper, what have we got here?"

The constable glanced at the two women as he spoke quietly to the sergeant. He pointed at each in turn, shook his head at some questions from the sergeant, shrugged at others, and frequently raised his open palms. Meg wondered if it were some form of police sign language.

The sergeant called them up to stand before his desk and instructed each to give her version of events, beginning with Mrs. Gold.

"I was on my way to the shop – the Ladies Clothing Emporium – you may know of it."

The sergeant nodded that he did, and swapped a quick glance with the constable.

Lady Muck, Meg thought, a common term from home for any woman pretending to high place. *From top of t'hill. Niver shit an' niver will.*

"I was attacked by a man—"

"A *boy*," Meg interrupted her. "It was a boy, not a man. The *man* attacked *me*. And the boy did not attack you, you tripped over me where I had been knocked down – into the horse shit."

Constable Pepper had a sudden need to clear his throat.

"And it was then that he stole your necklace."

"And rings, torn from my fingers! Obviously you knew what was happening, you must have been part—"

Christ Almighty! Sorry!

"I *saw* what was happening." Meg turned to the sergeant. "I told the officer – I have never been in London until today. I did not know these people. I was robbed just as she was. And thumped," she added, pointing to her face where a swelling had already risen from the blow she took. "And my clothes ruined." That much was obvious, on both women.

The sergeant said, "There's all kinds in London these days with different ways of talking, you might have been here longer than you say. Where do you live?"

"Nowhere, yet. I just arrived off the train. I'm going to be looking for—"

The sergeant waved her to be quiet. He wrote and murmured as he did, "No fixed abode." He said, "Arrived from where?"

Meg told him.

The sergeant shrugged. She might as well have said Bombay.

"And going where?" the sergeant asked.

Meg wondered if it really was any of his concern where a person was going, but she decided not to ask. Instead, she told him. "I'm going to meet Baroness Angela Burdett-Coutts."

Mrs. Gold snorted, "The Baroness, indeed!"

The sergeant smiled, humouring. "And is the lady expecting you?"

"Not exactly, but if I can find her, she is helping young women–"

"Get off the streets, out of prostitution." Mrs. Gold interrupted. "I might have known."

"Emigrate," Meg said. "She is helping women immigrate to Vancouver's Island. I am going to be one of them."

The sergeant nodded. "I have read of this plan."

Meg's face suddenly brightened. She reached into the pocket that held the gold sovereigns. She found the train ticket that Sarah had purchased at Whitehaven. It was stamped with the time and date of purchase, and showed the stops she had had to make along the way to change trains. She handed it across the desk.

The sergeant examined the ticket. "I see," he said. He handed the ticket to Pepper, who studied it carefully, then smiled.

"Well, Miss – what was it again – Tyson?"

"Yes. Meg Tyson."

"It seems that you might be telling the truth."

The sergeant appeared to address this as much to Mrs. Gold as to Meg.

Mrs. Gold scoffed. "They use all kinds of tricks. People throw used tickets on the ground all the time. No doubt she found it."

"Christ Almighty!" This time aloud. Then to the sergeant, "Sorry."

Constable Pepper turned away, busy adjusting his helmet.

A commotion at the door interrupted the debate. A constable had a boy by the scruff and was struggling to keep a grip on him as the boy turned and twisted and yelled, "Bleedin' peeler! Gerroff me!"

Meg recognized the boy as the one who had grabbed her purse. The same thin face and the white scarf at his throat, the straggling dirty blonde hair. The constable slapped the boy, who yelped. He looked up and straight at Meg, whom he recognized immediately. Any bravado was now gone, in its place quiet tears from the slapping, and fear.

Mam would say the lad needs some meat on his bones, Meg thought.

"I caught 'im dippin'," the new constable said. "He was after a gentleman's lace handkerchief."

Good God, shades of Oliver Twist!

The boy raised both hands, open and appealed to the desk sergeant. "I wasn't doin' nuffin' yer 'onour. I 'aven't got anyfin'."

The sergeant had caught Meg's examination of the boy.

"Do you recognize him, miss? Is he the one who robbed you?" He began stuffing a clay pipe with tobacco, then lit it with a match and puffed it into life while he waited for Meg's response.

Meg turned to Constable Pepper and asked quietly, "What will happen to him?"

"If it's him, he'll be committed for trial and will go straight from here to Newgate, where he'll stay until it's his turn in front of the beak. If he's guilty, maybe they'll hang him. If they're still doing that with young'uns. Workhouse, if he's lucky."

Meg wondered if some of that might be an exaggeration, or possibly a policeman's wishful thinking. Pepper's face offered no clue to either.

The boy had heard the mention of Newgate and his face twisted. Mrs. Gold also heard it and she nodded firm approval of the idea. Meg wondered if perhaps the woman attended and enjoyed the public hangings that were held outside the notorious prison. She shuddered at the recollection of how Dickens had described the conditions in Newgate prison in the materials that Sarah produced for her history lessons. She had read and shown her small class descriptions of the prison from old copies of Charles Dickens' *Sketches by Boz*. Meg had wondered if it had been Sarah's way of encouraging her pupils to stay on the straight and narrow. She recalled especially a passage that referred to a room of prisoners condemned to death and awaiting their trip to the gallows. One of that company had been a boy aged fourteen who was to be hanged for burglary. Another passage had described a room of boys under fourteen who had been convicted of pickpocketing or dipping. Some were barefoot, others dressed, barely, in rags, and while a trip to the gallows was not mentioned, one sentence of the author's had stayed with Meg: "...we never saw such hopeless creatures of neglect, before."

Hopeless creatures of neglect.

Meg realized that the description had been of conditions two decades earlier, but had no way of knowing what, if anything, had changed at Newgate. She could only imagine what might lie ahead for the boy.

"What about you, Mrs. Gold?" The desk sergeant switched his question.

The shop owner huffed, "He has the stook, as I described, and he looks like what I saw of the thief."

The boy seemed stricken. He looked to the door and struggled in the constable's grip.

Meg said, "You couldn't have seen much at all, you were lying on your face in the shit."

Mrs. Gold gasped, "Why, you—"

45

Sometimes you have to tell a white lie, to save harm.
Lizzie Tyson.

They had been picking blackites on the top of the old quarry at the south end of the village, where the Morthwaite women hung their washing to dry on good-weather Mondays. Meg's fingers, lips and tongue were stained with the juice of the fat black bramble berries. Lizzie had just suggested that Meg might eat fewer and pick more for the baskets they carried, when Elsie Briggs called to them, asking if they had seen her husband, Peter.

Elsie Briggs was a domineering shrew. She bullied her husband and her two sons, all of them hard-grafting colliers. She screamed at them in public if they were seen entering or leaving t' Dog. She marched them to Distington every Sunday to attend the cold, stone-built Methodist Chapel. She made it clear to all that she, at least, had come from better stock than the rest of Morthwaite, and that she held her men to higher standards than others.

Meg had been about to point to Moira Dixon's aging cottage on the edge of the quarry field, where she and Lizzie had noticed Peter Briggs knocking on the door and going inside a few minutes earlier, but Lizzie had spoken first.

"No, haven't seen him, not today, Elsie."

A look from Lizzie had silenced Meg.

Moira Dixon lived alone in the old cottage, which belonged to her farming family who visited her occasionally, but mostly left her to herself. Moira was acknowledged to be not the full shilling, but she was not quite as daft as many judged, and for men like Peter Briggs, who received little wifely comfort at home and who had a few spare coins, or indeed a bottle of the stout that Moira fancied, the cottage was a haven.

"She would kill him, if she knew he were in there," Lizzie said when Meg asked her mother why she had fibbed.

"It's called a white lie," she said. "A little fib that does nobody any harm and saves somebody a lot of bother."

Like getting killed!

Meg spoke over Mrs. Gold to the desk sergeant. "No, this is not the same boy. The one that robbed us was much taller than this, and he had ginger hair. I saw him quite clearly. I would know him anywhere. This is not him."

The boy stopped his struggling. He stared at Meg for a second. Then he grinned and turned back to the desk sergeant. "To'd y', didden I?"

Mrs. Gold snapped, "She's lying."

The constable holding the boy said, "Sergeant?"

The sergeant placed his pipe on the desk before him. He looked at Mrs. Gold. "You can't be sure," he said. And to Meg, "But you seem very sure."

Meg said, "I am very sure. This is not the boy."

Mrs. Gold glared at her and sputtered a protest.

Meg thought, *If looks could indeed kill, I would be a goner.* She looked resolutely at the sergeant. He held her gaze for a moment, almost smiled, but stopped himself, then, "You," he pointed a stern finger at the boy, "consider yourself lucky – this time." He nodded to the constable holding the boy. "Let him go."

The boy laughed. "Thank you, lady," he said to Meg. "It's nice to meet an 'onest person for once," and he was gone out the door.

The sergeant said, "Mrs. Gold, give us a description of your missing items. We will check in all the pawn shops in the area. Otherwise I'm sure that you would like to get home and change your clothing."

Meg looked down at her own stained and stinking frock. Her second frock was still in the bag that she had clung to in the attack.

"Is there somewhere I could wash and change?"

"There's water at the back of the station," the sergeant said. "Constable Pepper will show you."

It was a trough with a water pump. Meg thought it likely that the horses were watered here, but it was better than having to remain in the state she was. Pepper turned his back while Meg changed her frock and washed her hands and face. There was a bin for rubbish nearby. She folded her ruined frock and dropped it in. Then she left the station by the side entrance.

***

Meg chose the vehicle with the name 'Kings Cross Omnibuses' on its side and which charged sixpence a mile, after enquiring of the driver how far it was to the Charing Cross Road address and being told two miles. A hackney cab would have cost twice as much, and Meg decided anyway that she would prefer to have company than be alone in this mad place. She paid the money to the conductor who occupied a small platform at the back of the vehicle. She took her place on the end of one of the two bench seats next to a friendly woman with two children on her lap for whom the woman apparently had had to pay no fare.

"Good job these young'uns travel free if they're on my lap. Where you from ducks? Where you off to? Just off the train are we? Shurrup an'wipe yer nose." This directed at the boy crowded next to his sister on the mother's knees.

The flurry of words in an accent that Meg could barely decipher proceeded uninterrupted while Meg stared from the back of the omnibus at the masses of people and vehicles moving through London's streets. She took fleeting notice of the names on street signs as they travelled – Eversholt Street, Euston Road, Gower Street…

"Next stop Charing Cross Road!" the conductor shouted above the city's din. The horse and bus clattered to a stop and the woman bade Meg, "Cheery-bye, darlin', you tyke care, now," and went back to berating the snot-nosed boy as Meg stepped down.

Meg checked the address on the door facing her, and entered into a tile-floored hallway. Ahead was a door with the name in gold lettering on the glass upper half: **Columbia Emigration Society.**

She could hear voices inside. She knocked twice lightly on the door, and waited. There was no response. The voices continued.

'Assert yourself.' Sarah.

Meg rapped the door four, six times, until her knuckles stung. The voices stopped, then a voice: "Enter."

Meg turned the brass door knob and walked into the office. Facing her, a man Meg guessed to be in his forties, wearing a black jacket, a high stiff-collared white shirt with a black floppy necktie and a severe expression, sat behind a large dark-wood desk, a sheaf of papers in front of him and a pen in his right hand raised as if about to record a judgment. In the furthest corner a well-dressed man seemingly a few years older than the one at the desk, with an untidy, wiry beard and long but receding grey-brown hair, stood with a woman dressed in what Meg decided was the height of expensive fashion, with a full-skirted light blue hooped dress, a short, buttoned black coat tightly tailored at the waist, and a dark blue silk hat worn slightly to one side and adorned with what Meg recognized as the tail feather of a cock pheasant.

The pair examined Meg. The man nodded, and smiled.

So far, so good.

The man behind the desk said, stiffly, "Good day. May I help you?"

Before Meg could reply the woman stepped forward. "What happened to you, child?" She nodded to the obviously fresh bruise on Meg's face and the swollen lip.

Meg described the attack and the police involvement.

"And this boy, the one they brought in. You were sure that he was not the one who robbed you?"

Meg hesitated. She did not want to get off on the wrong foot with these people, whoever they were, though clearly they were connected to the emigration society. On the other hand, she had already told her white lie to the police and the lad was on his way, for better or worse.

"Sure enough," she said.

The woman nodded, a hint of a smile. From her expression Meg was sure that she had guessed the truth, but it did not seem to upset her. For Meg the matter was closed. It was time to get on with her mission. She addressed the man at the desk.

"My name is Meg Tyson. I'm eighteen years of age. I am – I was – a screen lass at Morthwaite in the county of Cumberland. I will not be going back there and my friend – my teacher – Sarah Teasdale, said I should enquire about going to Columbia under the society's emigration plan."

The couple exchanged glances and the man smiled.

The man at the desk said, "A screen lass – what on earth—"

"Young women who work on the pit tops, Mr. Payne." The man of the couple had spoken. "They do very demanding work for long hours. Work that would tire any man. They sort the rock and slate from the coal on a long table. I have seen the same work in the mines of Lancashire, south of where this young woman comes from." He nodded at Meg, a kindly look.

Payne, the society's chief clerk, looked from him back to Meg. "And what made you leave Cumberland, if I may ask?"

Meg saw the woman frown as Payne spoke.

"I have done nothing wrong," Meg said. "I have done nothing to be ashamed of. This," touching her face, "was none of my doing. "

The woman said, "Never mind that, Mr. Payne."

"Milady." Payne inclined his head.

Meg said, "I read a Mr. Garret's letter to the *Times* newspaper. I think that I could be one of the girls he talked about in that letter. The ones you say there are jobs for."

Meg referred to the section of the letter where John Garret, 'Vicar of St. Paul near Penzance and Honorary Secretary to the Society' had specified who would and who would not be candidates for the Columbia society's plans.

He had written: 'Two principles will guide us for selecting women suitable for emigration. First, we could not guarantee suitable homes on reaching the colony to women who should depend upon the use of their brains alone for support. Nor does it seem desirable to withdraw from their sphere of valuable occupation in this country those women who have received sufficient education to place them in situations as teachers in families and schools at homes. Those who go out under the protection of this society will agree to take service on reaching the colony in such situations as the governor and bishop and those acting with their authority may consider best suited to their several cases, and may have open and ready to give them an occupation and a safe dwelling on their landing in Columbia.'

"So you can read?" Payne.

"Anything you like. *And* write," Meg said. And after a second's thought, "*And* I can add, subtract and divide and multiply numbers."

The woman raised a gloved hand to her mouth.

Payne asked Meg a few more questions, jotting notes as she answered,

Finally, and after a glance from the woman across the room, he said, "I believe we may be able to help you, Miss Tyson. In the meanwhile, where will you be staying, so that we might reach you at the appropriate time?"

Meg said, "I believe there are lodging houses where the rates are reasonable. I can pay for a time, and I can look for work until—"

"There will be no need for that," the other woman broke in. "Just one moment, my dear." She turned to the man, and they held a brief and quiet conversation before he picked up a top hat and a pair of leather gloves from a side table and turned to leave. The woman said, "Thank you, Charles." And he replied, "Angela, my pleasure."

"Miss Tyson," he said, as he drew level with Meg. "I wish you well."

Meg froze. *Angela. Milady. Charles. Christ Almighty! Sorry!* The reports in *The Times:* Lady Angela Burdett-Coutts, and her supporter, Charles Dickens!

"Mister Dickens!" she exclaimed. "You are Charles Dickens!"
He smiled. "I am."

Meg was speechless, but only for a moment. "I have read your books," she said. "Most of them. I have not yet finished *David Copperfield,* in fact I had just begun the story when I had to…" Meg's voice faltered, but after a moment she continued. "I have it with me." She touched her small bag of belongings.

Dickens held out a hand.

Boot blacking labels?

Meg quickly opened the cloth bag and drew out the book. Dickens took it and smiled as he examined the well-worn cover. Dickens had said in newspaper interviews that this was his favourite of his stories. The book had been described as being partly autobiographical, and was said to have been inspired by the death from consumption of his favourite sister Fanny in 1848 and of her young son a year later. He turned to the secretary. "A pen, Mr. Payne, if you would," he said.

Payne was now enjoying the interplay between the celebrated author and this 'screen lass' whose past he could only vaguely imagine. He dipped his pen into an ink well, shook off the excess ink and handed the pen to Dickens, who opened the book to the page with the title. He laid the book on the desk and wrote in the white space, 'To Meg Tyson, with wishes for a successful journey into a new future. Affectionately, Charles Dickens.' He carefully blotted the words and blew gently on them to be sure the ink had dried. He closed the book and handed it back to Meg, who by this time was barely aware that she was holding it.

Dickens' brow creased as he looked at Meg's outreached hand and noted the legacy of her work on the screens. He touched her hand. "Good fortune, my dear. I am sure that you will prosper." With a final nod to the woman, "Angela." – *'Angela', the Baroness!* – He turned and left the office.

Meg opened the book and stared at the signature. What would Sarah have said? She almost laughed at the thought.

"Meg," the woman, the Baroness, said, "That would be the short form of Margaret, I believe?"

"Yes, but I have never been called anything but Meg."

She noticed the man Payne, behind the desk, frowning at her, and slightly shaking his head.

"Miss," Meg added. As she always addressed Sarah in the early days, before teacher-pupil advanced to friends.

Payne raised alarmed eyebrows and shook his head, no, no, no!

He had addressed the Baroness as 'Milady,' Meg recalled, and realized that he was admonishing her to do the same.

Meg had never called anyone 'Milady.' Had never met a woman she considered qualified to be so addressed by a Tyson. She knew that the Benson matriarch was known as Lady Benson, just through her husband being Lord Benson, and that her dad had had no time for either the titles or the behaviour of people bearing them.

'They bought them, lass, on the backs of folk like us. They're nowt special, they've done nowt special, wattiver they think a' their sels… Ah' wouldn't gah oot to see the bugger if he wuz in oor back yard.'

The collier and the Earl.

Meg had the feeling that this woman was a far cry from the Bensons.

Payne was poised to speak, but the Baroness waved him down. "Thank you, Mr. Payne." To Meg, she said, "I'm very pleased that you were able to meet Charles. He is always happy to meet a reader – as indeed he should be, they being the ones who keep him in wine and fine clothing," and she smiled broadly at Meg's laugh.

She touched Meg on the arm. "Come with me." They walked side by side from the office and out of the door onto Charing Cross Road. It was cold, the yellow fog was as thick and stinking as ever – *how did people live in this, day after day?* – and a murky drizzle had started. Immediately a coach drew up from further down the street and stopped in front of them. With a tall black horse between the shafts, it was not unlike the hackney cabs on the street, but was highly polished, had a folding hood of soft material, and what seemed to be a diamond-shaped design – a coat of arms, Meg realized – on the door which now was opened by the driver, a man in top hat and smartly clothed. He lowered a folding step, bowed and said, "Milady."

"Thank you Jackson," the Baroness said. She gestured to Meg to step up into the coach and held her arm as she did. Meg realized that she was going to be riding alongside the woman whom she had read was the wealthiest woman in England, a woman who so far hardly behaved as someone of that status might be expected to. Meg settled herself on one of the richly upholstered velvet-covered seats. The Baroness arranged her dress and sat opposite her.

Jackson pulled the folding hood over the interior, saw that they were comfortable, then reached over the closed door and placed a small wicker basket on the seat beside the Baroness.

"Are we ready milady?" he said.

"Ready indeed, Jackson. For home." To Meg, she said, "We have about four miles to travel to Holly Lodge, an hour or so." She raised the lid on the wicker basket. "And we must sustain ourselves." She handed Meg a napkin on which she placed two small pastries, one of which turned out to be filled with some kind of spiced meat, the other with a sweet jelly. Meg had last eaten at one of her stops on the train journey, hours ago, and wasted no time in finishing the snacks. She wiped the crumbs from her mouth with the back of her hand, and said, "That was very good, Miss, thank you."

The Baroness chuckled. "I'm pleased you enjoyed them, Meg."

The coach threaded its way through the city's crowded streets, with Jackson calling out to "make way" and urging the horse on. Twice hackney cabs pulled over to the side to afford them a clear passage, and each time the Baroness nodded and called, "Thank you," to the drivers, who responded with a slight inclination of the head and a salute with raised whips.

As the coach rattled and swerved through the bustle of people and vehicles, Meg was dazzled by the sheer scale of everything, the numbers, shapes and colours of shops and inns, the incessant noise from clattering horse shoes and rattling wheels, the calling of sellers of everything from cooked foods and fruit to newspapers and ribbons. She saw a black man, the first she had ever seen, in a handsome blue suit with white piping, opening the door of a coach similar to the Baroness's for a man wearing a long cape and carrying a sheaf of papers tied up with a red ribbon. She saw young – and some not so young – women in gaudy frocks calling out to male passersby, and realized they were prostitutes, like the several known to frequent the dock area of Whitehaven looking for sailor clients.

They soon left the clatter and crowded parts of the city, and for a good while travelled through countryside, lush meadows with cattle, and wooded areas. The yellow fog and its foul smells had thinned somewhat.

When finally they arrived in the part of London known as Highgate, Meg could only stare at the building before her: Holly Lodge, the Baroness's home. The word 'mansion' hardly did the building credit. *More like a palace*, Meg thought as she took in the massive structure with its canopies and decks and towering windows. It was set amid trees most of which Meg could not have named. There was an expanse of perfectly tended lawns and flower beds that were now a quilt of purple, white, and yellow crocuses. Other buildings, houses, sat apart in the grounds that stretched to surrounding high stone walls.

The Baroness led Meg through a set of massive double doors to a hallway that branched off into rooms and staircases, whose walls were filled with portraits mainly of men in military or formal business-like dress.

A woman wearing a black dress with vertical blue stripes, and with her hair carefully arranged in ringlets and held in place by a blue ribbon at the back, appeared and relieved the Baroness of her hat and outer coat and the fur hand-muff she had worn during the coach ride. Meg guessed the woman to be about Sarah Teasdale's age.

The Baroness had explained, as they travelled to Highgate that Meg, if she wished, could stay at Holly Lodge until arrangements were in place for her to continue her journey.

"You would be as well to stay here as in some rooming house in the city and search for employment. It will be several weeks before you leave for Dartmouth and the sea journey. Those details are still being arranged. You will be expected to do your share of some of the work at Holly Lodge, for which you will of course be paid the same wage as the rest of my staff, and it is a place where you will be safe until you leave."

Meg was registering the information and her thoughts were reflected on her face. The Baroness laughed softly. "It will be your choice, Meg – we are not kidnapping you! If you wish to make your own way and return in some weeks, that is up to you. However, if you do take up my offer, there is the guarantee that you will indeed be one of the women who will sail under the society's protection."

And that, after all, had been the purpose of coming here, hadn't it? She had found the people Sarah had told her to find, and she was not likely to have a better offer than this.

"Thank you, Mi—" she paused.

The Baroness finished the sentence for her. "'Miss' is perfectly all right, Meg," she said. "I believe I recognize the respect that attaches to it, and I am honoured. Besides," she added,

"'Milady' has a servile ring that I believe would not suit you, and too often I find it fawning, which is not an admirable trait."

They had reached an agreement without further discussion. Now, the Baroness said to the young woman with the ringlets, "This is Miss Tyson, Hannah. She prefers to be called Meg. She will join Nancy on the lower floor and once she has settled in, in a day or so, you may assign her the usual household duties."

To Meg, she explained, "It will not be easy work, but these will be the kind of duties that you will very likely find a need for when you arrive in Victoria, and which should help you find a position with a good family."

Meg thought of saying that she was no stranger to either hard work or household duties, but thought better of it.

The Baroness turned back to Hannah, whom Meg had correctly guessed held a housekeeping role.

"I believe Meg would benefit from a warm bath and a change of clothing, if you could see to that."

"Milady," Hannah said. The Baroness widened her eyes a fraction at Meg, and smiled.

"This way, Meg." Hannah said.

Meg was wondering who Nancy might be.

"First, your room," Hannah said, as they descended a flight of stairs into a corridor with several doors on each side. Hannah opened the second one on the right and signaled Meg to enter. The room held two beds, both made up and with flower-patterned coverlets. On the far wall were two windows that looked out onto Holly Lodge's grounds. The windows had curtains with patterns to match the bed covers. Beside each bed sat a small chest with two drawers, and on the wall across from the beds to Meg's right, were two plain wood wardrobes. Hannah indicated the bed furthest from the door. "You will sleep there, Meg," she added, indicating the room and its furnishings. "There are not many big houses where the maids are as comfortable as here. Now for that bath. This way."

She left the room and Meg followed her to the next door along the corridor. Hannah opened the door and Meg followed her in. A deep tub about six feet in length occupied the middle of the room. At one end of the tub were two taps. Beside the bath was a stool holding several folded towels.

Hannah touched one of the taps. "Hot," she said, and the other, "Cold." She turned the taps slightly and water trickled from each.

Meg had read in Sarah's newspapers of the luxury of hot and cold running water at the turn of a tap. She thought of the tin bath hanging on the back door at home, and the three taps in the lane that served all the houses on the row. Another world.

"The Baroness insists on personal cleanliness," Hannah said. "And while the water is running," she beckoned Meg to follow her once more into the corridor. She opened the next door along, into a much smaller room.

"The water closet," she said. A porcelain bowl-like structure with a curved wooden seat stood against the wall. A pipe led from the rear of the bowl several feet up to a metal tank, from which hung a length of chain with a handle attached. Hannah pulled on the chain and a gush of water rushed from the tank and into the porcelain bowl and ran away through the bottom section and disappeared.

Hannah looked a question at Meg, and said "Good" when Meg nodded that she understood what the equipment was for. Meg had read of the popularity the flush lavatory had gained since it was introduced to and used by the public at the Great Exhibition of 1851. The convenience had not yet reached Morthwaite.

Hannah left Meg to it. She used the lavatory, then returned to the other room where the bath had partly filled. She experimented with the two taps until the water was a comfortable temperature. She undressed, climbed in and settled herself. A small metal basket hanging from the side of the bath held a bar of smooth soap which smelled of violets, a difference from the coarse blocks of off-white stuff they used at home. This was how the well-off lived. No, this was how the well-off's servants lived!

The bathroom door crashed open. Meg instinctively crossed her arms over her chest and sank lower into the water. She realized that she could have and should have locked the door for privacy.

"Who the fuck are you?"

The demand was put by a skinny girl who stood in the open doorway and glared. She wore a floor-length black dress, white apron, high-necked white collar, and white cotton cap perched atop a blaze of chestnut hair tied back in a bun. Before Meg could respond, the housekeeper Hannah appeared behind the girl and took her by the shoulders.

"Get out, Nancy. And watch your mouth. You have been warned about that."

She pushed the girl out into the corridor, crossed to the bathtub and handed Meg a towel from the stool. "You should dry off now,

Meg, and get dressed. I've brought you some other clothes." She indicated a folded black frock on top of which sat a white cotton pinafore and white cap. "This is what all the maids wear."

She added, "That was Nancy. She can be a bit of a handful. She has the other bed in your room. And she will be going on the ship with you."

Meg got out of the bath, dried herself, and dressed in the clothing Hannah had left over her own clean set of underclothes. She smiled as she wondered what she would look like to anyone from Morthwaite who knew her as a screen lass in thick trousers, old coat and cloth cap. She left the bathroom and entered the bedroom. Nancy sat on the bed nearest the door, a truculence about her, as they examined each other.

Meg guessed that Nancy was a year or two her junior.

"I'm Meg. Meg Tyson," she said.

"A' know. She telt me." Then, "Y' should've shut the door. I could see y' tits when a' went in. I was on'y cummen in to clean, like. I mean, fuckin' 'ell – yon Hannah should've telt me y' were in there."

A mixture of defiance, justified complaint and grudging apology, Meg thought, and the initial hardness Meg had seen in the girl's face had faded some. She said, "I agree, she should have. And I should have locked the door. And you are Nancy."

A scowl. "Aye, Nancy Lowther."

"Where from?" Meg asked. "Not from London, not with that accent."

"No. Not bloody London." A pause. Then, "Around Manchester – outside of it – before I come south." Another pause, and progress: "What about you?"

Meg told her.

"Nivver 'erd of it."

"Not many have, I would think. It's that little. Just a spot on the moors."

"What did y' do there?"

"I was a screen lass, at a pit."

Nancy nodded. She looked at Meg's hands. "I know about them. Hard work."

"And all there was for lasses. What about you?"

The hardness was back, a defiance on Nancy's face and in her voice when she replied.

"I was on t' street."

And when Meg clearly did not immediately comprehend: "I was sellin' it. For money." She touched between her legs. "It was that or back to t' workhouse wid me mother, and I'd 'ad enough of 'er, and the bloke she took up wid – 'e didn't even give me money for it."

Good Christ!

"That Hannah stopped me in Covent Garden one day. I went there every day wid t'others from me room and took a pitch, y know, waiting for blokes wid money an' do them in a corner or a room they 'ad mebbe, or sometimes in a 'ansome cab, for the gents. But wid them it was a bit for the driver an' all, after them, for free. 'Bend over that seat an' drop your drawers.' Fuckin' idiots, why would we be wearing drawers – even if we 'ad any? Bastards. Then I 'ad to give me money to Charlie, he 'ad five of us going for 'im. Sometimes we got a tanner back, sometimes nowt, more likely a slappin' if we 'adn't made enough, but 'e would get us some bread and cheese. An a' course 'e always wanted 'is turn an' all."

Meg was trying to imagine the life the girl described, comparing it with warmth of family she had known and had to leave. She shuddered, started to say something, and stopped. What *could* she say?

Nancy continued. "Anyway, this one day I was talking to a bloke and arguing a price for what he wanted, which I didn't want to do, the dirty sod, but I was hungry…the last one had had his fuck and then took back the shilling he give me and bashed me. Anyway, Hannah told this one to piss off – I think Hannah might have been what she calls a spoiled dove 'erself, once. I think the Baroness collects them. Then she just grabbed me by the arm and said I was goin' wid her…an' she brought me 'ere. An' I'm glad she did."

Meg sifted through the images of the girl's life. Bloody hell!

She said. "So am I."

"Were you – did you? I mean after you came down to London?"

"No."

"But you have done it – mebbe not for money…"

"No."

"Nivver?"

Almost. Outside the welfare after a Saturday dance a year ago, Dougie Blair kissing her and Meg responding. His hands inside her frock stroking and raising her nipples, then one hand down inside

58

her underpants, Meg becoming wet, gasping, forgetting everything her mother had told her. Dougie Blair suddenly groaning, gasping, "Ah, fuck!" Spinning away, grabbing himself as he finished off in his best trousers. Meg finally collecting herself, realizing how close she might have come to cementing the kind of future she feared most.

"Not all the way."

"Bloody 'ell."

"A man tried."

"And?"

"I stopped him."

Nancy considered that, and smiled. "That's why you had to leave Mor – whatsit – your village?

"Yes."

"Christ, did you kill him? I 'ope you did!" Nancy's eyes shone.

"I don't think so, but yes, I hurt him." She described the episode with Benson, and how she had left.

"Fuckin' 'ell. Mebbe he died," Nancy said. "I 'ope so. The bastard. You're a bloody 'ero!"

Like an excited child.

"How old are you?" Meg asked.

"I'll be fifteen next birthday, in November."

"And how long were you—?"

"Two year." She looked down. "Mebbe a bit more."

Since she was about twelve, maybe younger. Poor little bugger.

She smiled. "Things will get better, Nancy."

Nancy's eyes filled for a moment, but she returned Meg's smile and said, "I fuckin' 'ope so, Meg."

Meg laughed.

Nancy watched Meg, then she said, "Can we be friends?"

The hard exterior had gone. Meg saw just a little girl in need.

"For as long as you want, pet."

She went to Nancy, put her arms about the girl and hugged her.

Chapter 6

The Baroness explained the society's plans to Meg and Nancy one evening after the two of them had helped clear away the remains and dishes from a dinner that Burdett-Coutts had hosted for a group of her friends. The Baroness had directed Meg and Nancy to a sofa opposite the plush wingback armchair she occupied. She showed them an advertisement in the *Times*. The steamship *Tynemouth,* under the command of Alfred Hellyer and bound for Victoria on Vancouver's Island, would leave London Docks on May 24, and take on passengers in Dartmouth four days later. The ship would make one stop at the Falkland Islands for coal and re-provisioning, and would call at San Francisco if required.

Meg read from the advertisement, "The accommodation for the several classes is of a superior description, the dietary scale liberal, and every means will be adapted to promote the comfort of the passengers."

She placed a finger on the passage and handed it to Nancy, who glanced at the page and gave it back to Meg.

The society would pay their fare. That was the agreement. Money had been donated for that purpose. Although Burdett-Coutts did not say so, much of that money was hers.

"The original idea came from a church man, Reverend Lundin Brown, in the Columbia gold fields. In its simplest terms, girls, his idea was to provide wives for the miners, men who resort to native women, and too often without the benefit of a church blessing.

"Add to that the fact that this country of ours has too many girls and young women without any prospects – we are told there are six hundred thousand more young women than men – and in danger of ending up in a dire condition, and you have the situation we face."

At a look on Meg's face, she added quickly, "No, you will not be required to marry a miner, or any man, unless you choose to. You will have the opportunity to work among decent people and for a decent wage in a new country. It will be up to you what you make of that opportunity."

It could have been Sarah speaking, Meg thought.

"I understand, Miss," she said.

"So do I… Miss," Nancy added, and smiled slyly at Meg.

The Baroness laughed softly.

"I am sure that you will both do very well," she said.

Meg and Nancy fell quickly into the routine and long hours of housekeeping under Hannah's often brisk but mostly kindly direction. The pair received eight shillings a week each and had Wednesday from noon and some Saturdays free, as well as their room and board. In their free time they travelled into London, taking one of the omnibuses that had a regular stop nearby.

On their first trip into the city Nancy said, "We'll go and see Jimmy," and Meg had her first taste of coffee, at a stall on Oxford Street, where they paid a ha'penny for a cup.

"Orright then, Nance?" said the portly man behind the table. He nodded to Meg, "Orright, darlin'?" Just a Londoner's rhetorical hello, and he gave each of them a ha'penny cake and a huge smile to go with the coffee.

Further down the street Meg pointed to two boys carrying baskets and picking up of the street what looked very much like…

"Dog shit," Nancy said. "They call it 'pure', don't ask me why, and them kids are pure-finders. They sell it to the tan-yards, summat t' do wid cleanin' leather, believe it or not."

Nancy always took the lead on their excursions.

"Christ, Meg, don't look at the men like that, they'll think you're on the fuckin' game!"

"I'm just curious. I've never seen so many people so dressed up. All these frocks and top hats."

At the same time Meg became acutely aware that despite the outward show, most of London's street population did not share Baroness Burdett-Coutts' preference for personal hygiene.

"You have to hold your breath when they get close."

Nancy laughed. "You should get whiff of them when they're *indoors,* and wid their pants off!"

She took Meg to her previous home, a ramshackle building on St. Giles High Street.

"They used to call it the Holy Land 'round 'ere. Cos of all the Irish, I was told. Wasn't much holy about it in our room. Charlie rented two beds, mattresses anyhow, for us on the floor an' that was it. We all piled in, lads an' lasses, young'uns that adn't been broke in yet – mind, that didn't last long – and t' rest of us. Mebbe six or seven at a time. Everybody doin' everybody else. Charlie's mate had a mattress in another corner, same thing there. It was mad."

Nancy led them to her old pitch at Covent Garden. It was early on a Saturday, always the market's busiest day, for girls and their clients as well as for the buyers and sellers of produce who packed the streets around the market from Long Acre and The Strand on one side and from Bedford Street to Bow Street on the other. Stacks of vegetables, cabbages, cauliflowers, broccoli, waited to be moved to stalls, and the flagstones underfoot were slippery and green from crushed leaves. Flower girls prepared their trays of violets, the flowers at this time of year coming from hot-houses or from the milder climes of the Scilly and Channel Islands or the south of France. Women with head-baskets loaded with apples from America, and red-faced with their efforts, pushed between towering hills of potatoes and turnips. At one corner a pony had gone to its knees under a load of imported oranges that had spilled over its haunches. At another, three boys at the bird-catcher's stall gazed and laughed at the fluttering caged larks and linnets. And everywhere, ragged street urchins shrieked and competed for bruised and fallen fruits which they grabbed from the road's filth and gobbled them down as fast as they picked them up.

In an open space Nancy was mobbed by groups of girls apparently delighted to see her again.

"Nance! How y' doin', girl? Look at you all done up an' clean. You found a bloke? Who's this one wiv y'? She chargin' top price, is she? "

To Meg the girl with the rattle of questions seemed as if she had enjoyed neither a wash nor a decent meal in recent days, but she had spared no excess in painting herself. Her mouth was a crimson slash, her gaunt face rouged and heavily powdered over. A paste filled the hollows where scabs from some disorder had formed and fallen away. *Her eyelids might have been rubbed with soot, like any screen lass after a long shift,* Meg thought. She and her mates were caricatures of the doxies that they saw dismounting from carriages and coaches on the Strand and in front of Drury Lane and the other theatres, the ones they envied and strove to emulate, the ones who practiced the same commerce as they did, but for golden guineas and even fine homes with their bastard offspring, instead of their own sad fares of shillings, tanners, and thruppenny bits.

Meg had never applied embellishment. Not in Morthwaite! Not unless you wanted a 'name.' She doubted that this made her any better than these poor little buggers. Just more fortunate in her parents and where she was born.

Nancy said, "Meg. She's my friend. We live at the Baroness's place."

"'course you fuckin' do, darlin.' An' me dad's the Queen's 'usband."

"Piss off, Sal, y'daft twat. I'm tellin' y' the truth. Meg an' me are waiting to go to thingamajig – Victoria – 'cross the sea. No more sucking dirty cocks for a bob a go f' me. Proper job when I get there, in a big 'ouse, wid wages an' everything."

A coarse laugh, and, "Whatever you say, Nance." But a wistful look at Nancy and her new friend as they departed.

Meg studied myriad street vendors.

"Fine pears, six a penny!" cried a boy of about eight years. "'ot chestnuts, ten a ha'penny!" from a tiny girl standing next to a bent-over man tending a portable brazier. Baked goods, writing paper, oysters and grapes. Boot laces, matches, and bonnets for four pence. The variety of goods for sale was endless and offered in a shouted babble of tongues by a jumble of races. Indians in long gowns and turbans offered spiced meats, and vied with weathered Irish women with oranges two for a penny, while the whole was overlaid by the sound of a bare-chested black man playing a violin and showing a card that said he was blind, and a kilted Highlander wailing on a set of bagpipes.

One day Hannah presented them with two tickets to the World Fair – "A gift from the Baroness."

They spent the day fascinated and astonished by a dizzying array of displays and attractions. Nancy laughed and pointed at one display, a pile of coal on a platform. "Mebbe from your spot, Morth…whatsit," she said. "Bloody coal, I ask y'!"

They walked closer. Meg pointed, "Look what it says though." The information read that the six tons of bituminous coal was from a place called Nanaimo. "It says, 'On Vancouver's Island!' Imagine that!"

Nancy said, "It's still only bloody coal."

One Saturday night as they reached a crowded Cleveland Street in the west of the city, Meg suddenly stopped.

"Look at that sign."

Nancy looked to where Meg pointed along a row of brightly lighted shops.

"There's all sorts of signs."

"The one that says 'Malin's – fried fish.'"

Nancy followed Meg across the street. Meg read from the printed sign in the window: "The finest fried fish, with fried chipped potatoes, five pence per portion."

Nancy said, "A family called Lees had a shop just like this when I lived in Oldham. Lees Fish and Chips, they called it."

"Are we hungry?" Meg laughed.

Five people were ahead of them in the shop where the smell of the fish dipped into a flour-and-water batter and dropped into a deep pan of boiling lard thickened the air.

"Luvvly, that is," Nancy said.

"Hello darlings, one each is it?" The man behind the counter smiled a welcome below his thick black mustache. "Very nice fresh haddock tonight."

He picked the pieces of crisp-battered fish from the smoking-hot lard with a wire basket, scooped up fried potato pieces from a small pile just cooked and deposited each portion on a square of newspaper laid on the counter.

"Salt and vinegar?" he asked.

"Yes, please," they said in unison.

Outside they opened the packages and ate with their fingers as they walked towards an omnibus stand.

"This is a new use for the *Daily Telegraph*," Meg said.

"The what?"

"The *Daily Telegraph*," She pointed to the newspaper. Her meal was wrapped in the front page of a copy from the previous week. Meg placed her finger where the name stood out boldly.

"Oh. Aye."

Meg was certain now of what she had suspected for some time. The name-cards they had been given for dinner settings at Holly Lodge were wildly misplaced, and Nancy was shrugging it off as a mistake; she was flipping through *David Copperfield,* but not stopping on any page; and shrugging off the information about coal from that place Nanaimo, at the Fair…

"It's nothing to be ashamed of, Nancy."

"What? What am I ashamed of?" Looking down the street, away from Meg.

"You can't read, can you?"

Nancy turned and glared. "So fuckin' what?"

"I didn't mean—"

"My arse you didn't! You mean I'm stupid. Not like you, miss fuckin' lah-de-dah wid y' Charles Dickens this and Charles Dickens that. An' laughin' behind me back all the time. Well fuck you *and* Charles fuckin' Dickens! I know when I'm not wanted. I'll go back to them as I don't give a fuck about readin'! Or writin'!"

She stormed away among the crowd of pedestrians, tossing her wrapped supper onto the street as she went.

"Nancy! I never thought anything like that! Come back! My own father can't read!"

Meg was stunned. She had had no idea that the girl, her friend, had been nursing such feelings. And there was a sudden and crippling guilt that her words had had such an effect.

Nancy had disappeared, her slight form taken easily into the swirling crowd. Meg rushed after her, but was buffeted and cursed at as she collided with bodies. It seemed as though half the population of London had suddenly conspired to place themselves between her and the fleeing girl.

She pushed her way on, still calling, "Nancy!" A scowling hulk of a man growled "cunt" at her and his shoulder connected hard with the side of her head. Meg staggered and went to her knees, scattering her fish and chips in the muddy road. She struggled to her feet and pushed her way to the side of a shop, where she leaned against the stone and caught her breath. She searched for Nancy, stretching to see over the hats and bonnets of those massed around her, but saw no sign. *Christ Almighty!*

"What's this, my dear?"

A woman, a motherly type, had stopped in front of Meg. She was of middle age, Meg guessed, and was dressed if not in expensive clothing, certainly in decent style and with a silk hat sporting a small feather. She fended off two scruffily dressed young men who had stopped to examine Meg and who clearly were the worse for drink.

"On your way, the pair of you," she said, and she raised a shiny black wood walking cane in their direction. "Or I'll call a policeman."

"What will you call him?" The one said, and he guffawed as his partner howled and slapped him on the back.

The woman raised her stick and swatted the wit on the leg. She looked behind them and called, "Officer!" Meg looked, but could see no policeman. Nevertheless the woman's cry was enough to see the louts off, muttering, "Old bitch," as they staggered away.

"Scum," the woman said. "Drunken scum. Disgrace to the city."

She placed a hand on Meg's arm. "My dear, you are shaking. What on earth has happened? Are you hurt?"

Meg smelled flowers as the stranger spoke, the scent from a nosegay of blooms fastened by a silver rose-shaped brooch to the woman's coat lapel.

Meg shook her head no. "I'm all right. It's my friend. We argued and she ran off and I'm worried for her."

"I think you need to sit down," the woman said. "Some tea, perhaps, or even a touch of brandy. You seem quite shaken."

"I'll be fine in a minute," Meg said. "But thank you."

"Well-mannered, too. Obviously from a good home. And where is that – your home?"

"A long way from here. But—"

"Yes, I can tell. I have travelled." She smiled. "I live on the next street. Come along, and we'll get you straightened out before you get on your way."

She took Meg by the arm and eased her away from the building.

There was movement beside Meg, and a familiar young voice.

"You mean you'll get her turned out. Fuckin' Lavender Lil," Nancy snapped. She raised her finger and shoved it towards the woman's face. "Piss off, you old cunt, and leave our Meg alone."

Nancy stepped between Meg and the woman, pushing the woman away.

'Our Meg.' That's family talk. Meg laughed.

"She smells nice," Nancy said. "But she's rotten behind the lavender. The old cunt has cribs all over the place and that's where she'd like to have you, right after her so-called 'brandy' – on yer back wid yer legs open for all the Fancy pigs that go to her spots. Leave you wid the clap and whatever else they've got, and 'er wid the profit."

"Nancy Lowther," the woman said. "Still the dirty-mouthed little slut that you always were."

"Fuck off, Lil."

And to Meg, "Let's go 'ome."

Nancy looped her arm through Meg's and pulled and turned them both away from the woman who was fuming but now silent.

"Can't leave you alone for a minute without you finding some sort of bother, can I? Some folk shouldn't be let out on their own. Bloody 'opeless, you are. Come on." She pushed back into the crowd along Cleveland Street. "There's a bus stop back there."

66

Relief flooded Meg's being. She stifled a laugh at Nancy's unique way of making amends, and she tightened the hold that their two linked arms had fashioned.

Nancy said as they made their way, "An' seeing as you're so fuckin' clever, you can teach me."

"Teach you?"

"To read."

"Right. I will. And you will start watching your mouth."

"Yes, Miss."

Their burst of laughter raised heads and brought smiles to those nearby.

***

Meg wrote letters home, making sure that the tone was positive:

'I have become good friends with Nancy Lowther, a girl younger than me, from Manchester. Nancy has had a hard life for her years, and I am glad to be her friend. She lives and works here at Holly Lodge with me, and we will be leaving together for Victoria when the time is right, which I believe will be quite soon.'

In early May her letter ended with, 'Today, Baroness Burdett-Coutts brought in a man with a camera and had him take photographs of me and Nancy. She has promised to send you one of these photographs, so you will be able to see for yourselves that I am getting along quite well. Also, it seems that we now have a date for when we will be leaving, which will be at the end of this month when we travel to the town of Dartmouth in Devon.'

The Baroness had told them of the company they would have on the *Tynemouth*.

"There will be many others with you. Our society will be supporting forty girls and women like yourselves. Another society has recently been formed, called the London Female Middle-Class Emigration Society—"

Nancy raised her eyebrows and made a comical face at the wordy title.

"—and there will be twenty of their members who will pay their own passage, or who may have been assisted but will sign an agreement to pay back the amount."

Not destined to be housemaids, Meg thought.

"As well as the sixty of you, the ship will carry an assortment of others who are emigrating, or even just visiting the colony."

On the day of their departure from Holly Lodge, the Baroness stood with them while the coachman Jackson readied his carriage which would deliver them to the train bound for Dartmouth.

The Baroness shook their hands, then gave each a quick hug before they mounted the carriage.

"Make your families proud," she said.

Nancy grimaced.

Meg said, "We will do our best, Miss."

Chapter 7

September 18, 1862.
Aboard the Tynemouth.
Dear Mam and Dad, Thomas, Matthew and Sarah,

I trust that you received the letter that I left to be sent on from the Falkland Islands where we broke our journey in August. Tomorrow we will leave the Tynemouth. It is said that positions with decent wages are being arranged for us as domestic servants in homes in Victoria, where the ship will anchor in the morning. At present we are in calm waters in Esquimalt Bay, which we reached yesterday, and where the Royal Navy has ships in and out. We understand that the city of Victoria is but a short sail from here, and only three miles by land. I am well, although each day there are moments I feel heavy-hearted when I think of you and what you and Dad and the lads are doing at the very moment...

It had been more than three months since the three-masted, steam-assisted sailing ship *Tynemouth,* after some delays, finally left Dartmouth on June 9. There had been moments from the very start that the three hundred souls aboard had wondered if they would see another day.

The closest Meg had been to any ship before this was when she had walked along the walls at Whitehaven harbour, and looked down on the tied-up fishing boats and coal carriers. The *Tynemouth* was much bigger than any of those, but seemed to have as much rust on and damage to its fittings as any of them. Perhaps that was just the way with ships after time at sea, she thought, as the tender brought them close to the ship.

Nancy had stayed at Meg's side since they left Holly Lodge, and she held on to Meg's arm during the brief trip to the *Tynemouth* through a heavy rain and a rising wind.

On board, they were directed to one of a row of third-class cabins within a roped-off area on the deck and under the ship's funnel, which already belched smoke and soot. The cabin, less than half the size of the room they had shared at Holly Lodge, held six bunk beds. When four other of the society's girls found their way to the cabin, it became a challenge for any of them to turn round when out of their bunks. Changes of clothing for night and daywear eventually were completed one-by-one by consensus.

Other cabins in the row, and still within the roped-off area, were occupied by independent fare-paying women and those of the London Female Middle Class Emigration Society. These had the relative luxury of travelling two to a cabin.

The last two cabins in the row went to The Rev. Richard William Scott and his wife, Harriet, and their two young daughters. Next to them were Mrs. Isabella Robb and her husband, James, and a son and two daughters. Mrs. Robb was designated chaperone to the single women.

"Chaperone?" Nancy said, after Mrs. Robb denied any of the women access to any part of the ship beyond their roped in area and given them a long list of what would and would not be permitted during the voyage, including a stern warning against fraternizing with any of the male passengers or members of the crew. "She's worse than a fuckin' workhouse matron."

Meg had come to recognize that Nancy's cursing was as natural to her as were his daily prayers to the Rev. Scott. Although she conceded that Nancy was making an effort, after she added "the old c—" and paused and made it "cow," in her critique of Mrs. Robb.

An hour after they had settled into their cabin, the ship shuddered, and sounded a series of blasts on its horn. She backed away from its moorage, and aimed its prow toward the English Channel.

Meg and Nancy hurried out onto the deck. As they watched the Devon shoreline recede and caught sight of the approaching open water and tossing whitecaps, Nancy moved close to Meg.

"Well, Meg Tyson, we've done it now, 'aven't we? Bloody 'ell."

Meg laughed. "Yes, we have, lass. No turning back." She added, "We'll be fine, Nancy."

"Aye. You an' me," Nancy said.

As she spoke, the ship felt the first thrust of a wind that appeared to have been poised, waiting for them to reach the Channel, and was relishing the fact that they had. Nancy gasped as the vessel rolled and righted itself and rolled again, competing with a rising swell for the right of way. Many others of the girls and young women who had ventured out onto the open deck, and who like Nancy and Meg were experiencing their first sea voyage, screamed and clung to each other as the ship was buffeted by consecutive waves, and the ever increasing wind howled in their faces and spattered them with spume. Suddenly, against the ocean's power, the *Tynemouth* did not seem as big as it had while sitting quietly at moorage. A small group of five or six people who had been standing at the ship's rail, outside of the women's roped-off area, turned and hurried toward an open hatchway and went from sight below deck level.

"Steerage passengers," Mrs. Robb said as she passed behind them. "Riff-raff."

As another wave challenged the ship and the *Tynemouth* rose to meet it then fell away and crashed into a trough, Meg saw two crew members, on the other side of the ropes, exchange a quick glance. One of them, a lad with blonde hair sweeping from under a black wool cap, caught Meg's eye. He winked and called, "You all right, sweetheart? Maybe we'll see you later, eh?"

He was about to say more when a wave bigger than any before slammed into the ship and poured onto the deck. Nancy screamed. The crewman's mouth opened in a shout that was lost in the storm, but he waved at the girls to get inside their cabin. Meg grabbed Nancy and shoved her towards their door as it crashed back and forth in the wind, which was now a gale.

The sound of splintering wood toward the front of the ship was accompanied by the bellowing of a cow that had been tied in a flimsy stall. The stall had collapsed as the cow skidded across the deck and crashed into the wooden frame. The ship lurched again and the cow was gone, over the rails and into the churning ocean. Several pigs that had been poorly contained on deck were loose and they slid around, squealing, until they too were washed overboard.

Meg shoved Nancy into the cabin and fought to close the door. She was relieved to see that the other four girls had stayed in the cabin. They were all younger than Meg, two of them no older than Nancy. All had been employed in Lancashire cotton mills before the supply of raw cotton from America had fallen due to that country's civil war. Mills had closed and the choice for these girls, as it had been for Nancy, was the workhouse, the streets, or where they were now – terrified and clinging to each other, but possibly with a future.

"Get onto your beds and hold tight," Meg ordered. Nancy went first and the others obeyed in quick fashion. This way, at

71

least, there was less danger of them being tossed around as the ship fought the storm. They stayed that way for half the night, until the wind gradually abated and the ship made headway into a calming sea.

Within a day the storm was behind them. The ship's complement began an uneasy routine, and Meg took charge of the cabin. It had not taken long for her to realize that the advertisement that she and Nancy had been shown from *The Times* had been less than candid, that the claim that 'accommodation for the several classes is of a superior description, the dietary scale liberal, and every means will be adapted to promote the comfort of the passengers,' was at best an overstatement.

Those in second class, which was the best level of service, there being no first class, were served meals in a dining room. This included the women from the London Female Middle Class Emigration Society in their two-to-a-cabin accommodation. The rest, including Meg and Nancy and their cabin mates, were third-class passengers. They were not served meals. Rather, Mrs. Robb each day collected carefully measured rations allotted for each meal. The girls would help prepare the makings which then were taken to an area on the foredeck, where a designated crew member would do the cooking. The other younger girls in their cabin were happy to be organized by Meg into a daily schedule.

The people below decks in steerage were much worse off, Meg realized, after meeting a few of the pale-faced women who had climbed up to take air at the ship's rails. They were doled out their rations in groups and told to get on with it, using fire pits and communal cooking pots.

The contact with the crew member cook would be as close as any of the sponsored girls and women from both societies would get to any males on the ship, other than the curate, during the time they were at sea. Mrs. Robb seemed not to need sleep as she patrolled the cordoned off area that was their world, and the Rev. Scott was ever present with prayers and admonitions.

In her letter Meg made no mention of the challenges the ship and passengers endured on the voyage, of the two mutinies by a short-handed crew over working conditions, in which the captain, Hellyer, was held over the rails and punched repeatedly by the mutineers before others of the crew, assisted by male passengers, rescued the situation, and saw the main culprits manacled and sent to the brig. She described the relief that all felt when after six weeks the ship arrived at the Falkland Islands, and they could see green fields and fresh running streams, but omitted mention of the anger and frustration they had felt when Mrs. Robb and Rev. Scott had denied permission for any of the women to go ashore, for fear they might be led astray. Any mention of those experiences would only have worried her mother and Sarah. And anyway the memories would fade. What mattered now was what lay ahead.

Chapter 8

"Behold, ladies. Your new home!"

Captain Alfred Hellyer made his announcement and spread his arms wide as Meg and the other women stared at the wharf in the inner harbour of the city of Victoria, on Vancouver's Island. The passengers had been told to prepare for disembarkation that morning, and the Royal Navy gunboat *Forward* was alongside waiting to deliver them to a smaller craft and thus ashore.

On the brief trip from Esquimalt Bay, the passengers had marveled at the closeness of the towering forests of cedar and fir and the scents that carried from them to the ship. Nancy had pointed to the top branches of one tall tree where a huge bird, with a chocolate-brown body, a pure white feathered head and a bright yellow hooked bill was perched, appearing to examine them. It took flight as they watched, soaring and displaying tail feathers as white as those on its head.

Meg had occasionally glimpsed a golden eagle in the sky over Morthwaite, but this bird was bigger.

"Sea eagle," a passing sailor said. "Some call it a bald eagle. And look there." He pointed to the beach where a doe and two yearling fawns browsed on low shrubs, oblivious to the passing ship.

Now they watched small boats crisscrossing the harbour, some driven by sail, others being rowed. Meg stared intently at two canoes occupied by dark-skinned men with long black hair. This was their first sight of native Indians, she realized. The canoes glided to a stop at the far side of the harbour. The dock was crammed with people, hundreds of them, curious, indeed many anxious, to see the new arrivals.

"They're all men," Nancy Lowther said, and giggled as she squeezed Meg around the waist. "Which one do you want, Meg? It's said you can have your pick."

Nancy was almost correct in assessing the crowd on the dock. The great majority were men, some in formal day clothes, others in rougher apparel, heavy work trousers and boots, and a variety of headgear from beaver hats to woolen caps. In one case a length of brilliant blue ribbon tied back a cascade of flame-red hair on a giant of a man in rough working clothes who waved his arms over his head and cried out, "Come on, my lovelies, come and get me!"

"Not that one!" Nancy laughed out loud and waved back at the crowd, and Meg laughed with her and with pleasure at her young friend's spirited recovery from the trials of a journey that had at times seemed would never end.

"Shush. Behave yourselves!" A voice from behind them. "What on earth do you expect people to think?" Mrs. Robb stood close to them by the ship's rail, attended by her husband and their three children.

Nancy turned to Mrs. Robb. "They can think what they like. An' you can bugger off. We're done with you. You can't tell us what to do anymore. We're here now."

One of the girls glanced at Meg, opened her eyes wide at Nancy's impudence, and grinned.

Mrs. Robb flushed and glared at Nancy, "Mark my words: You'll come to no good."

Meg said, "Leave her alone. She's right. We're out of your hands. We're on our own now."

Mrs. Robb sneered, "And you're no better." She stalked off.

Nancy stuck out her tongue and laughed.

Beyond the wharf, what they could see of the city of Victoria seemed to be mainly wooden buildings along muddy streets and a few plank boardwalks. Looking towards the dock and off to the right (*the west?* Meg thought) was an odd-looking structure that reminded her of a picture she had seen in Sarah's encyclopaedias of a Chinese...pagoda, that was it. Maybe a church or something.

"It's the birdcage." The sailor who had told them of the eagle. "That's what people call it anyway. It's the government offices, the legislature." He went off about his duties.

As their small boat reached the wharf, the crowd jostled for position. They closed in on the women, who were unsteady on their feet on firm ground for the first time in months, as they stepped ashore. Some of the bolder men reached out to touch them, but they were pushed back and given gruff warnings by six Victoria police constables, who were in blue uniforms similar to those of the Bobbies in London, and four young scarlet-coated Royal Marines who had been assigned the task of seeing the women safely ashore. Even so, the escort was unable to prevent the sudden leap from the crowd of the big red-haired man, a gold miner from the Cariboo, who had his eyes set on Sophie Jenkins, a slight, pretty 16-year-old girl from Birmingham who had been in the cabin next to Meg and Nancy.

The miner dropped to one knee in front of Sophie.

"Marry me and make me happy, my sweet," he said. He offered the astonished girl his right hand, which held a thick bundle of bank notes. "I have more of this and I will take care of you."

The crowd roared its approval. One of the Marines stepped in and tried to bring the miner to his feet, but the big man brushed him away and was cheered by the crowd, who pressed ever closer to the pair.

"I 'ope she says yes," Nancy said.

"I think she just did," Meg said beside her, as Sophie reached out, took the money from the huge work-hardened paw, examined it for a few seconds, then smiled and tucked it into a pocket on her shabby, worn dress. The crowd cleared a pathway and the triumphant miner and his wife-to-be left to a chorus of laughter and cheers. When the wedding took place, at the earliest that convention allowed, Sophie would wear a gown that the groom insisted cost no less than £400.

***

From the wharf, the girls and women from the *Tynemouth* were directed in pairs to an area where tubs of hot and cold water and a supply of soap awaited them. It was the first fresh water, other than for drinking, that they had seen for the duration of their journey. They had been restricted to sea water for washing of themselves and their clothing. The result had been garments caked in salt, which much of the time remained damp, and eruptions of boils on the body which had proven too much for many of the women who had simply stopped washing their clothing and, as became increasingly noticeable, themselves.

They attacked the washtubs with a zeal that delighted the male spectators who had followed their progress along the wharf and now were treated to displays of bared arms, shoulders and even thighs as the younger ones abandoned all cares of modesty, stripped off their outerwear and dumped the pieces in the tubs. They then proceeded to give themselves a thorough washing, dipping their hair into the luxury of soap and hot water and repeatedly rinsing while laughing and splashing each other from sheer joy.

Meg and Nancy joined in. Nancy tossed her soiled, salt-stiffened frock into a tub of hot water and leaned in over the side to soak her hair, and Meg followed suit. They soaped each other's hair, then filled buckets with the clear hot water and poured it over their heads to rinse. The male spectators cheered each move, and offered to help. The Royal Marines managed to keep them at bay.

They were told that until places had been found for them with local families they would be staying in a section of the nearby Marine Barracks already prepared for them, and they set out to walk there with the Marines escorting.

They had walked a short distance when Meg looked up at a cry, a mix of anger and pain, from the crude roadway off to their right. A heavily bearded, wild-haired man dressed in rough work clothes and high leather boots dragged a young woman at his side. His right arm was around her shoulders and neck, while he slapped her face with his left hand. The woman was Indian, her long, ink-black hair contained by a beaded head-band. She was dressed in an ankle-length garment of what appeared to be some kind of animal skin, and slipper-like hide shoes.

"Goddam stupid squaw," the man roared.

Meg and Nancy stopped and two girls bumped into them from behind.

The Indian woman yelled as the man continued dragging her along. She struggled to free herself and swung a fist towards his face, but he easily contained her again and pushed her along.

"Bloody hell!" Nancy cried.

Meg shouted, "Stop that! Let her go!"

The man stopped for a moment, looked at her in disbelief. He laughed and continued dragging the woman.

Christ Almighty!

Meg broke away from the line of girls and made towards the couple. The woman was bleeding from her nose and the flesh around one eye was swollen.

Meg spoke to the police constable closest to them as she moved.

"Stop him! Help her!"

The policeman pushed her roughly back into line.

"It's nobody's business but Sweeney's."

"Of course it's somebody's business! He can't do that to the woman." She tried to push past the policeman, but he kept a firm hold of her arm.

"She'll be with him by choice, for money or liquor," he said. "Move on."

Meg glared over at the man named Sweeney, who looked at her and laughed. The Indian woman had straightened up somewhat and she too was examining Meg. Meg smiled at her, raised her hands, sending a message to say – *This is wrong! I would help if I could.* The woman found a smile of sorts and nodded. Sweeney pushed her forward and they went from sight beyond the still jostling crowd.

The policeman's grip had tightened, and now he swung Meg around. "Get a move on," he snapped, and pushed her in the direction he indicated. Meg stumbled and almost fell.

Nancy grabbed the policeman's arm. "Take your fuckin hands off her!" She swung a punch, which he easily pushed aside and he grabbed her wrist.

"Little bitch," he muttered, and now he had a grasp on both girls, and appeared unsure of what to do next.

Meg pulled free and pushed the policeman away from her. The nearest Royal Marine, wearing the single stripe of a lance-corporal stepped into the fray.

"All right, Jim," the Marine said. "I think we're finished now. Let them get on."

"Let them get on? That little twat attacked me. She needs putting right."

By this time Sweeney and his woman were long gone. Meg and Nancy and the two in uniform were now the centre of attention, which the Marine decided they could do without.

"Let them go," he said. "They need to be moving on." He indicated the rest of the immigrant women who were now well on their way to the barracks. "And we need to—"

He was interrupted by a strident voice from the head of the line, "What is the holdup back there, you people?" Mrs. Robb.

"Piss off," Nancy muttered.

"That's enough from you!" The constable snarled.

"And you can as well," Nancy said.

The Marine stifled a laugh. "You really have to move on, girls," he said.

Meg glared at him. "We will. And thanks for your help with that lass! I'll bet your mother would be proud of you. And your sisters, if you have any."

Nancy chimed in, "Too bleedin' right! You big arsehole! All dressed up like a shilling dinner but useless!" And to the policeman, "And you're bloody worse!"

Meg laughed at Nancy's outburst.

The young marine blushed scarlet. "Look, I can't...I'm sorry...it's out of my hands."

"Bollocks," Nancy said, as they moved forward.

Chapter 9

They spent three days confined to the Marine Barracks. Mrs. Robb was still officially in charge, but gave Meg and Nancy a wide berth while the city prepared to receive the immigrants and help them with their new lives, which in most cases had meant entering domestic service.

A week after the *Tynemouth's* arrival, a notice in the city's *British Colonist* newspaper had advised that the new immigrant girls were available for interviews for employment in various roles. The Victoria Immigration Committee had recommended a wage of £25 or $120 per year, along with room and board, considerably more than what Meg and Nancy had been paid by the Baroness, although things generally were more expensive here.

The response from the wealthier of Victoria families had been immediate, and Meg had quickly recognized that she had bargaining power when she realized that there were more jobs than girls and women to fill them, especially as several of the sixty from the Columbia Immigration Society had chosen to make their own ways. A few had been offered marriage within weeks of arriving and had taken their chances. One was known to be in residence at a particular hotel on Broad Street, one of the city's several licensed 'dance halls,' which were in all but name brothels and, given the vastly disproportionate number of men to women in the colony, tolerated as such.

Meg had insisted that she and Nancy be hired together.

The first to offer them work was Mrs. Elizabeth Stubbings, a mother of four children aged from two to eight, who had said she would pay more than the recommended wage: $130 a year.

Nancy at first was all for taking it – "It's going to be scrubbing and polishing and wiping bums and snotty noses, doesn't matter where, does it?" – until it was clear that Mrs. Stubbings wanted the pair of them for that price.

"The wage is for a *position*," she insisted. "Not a person."

Nancy was quick, "Well, missus, we are together but we are *not* a position." Her response left Meg with no need to say anything, and Mrs. Stubbings affronted at the young commoner's insolence.

Mrs. Stubbings had affected to save face by looking deliberately down at Meg's hands, at the barely faded bruising and cuts. "Perhaps it would not have been for the best anyway," she said. "Standards, after all."

As she turned and stalked away, Nancy said, "Aye, we have them an' all." She stuck her tongue out at the departing well-dressed back, and added quietly, "Fuckin' cow."

Immediately afterwards they reached an agreement with Mrs. Louisa Campbell, a tiny black-haired, blue-eyed woman, with a ready smile and a soft Scottish voice, who hired them as individuals, on the $120 each rate, and it had gone well. Her husband Bruce Campbell was a Highland Scot, a giant of a man with untamed fiery red hair and beard, who worked for the British Bank of North America, was part-owner of two of the clothing and furniture stores in Victoria, and a Member of the Legislative Council. Meg guessed that the couple were in their early forties.

With the Campbell's five young children in the large four bedroom house on the eastern end of Johnson Street, it was hard enough work. Up before 6 a.m. to clean and set fireplaces, and start preparing breakfasts, cleaning and dusting the house from cellar to ceilings, making up the grocery lists and doing the shopping, helping make lunches and dinner and cleaning up afterwards. On Mondays were the most demanding of their chores – laundry, the frequent and uninhibited characterization of which by Nancy had persuaded Mrs. Campbell it was best to be away from the tubs and mangle until all was dried, wrung, and folded. Other than that, Louisa Campbell did a good share of the work alongside them. A week ago she had said, "I would prefer it if you would call me 'Louisa,' Meg. You are almost a grown woman, and while there are some people who pretend it to be, this is not Britain. We will always be British, of course, but somewhat different."

The money was sufficient and Meg spent little. Also, she had plans, which she shared with Nancy in the spring of the following year, 1863.

"I am not going to be a housemaid for the rest of my life, Nancy."

'A man's reach should exceed his grasp... And so should a woman's, Meg.'

'It is an opportunity for Meg to build a new life.'

Meg had been reminded of Sarah's words when a letter arrived in April.

January 15, 1863

My dearest Meg:

I write this in the hope that life is being good to you, and in response to your letter that you wrote while you were on board the Tynemouth and which we received in time for Christmas. We were thrilled to learn of your safe arrival in Victoria.

We had earlier received the photograph sent by Baroness Burdett-Coutts. What a fine pair you and your friend Nancy make!

The letter went on to say that life did not change much in Morthwaite, that Sarah had not yet found another pupil the likes of Meg Tyson – nor did she expect to again! She said she would be visiting her mother and siblings in Suffolk in the summer, when her brother Francis, the youngest, would be preparing to leave home to attend Oxford University, with – and thank the Lord for wealthy relatives! – the assistance of his aunt and uncle. He had decided he wanted to study divinity and follow his father's path into a life in the church.

(In which, she thought but did not write, she hoped he would fare better than our father – who art surely NOT in heaven, and hoped that none of the Rev. Samuel Teasdale's habits would be inherited by his son.)

The letter included a note from Meg's mother, sending her love, and that of her father and brothers and saying that everyone was well. She noted that Thomas, the younger of Meg's brothers, had begun to follow in his brother Mathew's ways and had won some contests in the booths at both Whitehaven and Workington fair grounds in the autumn.

'He wonders if you have any prize fighters in Victoria – or if you need any!'

Meg had laughed aloud as she imagined young Thomas climbing into the boxing ring, and the good mood stayed with her.

Sarah had added that Sandy Benson, on the now rare occasions that he was seen near the village, wore a black leather patch over his left eye and barely spoke to anyone. Meg put him out of her mind.

"Then I'm not always going to be a house maid either." Nancy said. And after a long pause, "So what *are* we going to do?"

Meg had arrived at that decision on the day that she saw the Indian girl for the second time.

"Meg, the Songhees girl Martha is at the back door with some salmon. She has just begun supplying us. Could you fetch it please?" Louisa Campbell had asked.

When Meg opened the door it took her a few seconds to recognize Martha as the one whom she had last seen being dragged along the street by the scruffy, bullying Sweeney. Today she wore a deer-hide skirt and tunic, each with various-shaped designs coloured crimson and black, and moccasins on her feet. Her ink-black hair was in a single braid tied with a thin strip of leather, decorated with bright blue and red beads.

Martha smiled, a bright, full smile of sudden recognition even after the months since Meg had shown her sympathy. Looking at her, Meg realized that Martha was in fact not much older than herself, if at all. She carried a woven willow twig basket filled with an assortment of fish, some plump Pacific salmon for which Mrs. Campbell paid twenty-five cents each, and several varieties of cod and snapper. It were these that planted the idea.

Martha had rudimentary English and assured Meg that she would be back again the following week with more salmon.

Martha bore none of the bruises that Meg had seen that first day, and she seemed pleased that Meg was interested in where she lived, which was in the Songhees village on the far side of the harbour. Meg took a bold next step.

"Sweeney?"

Martha's smile fell away and she looked at the ground.

"Sorry," Meg said. "Not my business, I know."

Martha looked up. "Is all right, Miss. Sweeney go for gold. Come back to start new winter." She added, "He good when not drinking."

Meg knew by now that male population of Victoria fluctuated with the seasons. During the winter the city bustled and rang with the presence of hundreds of miners who had returned from the deep snows and bitter cold of the gold diggings in the Cariboo region of the mainland colony of British Columbia. With the arrival of spring, they would return to the gold fields, full of hope and dreams of riches. A local man named Billy Barker, another immigrant from England, was among them, and was celebrated for having made a huge strike the previous year and become instantly wealthy at the time that Meg was still on the *Tynemouth*. She had read recently in the *British Colonist* newspaper that a new town was being built near where Barker had made his fortune and that it was thought it would be named for him.

Meg decided to say no more about Sweeney.

As she reached out to take the fish from Martha, she dropped the tea cloth she had been carrying and which had mostly covered her hands. The Indian girl frowned at the dark scars and the few cut-ridges that remained. She reached out and touched Meg's hands and murmured something in her own tongue. She smiled and patted both hands, as if comforting a child. As she walked away from the house, Martha quietly hummed part of a tune that Meg knew was familiar, but couldn't quite place and which soon faded and left her thoughts as she concentrated on preparing the salmon.

Later she mentioned to Louise Campbell that Martha's appearance differed from the other Songhees women – and many children – she saw around Victoria.

"Yes, she's not a flathead. Possibly brought up somewhere else, where they don't do it." She frowned. "I do not really know *why* they do it. Apparently it is to be admired it, but I can only wonder, by whom? Imagine, pressing the baby's head flat with a piece of board strapped to his forehead and making it tighter as the child grows." She sighed, "Things are different here, Meg."

***

In response to Nancy's query of "So what *are* we going to do?" Meg took that day's copy of the *Colonist,* which carried reports of world events: the war in America between the Federals and the Confederates, the marriage in London the previous month of the Prince of Wales and Her Royal Highness Princess Alexandra of Denmark. She read that item out to Nancy and was about to continue when Nancy said, "Wait a minute. That was on'y a month since, y' said?' Meg nodded. "Well it took us three months to get here and it takes that long for letters, so how does Mr. – what's 'is name – know about that for his newspaper? Do they 'ave pigeons? I know they used them in that war, to send messages."

Meg had asked the same question earlier of Bruce Campbell who said, "Fast ship across the Atlantic to New York, telegraph to San Francisco, four days to here. De Cosmos tells me that plans are being prepared for the extension of telegraph lines from San Francisco to New Westminster in the next year or so. Imagine that – one day something occurs in London, little more than a week later he has it on his news pages."

Meg imagined letters moving as quickly.

"And before too long there will be a working telegraph cable under the Atlantic and everything will be a matter of hours," Campbell said. "Our world is shrinking. Imagine the effect on business – on everything – with information so quickly available!" He described the first attempt to lay a sub-Atlantic cable, five years earlier, a venture which had succeeded. "But it worked for only three weeks, before the cable broke. They will succeed eventually."

She gave the explanation to Nancy, who shook her head and said, "Bloody 'ell. Fancy that."

Alongside the international news in the *Colonist* were columns of advertisement for various businesses, from hotels, banks and a butcher, to liquor and ale vendors, to boot and shoes stores. Everything a small but growing city could wish for.

Or, almost everything.

"Tell me what you don't see among the advertisements."

Nancy stared at the front page, which was all columns of businesses advertisements. She moved her finger slowly up and down and across the page as she read, sounding each word quietly. Meg had taken Nancy up on the matter of teaching her to read. They had had plenty of time during the three-plus months aboard the *Tynemouth,* and Nancy had proven to be a quick and industrious learner. While she had some way to go to full proficiency, she was able to make her way through most of the parts of the newspaper that interested her, and in her spare time, she was progressing through the Campbell children's library of titles such as the *Mother Goose* nursery rhymes, the stories of *Cinderella* and *Little Red Riding Hood* and most recently, along with the two older children, the twelve-year-old twins Ethan and Amelia, the story of *Robinson Crusoe* – ("There's lots of big words but we want to find out what 'appens to him. 'Es 'avin' all kinds of problems, wid 'is raft, like.")

"What I *don't* see?"

"Where can you go for a quick meal?"

Nancy checked the columns and read the names of places offering dining. The Washington Restaurant Coffee Saloon. The London Coffee House and Luncheon Bar. The St. James Luncheons and Dinners. The St. George Hotel…they went on.

"All sorts of places," Nancy concluded.

"All sorts of *sit-down* places," Meg replied. "Where can you get, say, fish and chips, to carry away?"

Nancy paused. Then, "Bloody 'ell, Meg!"

Chapter 10

Meg stopped on the sidewalk before a small wooden building, not much more than a shack, which sat between two much bigger buildings on Wharf Street south of the intersection with Bastion Street. One of the other structures was the towering Hudson's Bay Company retail store, and adjoining it a ship's chandlers. On the waterfront side of the street a clutter of ramshackle sheds clung to the small rise of land above the harbour, some of them appearing undecided about remaining or falling in.

The Hudson's Bay store dominated Wharf Street, in the way that the company, as Meg had learned, had dominated much of the trade in the Pacific Northwest for the past several decades. This she had learned from Mr. Campbell, who insisted that the new girls should know something of the history of the place they now called home. "You are going to be part of the future of this new land. You are going to be the citizens who will help determine that future. And you will become the mothers of those who will continue to grow and build this new country." Mr. Campbell had given the girls tests after his history lessons.

Nancy had rolled her eyes at the 'mothers' prophecy, but Meg listened carefully to Mr. Campbell and felt that there was sense in what he said.

Bruce Campbell had been employed by the company before joining the bank. He was a friend of Sir James Douglas, now the governor of both separate colonies of Vancouver Island and British Columbia. Douglas had been a fur trader for the Hudson's Bay Company and ultimately its chief factor, the highest rank in the company's field service. It was he who had selected the site for and ordered the construction of Fort Victoria, twenty years before the *Tynemouth* and its passengers arrived.

Where Meg stood now the streets had plank sidewalks, a feature still awaited in most of the rest of the city where at this time of the year the streets were largely dust. When the autumn rains started, and for months to follow, they would be deep in mud and stinking with run-off sewage from houses and taverns and the leavings of horses and cattle. Many of the latter would be bound for the slaughterhouse on Wharf Street owned by the city's mayor Thomas Harris, an Englishman and former gold-seeker who the previous year, when Victoria was incorporated as a city, had been elected its first mayor by a show of hands in the yard of the police barracks. Harris bragged of his weight which was said to be more than three hundred pounds, a bulk almost matching that of some of the bovines that came to meet their ends at his place of business. Victorians had been amused by newspaper reports of that same bulk causing the mayor's chair to collapse in pieces when he first lowered himself onto it. Harris also owned and ran a butcher shop, and Meg had his businesses in mind in connection with her own plans.

They city had grown in the past year. Meg had read in the recently published *British Columbia and Victoria Guide and Directory* that the population now sat at an estimated six thousand, and that investors and business people were arriving daily from around the world. And the location where she now stood was one of the city's busiest areas, with ships crews coming and going and waterfront labourers busy all day, as well as Royal Marines and sailors travelling back and forth from the flourishing Royal Navy port at Esquimalt three miles away. For many of the men the first stop was at any of the several drinking establishments within a block or two of the harbour. *Indeed*, Meg thought, there seemed to be more inns and public houses than any other single type of business in the city. Along Government Street alone were the Australia Hotel, The John Bull Hotel, The Brown Jug Saloon, and at least three more. Johnson Street had three drinking establishments, Yates Street had six, and there was Steele's Saloon on Bastion Street. Near these places was the right place for Meg to set up her venture, if she could make it happen.

The shack's narrow front and siding were of rough cedar planks. The whole front could not have been more than seven feet across including the door. Meg thought that from what she had learned, this might be to her advantage. One small window was set in the wall next to the door. A large neatly lettered notice on a square of white card pinned to the door announced 'Property to Let or Sell. For details see next door.' A neatly drawn arrow pointed to the Hudson's Bay Store, a five-storey red-brick structure. It was one of the few brick buildings in the city where most were wood-framed and fronted, a legacy of the rush of construction that had been prompted by the gold rush of five years earlier.

The notice had been there more than a week. Meg had passed the place on her walks around the city – leisurely walks which took in the whole of the city in less than an hour – in the months since she had told Nancy of her plans. Now it was early August and time to put those plans to work if she was to meet the deadline she had set for herself. It was late evening and the Hudson's Bay store was in darkness. She would ask Louisa Campbell for an hour away from her duties the next day and come down to ask about the cost of renting the shed. As she considered this, the front door of the Hudson's Bay store opened and a man whom she recognized stepped out. His dark brown hair was long under a tweed cap. He wore a neatly trimmed goatee and he was smartly dressed in narrow black trousers and a well-cut jacket over an embroidered silk waistcoat. His black leather shoes were highly polished. Meg guessed he was in his mid-twenties. He closed and locked the door behind him and started along the sidewalk. After a few steps he noticed Meg, and stopped.

"Good evening, Miss."

Meg returned the greeting and turned to leave.

"You are the Campbell's maid, aren't you?"

Meg turned back. "Yes, I am."

"And they think highly of you, I know. I have visited their home."

Meg said, "Yes, I have seen you there."

That was a few weeks previously when Mr. Campbell had held a meeting with other businessmen and the subject had been property values in and around the city. Meg had served the men drinks and food as they talked and smoked their pipes and cigars. Mr. Campbell had laughed at one point and said, "Remember those lot prices before 'Fifty-eight? You couldn't get five-hundred dollars for them. Then the rush happened and what did they go to – three thousand and more!"

This young man was the one who had said, "And aren't you glad you held on to yours at the time, Bruce?" which sparked general laughter. He had the same Scots burr as Mrs. Campbell in his voice.

Meg knew from her "history lesson time, ladies" with Mr. Campbell that the reference to 'Fifty-eight' was that of the gold rush that year on the Fraser River in British Columbia. Would-be miners had arrived in hoards in Victoria from all over the world, and especially from San Francisco. Victoria was the starting-off point in their search for riches and the city's population had exploded from its barely one thousand permanent residents to a mainly tent city of upwards of twenty thousand almost overnight. The new temporary arrivals had needed clothing, supplies and accommodation before they crossed the Strait of Georgia for the sand bars and canyons of the Fraser River. Victoria's citizens and businesses had profited.

Now there was the new gold rush, in British Columbia's Cariboo area. More people again were using Victoria as a starting point. Meg wondered if indeed the same thing was happening to drive up prices, and if the shack might be part of it.

"You were working late," Meg said.

"You know how it is – no rest for the wicked." He laughed as he spoke. Then, "I'm sorry, my name is Munro. Alan Munro. And you…"

"Meg Tyson."

"Happy to meet you, Meg Tyson." Something a little forward, a little bit cheeky, in the way he said it, Meg thought, but she liked the smile that came with it.

Nearby a door crashed open at one of the taverns nearby and a deep rich voice sang, *"O, my love is like a red, red rose that's newly sprung in June…"*

"O my love is like the melody that's sweetly played in tune…"

"Ah, another lost laddie," Munro laughed.

The song died and was replaced by a loud burst of laughter, among it a girlish shriek, followed by a torrent of profanity as the laughter stopped. The door slammed shut and there was quiet.

Munro said, "I am going in your direction. Perhaps I could walk with you."

He was acknowledging that this was after all one of the rougher parts of Victoria, especially when the drinkers began leaving the taverns, under their own steam or with assistance.

Meg recognized his gesture and was glad of it. "Yes, that would be fine," she said. She pointed to the sign on the shack door. "I am interested in that. Who would I speak to about the rent?"

Munro looked at her, curiosity on his face.

"Does Mr. Campbell wish to know? I would have thought that he would have—"

"No, not Mr. Campbell – me. *I* want to know."

"Good Lord."

Meg waited.

Alan Munro realized that the young woman was serious.

"I'm sorry…what do you…?"

"I'm going to open a business – a fried fish and chipped potato shop. Fish and chips. Good cheap food to be bought and carried away, eat it as you go if you wish. We did that in London. The meal was wrapped up in a sheet of newspaper. *The Daily Telegraph,* in fact. It was cheap and simple. And very tasty."

"Good Lord."

"The food, I mean, was tasty." She felt herself blushing. As if she could have meant the…oh, for heaven's sake!

Munro laughed, enjoying the moment.

"I'm sure it was," he said. "The food that is."

Then, "Sorry," he said, with a grin. "I couldn't resist it."

Meg laughed, and relaxed in the young man's company.

She said, "I have not told the Campbells about this yet. I was waiting to find a place. I will of course talk to them, if…when…"

Munro said solemnly, "I am sworn to secrecy." He placed a hand over his heart.

Meg laughed. "Thank you. So who is it I ask about the price?"

Munro gave a mock bow. "You are speaking with him this very minute. I am chief trader and in charge of some of the company's property management, and this happens to be part of it."

Meg pointed to the sign. "It seems to have been there for some time," she said.

Munro chuckled. "It seems that we are negotiating already! Very astute, Miss Tyson."

"It's 'Meg'," she smiled. "We are not in England anymore."

Munro nodded. "Very well, Meg. And please call me Alan. You are correct in thinking there has been no stampede to rent the place. It is very small after all, and narrow, perhaps too small for…but then I'm not to say…" Then, "Would you care to see the inside?"

Meg hesitated. The night was drawing in. There was one gas lamp that had just come on at the end of the street near the front gate of the old fort, one of just a few of the new lamps in the city, but the rest of the area was in deep shadow. She was alone with a man she did not know, other than that he was a friend of the Campbells.

Alan Munro read her hesitation. "Perhaps another time."

She dismissed unwanted images. "No, I would be happy to look at it now. 'She who hesitates…' you know?"

"Right then, just a moment." He turned and re-entered the store and soon returned with several keys on a wire ring.

He selected a key. "This one," he said.

Munro had to push the door hard before it moved slightly, then stopped. He put his shoulder to it. The door creaked and a gap opened near the top. Meg helped by giving the bottom a sharp kick. The door flew open and banged against the wall inside.

The air was musty and a pile of sacking lay up against the far wall, which Meg estimated was a good fourteen feet from the door, which made the room while narrow as Munro had said, certainly deep enough to...*if she had the cooking area on the wall to her right, with a counter in front, which might take up five feet or so of the available space and that would leave plenty of room for access from the outside, and customers would not be staying around anyway because it would be like the one in London, Malin's, where you were served and you left with your supper...yes, this could certainly work!*

"Potatoes." Munro said, bringing her back. "I mean, that's what the bags held. Perhaps a good omen," he added and they both laughed.

"What would you need to get the place ready?"

Meg started to reply, again envisioning an area for preparing the fish, for dipping them in batter – a pot, no, two pots big enough for frying both the fish and the potato chips...a serving counter. But first:

"I would need first to know what the rent would be and if I could afford it."

"Yes, well, let me see." He nodded his head now and again, as though calculating. "Hmmmnn..."

"Now who's negotiating? You must have a figure in mind, after all this time."

Meg had read in the *British Colonist* that monthly rent in the increasingly busy commercial area, which included Wharf Street, was from two to six dollars a frontage foot. Even the lowest number, which would mean fourteen dollars, would not be easily done. But the small shack was hardly a prime structure, as evidenced by the lack of interest in it so far.

Munro laughed again. "Touché. And yes, I do. I believe the company would be happy with, shall we say, seven dollars a month?" A bargain, by the newspaper reports.

It was just three dollars a month less than the wage she had started on at the Campbells almost a year ago. In the summer, an appreciative Louisa Campbell had increased that by one dollar, to eleven, for both Meg and Nancy. If she agreed to Munro's proposal, she would be left with four dollars a month and still there would be supplies and fittings to buy and work to be done on preparing the place, but she still had the three sovereigns from Sarah, and she had been saving most of her wages. In all, she counted that she had almost two hundred dollars. It would take most of that to get set up and, to be safe, pay for perhaps the first three month's rent. Then she would have to rely on profit to stay in business, but wasn't that exactly what she had been aiming for? And wasn't this her chance to do it?

Meg went over to the pile of sacks, kicked them and watched dust rise and a cat-sized, red-eyed rat emerge. It left tracks in a thick layer of dust as it scuttled to the open door.

"Ugh! My goodness!" Meg stepped back quickly and hiked her dress up over her shoes. Meg Tyson, who had kicked aside more rats on the pit-top at Morthwaite than she had put shifts in there. "Nasty things!"

After a few seconds Munro laughed, then offered an exaggerated sigh, one of capitulation. "Very well, Meg – seven dollars, with the first month complimentary because of a vermin outbreak? And we'll take care of that."

Meg took another look around the space, visualizing what could go where, seeing a line of customers at her counter. *Her* counter!

"Agreed," she said, and immediately felt both a lifting of spirit and a flutter of trepidation.

Munro reached out a hand and for a second Meg was flustered, until she realized that he was offering to seal the agreement like a gentleman.

They shook hands, with Munro clasping Meg's palm a little more tightly and for a little longer than a simple business deal might have warranted. Meg withdrew her hand.

"I will draw up a contract tomorrow, if that is suitable," Munro said. "It will be a simple agreement stating the use of the premises and the rent to be paid on the first of each month."

"Starting on the second month," Meg said.

"Of course!"

They turned and began walking in the direction of Johnson Street and the Campbell home.

A door banged open from a place on Bastion Street behind them, and another soulful Caledonian soloist offered,

Oh, ye'll tak' the high road, and I'll tak' the low road,
And I'll get to Scotland afore ye;

But me and my true love will never meet again
On the bonnie, bonnie banks o' Loch Lomond.
The place was a second Scotland!

She let him take her arm as they came to the end of the wooden sidewalk and stepped down on to the street. She released his hold as they continued walking.

Chapter 11

Meg announced her plans the next day.

Bruce Campbell met her news first with a surprised start, but then quickly with a smile and, "That is wonderful, Meg. That is the kind of spirit we need in this country, in this city."

Louisa Campbell was not so enthusiastic.

"But Meg, what will we do without you here? You see to so much—"

"I have thought about that," Meg said. "Until I open my business, I can still be here and do what needs to be done in the morning. Nancy for the moment will still be here all day."

Louisa Campbell did not lose her frown – nor her husband his encouraging smile.

A fierce look from Nancy prompted Meg to add, "Although, if the business succeeds, she will be my partner, and in time it is likely that we both will be occupied with the shop on a full-time basis." She also added, "I would not expect to be paid, of course. But for the morning work that I do, I would like to be able to keep my room."

Bruce Campbell smiled even more as he listened to Meg's confident plans, though his eyebrows rose slightly in surprise when Meg made her next suggestion, "I think that Martha would be an excellent replacement for me, especially at the start. She could be here at around the noon hour, which is when I would leave."

"Martha? The Indian?" said Louisa Campbell.

"I have already asked her about it. She would be happy to do it – and she would not be the first Indian to work in a white household."

"That is true," Bruce Campbell said. "Two or three of the new people have employed native women, inside and outside the home, and I have heard of no problems with them. In fact, the opposite. They are reliable workers, I understand, and are particularly good with children."

Meg said to Louisa Campbell, "She would not need to live in, of course."

"But remember also," Bruce Campbell said, "Helen is making plans to join us."

He explained to Meg, "Our niece in New York. My brother's daughter. She writes that she wishes to experience life on what she calls the western frontier and wants dearly to meet her young cousins and spend time with them. She will have taken the train across the Panama Isthmus, then steamer to San Francisco, and on here. She should arrive quite soon."

Louisa Campbell said, "Well..."

Nancy said, "I would help Martha to get started, get to know our routine."

Meg smiled her thanks to Nancy.

Bruce Campbell, clearly in favour, said, "My dear...?"

Louisa Campbell looked at the three faces. Finally she smiled. "Very well, we will give this a try. But if it does not work out..."

"Of course," her husband said, then, "Do you have a particular time in mind for opening your, ah, venture, Meg?"

"My fish and chip shop. Yes, I have."

***

Bruce Campbell had been correct when he said that the Hudson's Bay store probably would have most of what Meg needed. And Alan Munro was there to help. He first invited Meg into a small office behind the main counter. He had the rental agreement prepared and Meg quickly read and signed the simple one-paragraph document.

Meg looked around the Hudson's Bay shop, properly called the sales room, and wondered, as she had on previous visits to buy items for the Campbell home, at the vastness of the place and the range of goods available.

There was no attempt at ornament or decoration. The ceiling was simply the exposed joists and flooring of the second floor above. The roughly squared fir joists were studded with nails and hooks, from which hung various articles of trade. Along the side walls were box shelves that appeared to be a good two feet deep. The floor was piled with bales of various goods, some of which could only be guessed at. All of this was behind a counter which ran the length of the room. A small area was railed off near the door, large enough to hold perhaps twenty standing customers, the practice being that when that area was filled, remaining patrons must wait on the street until it was their turn to be served. At least two clerks usually would be on duty to serve those inside.

Meg had a good idea of what she needed. She described the shop arrangement that she envisioned and Munro led her through the store.

They passed deep shelves stacked with bolts of coloured cloth, others displaying footwear of all kinds from heavy work boots to children's shoes. A box of kid gloves sat below a display of ladies' bonnets. There was tea, sugar, calico, ammunition, fishing gear, blankets, and a thick kind of cloth called duffel. A section of the ground floor was devoted to saddles, bridles, and work-horse collars. Tools and utensils of all kinds hung from the walls and sat in boxes – scissors, scythes, spoons and spades. Stacks of various folded tartans declared their Scottish clan affiliations. Another area was devoted to marine goods – ships' cordage, oakum, and pitch and pieces of shaped iron. The goods collectively created a potpourri of scents that blended into…what, exactly? Meg wondered.

Alan Munro smiled as he watched Meg, her head lifted, her nose slightly wrinkled as she turned here and there.

"History," he said.

Meg turned to him. "Pardon?"

"That scent," he said. "The aroma. The best I can do is to say that you are smelling history. Some of it already made, and I would say, more of it in the making."

Meg smiled, nodded. "Yes…I think I understand."

He next stopped before a section where several items hung by chains from hooks sunk into the joists. He read from a written list he picked off a nearby shelf.

"Cast iron pots – eight, twelve, fourteen, or sixteen gallons."

To Meg they looked very much in shape like the set-pots that Morthwaite families used for the Monday washing and sheep's-head broth. They were just what she needed.

She imagined the size that would meet her needs – one for the fish, one for the potatoes.

"I believe the fourteen gallon size would do. Two of them. What price?"

Munro checked the paper again.

"Five dollars each, but four dollars and fifty cents as a discount for regular customers. When you buy the sawn planks you will need for your counter, you will qualify."

Meg thought that the regular customer price, perhaps, was a recent arrangement, as in just now and for her, but she was not about to ask.

She said, "I also need something smaller, for holding the batter for dipping the fish into."

Munro looked around, then pointed into the corner. "Kettles," he said. "Old fur traders' kettles."

Two objects, large iron bowl-shaped receptacles, also hung by chains.

"They're from the early prairie traders," Munro said. "Their women packed them along and used them for boiling meat – deer, elk, and so on – when the groups would be on the trail for weeks at a time, between the forts and meetings with the various Indians, looking for beaver. There's not a great call for them here."

Meg examined the bowls. "So the price would be reduced."

He laughed. "Down to two dollars."

"They'll do very well," Meg said. She brought out and opened up a folded square of paper from the reticule that she carried.

"This is a plan of how it will look. If we measure the area now, we can work out how much lumber will be needed."

Munro contained a smile at the 'we' that apparently now involved him in Meg's plan, but he seemed quite pleased. He said, "Of course," and led the way out of the store and to the shed.

It took just a short time using Meg's sketch to determine the amount of planks needed to build a three-sided counter with a small hatch set in one of the sides for entry and egress. Munro suggested a carpenter whose rates would be reasonable, and a bricklayer who would construct the bases that would hold the kettles and the fireplace beneath them. The fire would be concealed and accessed by a hinged iron door.

"What fuel will you use?" Munro said. "Wood or coal?"

At the Campbell house the fireplaces mainly burnt wood, which the family bought from a Chinese man, the first Chinese person Meg had ever seen. Mr. Lee hauled alder and maple logs in a handcart. But the wood had to be stacked and dried out after being cut, and Mr. Lee on occasion failed to show, which was connected to his affection for the opium pipe, so the supply could be haphazard. Also, Meg found that the seasoned wood burned very quickly compared with coal, which the Campbell's occasionally used as an alternative.

She had asked Mr. Campbell where the coal came from.

"Until a few years ago it came mainly from Wales. By ship, when it was used as ballast. The company invested considerable efforts to mine coal at outcrops at the north end of this island, at Fort Rupert, but what little they produced was of poor quality, so that plan came to nothing." Then he laughed and said, "There's a story that an Indian man was in the company's smithy here in Victoria and asked where the coal they were using in the forge came from. He was amused when told it came from halfway around the world and took three months to get here. He told the blacksmith that there was so much of it where he came from that it littered the beach. It seems that he was laughed at and told to go home. He did, and returned some weeks later with his canoe filled with coal. His claim of coal on the beach turned out to be true and now we get all we need from there. Nanaimo."

This was the town about sixty miles north on the Island's east coast, where coal mines had been established a decade or so previously. Meg had found out about the town after seeing an advertisement on the front page of the *British Colonist* for the Victoria Coal and Lumber Company for Nanaimo coal: 'English ton of 2,240 pounds. For steamers. Small, for blacksmiths. Screened, for families.' She had wondered aloud who might be doing the screening.

"Chinese workers to some extent," Bruce Campbell said. "And then there are the families of the Scots and English miners who were brought out to work the mines. Likely some of them."

Likely enough.

He said, "The mines have become a good investment. The company – the Hudson's Bay Company, that is – just last year sold its interests to the Vancouver Coal Mining and Land Company. I have some shares in it and some other interest in the area. With so many ship owners and the Royal Navy beginning to change from sail to steam, the demand for coal can only grow."

Meg answered Munro's earlier question about fuel, "Coal. I know there will be a steady supply. And I'm used to it." She had never held back details of her life at Morthwaite.

Munro smiled. "Of course. Good decision."

He jotted down figures with a silver-cased pencil on a page of a small leather-bound note book. He totaled the count and concluded that the cost of purchasing and setting up all of Meg's needs would be approximately one hundred and twenty dollars. Meg calculated quickly, said that was acceptable, and asked when the work could begin.

Munro put the same question that Bruce Campbell had asked, "Do you have a particular time that you would like to open? Maybe by the time the miners return from the gold fields? Possibly late October or early November," he said. "I'm sure that can be possible."

"No, before then," Meg said. "In fact, on September nineteenth."

Munro frowned slightly. "That is just—"

"A few weeks, I know – and exactly a year to the day that we sailed into this harbour from Esquimalt."

"Of course!"

Chapter 12

Nancy moved her finger on the page as she read aloud.

"People in our fair city will of course recall the company of young women from England who arrived here almost one year ago, aboard the good ship *HMS Tynemouth*."

"Company." Nancy snorted. "Last year they called us a bloody inventory – whatever that is." And "Good ship?" She said. "They should have been on board the f—, the thing!"

"Never mind that now, Nance. Read on," Meg said.

They were in the kitchen of the Campbell home with that day's edition of the four-page *British Colonist* open before them on the table.

"'Several of those young women remain who accepted employment in the homes of some of our well-known citizens.'"

"That's us." Nancy said.

"It is. Now read the rest."

"'One such young woman is Meg Tyson, originally from the northern English county of Cumberland, where she worked as a colliery 'screen lass' and who now does domestic duty in the esteemed Campbell family home on Johnson Street. We understand that Miss Tyson may not be much longer part of the family household, as she plans to open for business as the proprietor of what she calls a fish and chip shop.'"

"Bloody 'ell. How do they know that?"

"He," Meg said. "It's a he. Mr. De Cosmos, the newspaper man."

"Oh, him. The one what changed his name."

It was widely known that Amor De Cosmos, owner and publisher of the *Colonist,* had indeed been born William Alexander Smith in Windsor, Nova Scotia. Bruce Campbell, a friend of De Cosmos, knew more details of the man's history, both from De Cosmos, who had recently joined Mr. Campbell as an elected member of the Vancouver Island Legislative Assembly, and from incoming Americans who had known him in that country.

As William Smith he had travelled west across America, first by covered wagon from St. Joseph, Missouri, to the Mormon settlement of Salt Lake City, then alone on horseback to California. It was there that in 1854 he had had his name changed in a bill signed by the state's governor.

Bruce Campbell said, "There was speculation that his change of name was to escape vengeance from a group of California miners, for some unspecified deed." He laughed. "But how on earth would changing his name to De Cosmos have given him any way to hide? And there's the fact that he was living in a place called Mud Springs, which changed its name to El Dorado, so perhaps it was something in the water in both cases!"

The new name was generally believed to mean Lover of the Universe. De Cosmos had arrived in Victoria along with the gold-rush miners of 1858 and had started his newspaper almost immediately on arrival. Its original two hundred copies, three days a week had five years later become a daily press run of four thousand. The *Colonist* competed for readers with two smaller newspapers, the *Daily Evening Express,* and the *Victoria Daily Chronicle*.

Much of the interest in the *Colonist* was generated by De Cosmos's persistent criticism of the governance of James Douglas, which he saw as pandering to the 'ruling classes,' and on his personal feuds with individuals, many of which resulted in libel actions, and many others in confrontations and even fist-fights in the streets, all of which he reported on in great detail, usually assigning fault to the other parties. In one case where he had been ordered by the legislative assembly to apologize for publishing information the assembly ruled to be inaccurate, and before his own election to that body, he had amused Campbell and many others by writing, "I apologize for the publication of an article which I believed to be based on correct information."

Meg said, "Yes. He came to interview me. I think that either Mr. Campbell, or more likely, Alan Munro, told him about it."

De Cosmos had appeared at the shed door while Meg was inside discussing measurements with the carpenter recommended by Alan Munro.

A tall, pale-faced, full bearded man, dressed in a frock coat and top hat, carrying a heavy cane and a serious demeanour, De Cosmos had seemed at first just mildly curious but became more attentive as Meg gave him forthright answers to his questions and explained her thoughts about the customers she expected to have, from men from the Esquimalt navy base, labourers on the Victoria waterfront, and the miners when they began returning to the city from the Cariboo country.

Colonist readers had come to know that when De Cosmos settled on an issue, he spared no enthusiasm, and he clearly had been taken by Meg's story. So too, apparently, had the other two newspapers, each of which sent reporters to talk to Meg on the day her story appeared in the *Colonist* and ran almost identical reports the following day.

"Alan said a new business cannot get too much publicity," Meg said.

"Oooh, '*Alan*', is it?" Nancy raised her eyebrows.

"Shut up, Nance."

Nancy laughed and read on. "It says you are 'a shining example of what the colony should expect from new arrivals: Enterprising, forward-looking and with no doubt a bright future ahead of her.'"

Nancy read the rest and concluded, "Her venture will be called 'M and N's Fish and Chips' and will be open for business at 5 p.m. on Friday September 19. M and ?"

"Meg and Nancy's. Of course."

"Bloody 'ell, Meg, that's marvellous! Me name up!" She stopped and frowned, then offered a sly smile, "Why is your initial first?"

"Because it's alphabetical."

"Hah! I knew that! I was just checkin'."

"We'll need a sign, like the shops have, so…"

"I'll do it. I'll mek one!"

And though in doing so enthusiasm overcame artistry, she made one, using two cedar boards fastened together and painted white with the name printed in rich cobalt blue. There was just enough room for Meg to insert the apostrophe that Nancy had omitted.

The sign stood out dramatically from the rest of the structures on Wharf Street, due to Nancy graduating quickly from sign painter to shop-front decorator. She painted the front solid white and finished the door, window frame and the eaves in the same blue as the lettering on the sign.

Chapter 13

Meg was sweating. Soaking. It ran from her hair which had graduated from damp to slick and wet, onto her face and down her shoulders and arms. It trickled down her thighs beneath her long frock and created itches, which for decency's sake she was unable to relieve. She concentrated on dipping the long-handled wire basket into the bubbling lard and picked out another piece of crisp-battered fried cod. Beside her Martha did the same thing with the chips frying in the second pot.

"More batter, Meg," Martha said. She nodded to the iron bowl where the batter had been mixed and was now almost empty. Until now, Nancy had been in attendance each evening. She had not felt well earlier in the day, and Louisa Campbell had insisted she stay home. Martha had been happy to stand in.

Meg glanced at the queue which stretched to outside the shed and grew as a quartet of wharf labourers joined the end. It appeared that anyone in Victoria who could read had been taken by the articles written by Amor De Cosmos and copied by the other newspapers, and that those who did not read had heard about it in gossip.

Meg dropped the dipper onto the counter, shook another portion of flour into the bowl, added water and mixed the batter. Martha grabbed three more cod fillets, dipped them into the batter and plopped them into the hot fat. She grinned at Meg, then began slicing another potato into chips.

***

Raw supplies had been Meg's first concern after construction of her premises. She had decided from the start who her fish supplier would be and Martha had been delighted when asked. The potatoes, at twenty cents a sack, had come from the Wilson family farm just north of the city, and Meg had been promised a continuing supply even through the winter when the farm's deep root cellar with layers of straw and sand would handle her needs.

For the lard she needed, Meg had approached Thomas Harris, the genial and rotund butcher, and mayor of Victoria.

"I'm more a meat and spuds man myself," he had said, "but good luck to you and yes, there will always be a supply of hog lard for you, at a fair price."

On M and N's first night, Martha's perfectly filleted cod portions had lasted just long enough to feed the long and curious queue, plus two servings left which Meg had served with a flourish to Alan Munro and Amor De Cosmos, who had checked on the shop during the evening. De Cosmos had held up his grease stained square of the *British Colonist* as he finished the last chip and piece of cod.

"I must say that I never envisioned such an application for my product," he said.

Meg neglected to describe how more than one patron had commented that the newspaper had finally found a fitting use.

"That will be forty cents for the two of you," she said.

She had priced each serving at twenty cents after doing a rough calculation based on remembering Malin's price of five pence in London and totting up what her cost per portion would be.

De Cosmos laughed, and paid.

***

That first Friday night had been two weeks previous and with the exception of the two Sundays, when Victoria closed down other than for church-going, social outings, and tennis, there had been a steady line of customers. Most of these had been single men, generally smelling of liquor, though a few women had braved the company and said the experience would be a welcome change from cooking another meal.

Meg wiped her damp brow again. A few drops of sweat fell into the pan of boiling lard. It crackled and popped and bounced back onto her bare arm.

"Bugger!" she muttered.

Martha laughed and turned to add something, but she froze as her eyes settled on a man barging through the line of customers and reaching the counter.

"Sweeney," Martha said. She shrank back from the counter and closer to the fryer pans.

Sweeney was roaring.

"Martha!"

His red flannel shirt was across the counter, his hands splayed on the surface.

"Come here!"

He made to say more, but stopped.

He looked down, seemingly puzzled. His left hand, which had been reaching for Martha, now was impaled on a filleting knife which was sunk half an inch into the cedar-plank counter top.

Time had stopped for Meg when Martha called out. Everything had stopped, except for a flash of images that she had seemed to see, like a rush of reflections in a mirror. The first image was that of the Irishman dragging and clubbing the Indian girl while the bullying police constable and the marine had refused to stop it, and she and Nancy had offered their opinions on the Marine's character and shamed him.

In the second image she was back at Drigg Beck with Sandy Benson on top of her, his hand searching and a piece of slate lying at hand…just as now had been the filleting knife with its honed and pointed blade.

Meg had grabbed the knife and swung it downward.

The bladed penetrated the back of Sweeney's hand, through the web of pliant skin and flesh between the thumb and forefinger and continued into the wood.

Sweeney had roared again, this time in surprise, and pain.

Blood seeped and collected on the recently scrubbed counter top.

The crowd scattered away from the scene. Two women from the queue screamed and ran out of the door.

The marine, who Meg now knew was Lance-corporal Rhys Llewellyn, was at the back of the line with the policeman from that earlier day, Victoria Police Constable James Watson, who was in uniform, as he tended always to be. The policeman saw the incident from the moment Meg had reached for the knife until the blade entered Sweeney's hand and pinned it to the counter. He swore, and leaped forward. He pushed Meg out of the way and grabbed Sweeney's arm while Sweeney howled.

"Don't wiggle it, you dopey bastard, pull it straight out!"

Sweeney howled again and tried to free his hand. He roared louder as steel moved and grated on bone.

Watson yanked the knife from the wood and freed the blade from Sweeney's hand.

Sweeney spun away, wailing.

"Shut up," Watson said. "You're like a fucking girl. Go and pour some whiskey on it and get it bandaged."

The Irishman turned back at him. "Fuckin' copper, you don't understand! I was—"

"I said get going! I'll talk to you later."

He bundled Sweeney across the shop floor and out of the door.

He returned to where Meg stood staring at the knife and at the blood on her counter.

"Miss Tyson."

No familiar 'Meg.'

"Miss Tyson?" He put a hand on her arm.

Meg pulled back.

"You just committed a crime. A serious crime"

"He was—"

"Shouting. He was shouting, that's all. And you stabbed him."

"He was after Martha! He would have—"

"He was on this side of the counter. He hadn't touched her, or you."

Llewellyn was beside them. "Jim, you know what Sweeney's like. I don't know what in hell he's doing back this early in the year anyway, but—"

"She attacked him with a knife," Watson insisted. "That is a serious crime, and we have at least twenty witnesses." He swept a hand toward the remaining customers, most of whom now were enjoying the drama. Watson was at his officious best by now, given a rare chance to shine in public. "This has become a police matter – it *has* to."

He spoke to Meg, "Meg Tyson, I am arresting you."

"Arresting—?" Meg gasped. "He was going to—"

"I am charging you with assault and intent to harm with a deadly weapon."

"*What?* That is—"

"Be quiet. I don't want to put handcuffs on you, but I will if you resist."

Llewellyn protested, "Christ, Jim!"

Watson shook his head. "I have no choice. She stabbed a man in full view of witnesses, including yourself. She could have killed him. It's that simple."

"But the cuffs?" Llewellyn almost laughed. "Where do you think she's going to run to?"

Watson ignored him. He said to Meg, "If the grand jury can be convened tomorrow you will go before them and they will decide what's to be done."

"And if they're not available tomorrow?" Llewellyn asked.

"She'll have to wait until they are."

"Wait?" Meg said, regaining some control and starting to see how things looked to Watson, a man who was never shy about declaring his goal of advancing within the city police force, or getting his name in the columns of the *Colonist*, which this certainly would do.

"Wait where?"

Watson shrugged, as if the answer should be obvious. A new police barracks and gaol had been constructed on Lower Bastion Street inside the shell of the old fort, the previous year.

Meg – minus handcuffs but with Watson maintaining a firm grasp on her arm – was walked the two blocks from her shop to the gaol. People on the sidewalk stopped and gaped.

"Meg?" a puzzled young woman said. Meg shook her head and kept walking, through Bastion Square where – and she cringed at the thought – back in the spring there had been a public hanging of four Indians convicted of killing three white men and a fifteen-year-old girl. *Criminals.*

Inside the gaol Watson completed a form which charged her with the crime, had her sign it, and directed her to a cell opposite the door.

"I assume you will want the Campbell's to be advised," he said, as he closed the steel barred door and turned the key.

Rhys Llewellyn was ahead of him on that, already on his way at the marine double-time, up Johnson Street.

Meg's mind was in turmoil.

Yes, she had stabbed Sweeney, but she had done it without stopping to think, to protect Martha. Surely anybody could see that? It had been a spur of the moment thing, not something planned like the crimes committed by the Artful Dodger and his friends, though even they had Fagan to blame, and Oliver Twist had everybody to blame, but none of them had stabbed anybody...*Christ Almighty! Stop it or you'll lose your mind.*

She forced herself to be calm. Deep breaths.

She was in gaol. Maybe to become a convict and stay in gaol. For how long? What was the sentence for assault with a deadly weapon?

She sat uneasily on the wooden bench that she supposed would serve also as a bed if she was to be kept in gaol which, if Jim Watson's attitude was anything to go by, she would. He was doing his duty, she acknowledged, though he seemed to be getting an undue amount of satisfaction from it. Probably he remembered their first meeting on the dock. And that both Meg and Nancy had since declined his invitation to walk out with them.

"Not an 'ope," Nancy had said.

"But it was kind of you to ask," Meg added to her own polite refusal, though this had seemed only to salt the wound of Nancy's flat rejection.

She could hear Watson now in conversation beyond her sight, at the entrance to the building.

"No one else is here and I do not have that authority. Visiting has to be approved by…" The voices were cut off as the door was slammed shut.

Meg guessed that an hour passed before anyone else appeared. This time it was Bruce Campbell, accompanied by Alan Munro and a man she recognized as Victoria's Police Commissioner Augusts Pemberton, a man usually with a friendly greeting, but who at this moment was nothing but policeman.

"Miss Tyson, this is a disturbing event. And a surprising one, if I may say so. A knife…a stabbing…"

He frowned as he studied her. Meg held his gaze, decided this likely was a time to remain quiet, especially with the looks she was receiving from Bruce Campbell. No doubt it was his influence that had brought the Commissioner to her cell.

Pemberton turned to Campbell.

"This is going to take some time. There is a grand jury that was convened for some earlier business, but I believe that given the eye-witness account from a member of my own police force" – he nodded at Watson, who seemed to strut though standing in place – "that this case can proceed directly to supreme court, and that is what I shall suggest."

'Criminal!'

"And a judge?" Campbell asked, knowing that colony's chief justice David Cameron did not have authority to conduct a criminal trial. Cameron was a man with no legal training or qualifications, but who had the full confidence of Governor James Douglas – his brother-in-law – who had appointed him, though without jurisdiction in criminal matters.

Pemberton continued, "I hope for Chief Justice Begbie, from British Columbia. I have already sent a message to New Westminster. We know from the newspapers that the judge is due back within a day or so from his Assize courts at Lytton and Lilloet. He enjoys nothing more than a few days in Victoria so no doubt he will agree to make the trip across to hear this case."

"In that case, we ask for bail until—"

"I have considered the question, and I believe in this case I can take it upon myself – with your commitment to stand surety – to agree."

To Meg, he said, "Miss Tyson, until the time that you appear before the court on this charge, you will remain in the Campbell home. You will not attend your place of business or be seen on the streets of this city. You will have no connection with anyone who might be a witness to the incident, including your assistant, the Songhees woman Martha, or especially with the apparent victim, Seamus Sweeney."

Meg blurted, "As if—"

She stopped as Alan Munro shook his head at her. He said to her, "Nancy will handle the business, with Martha. And I will help keep an eye on both of them."

Pemberton said, "I believe that concludes our business for now."

He shook hands with Campbell and Munro.

"I wish you well, Miss Tyson," he said, shaking his head as he left.

Chapter 14

The news of Meg being charged – and the fact that the celebrated Matthew Baillie Begbie would conduct her trial – sped through the city. The career of the Cambridge-educated Begbie had been regular fodder for the newspapers of both colonies since he had arrived at Esquimalt five years previously with a commission from Queen Victoria that appointed him the first judge in the colony of Columbia and decreed the attachment of 'British' to that colony's name. The commission also appointed James Douglas its governor, as he already was to the colony of Vancouver Island. Begbie read the commission in a log building at Fort Langley, to where he travelled the day after his arrival at Esquimalt the immediacy of that trip serving notice that he was here to do business.

The newspapers had assigned correspondents to travel with the judge as he took British law and his determination of what constituted justice to the rough and tumble and frequently violent camps along the sand bars of the Fraser River, and on into the gold fields of the rugged Cariboo country. Applying the established principle of English law – the belief that the accused should be tried by their peers in the locality of the alleged crimes – he held his hearings in a court room where one existed, otherwise where it was convenient: in a miner's ragged tent, in a crudely built bar room, and when necessary on a tree stump on the banks of the Fraser River. It was reported that in one case of an Indian charged with murder, the witness was an Indian girl who spoke no English. The one person present who understood the girl was a man whose only other language was French. The bilingual Begbie became his own court interpreter. His visits by horseback and on foot to the remote sites frequently required a round journey of several hundred miles. He kept a sketch book that he filled with illustrations of his travels, and his Bench Book with his Gurney's shorthand provided a recorded of events.

A *Colonist* correspondent just the previous week, after accompanying Begbie on one of his peregrinations, had written of 'the wholesome presence of Judge Begbie who seems to be a terror to evildoers and a sworn enemy to the use of the knife and revolver.'

***

Meg pointed to the last words, her finger wavering.

"That is just the word of a newspaperman trying to impress his readers," Michael Blacklock said, waving aside the copy of the newspaper. "Judge Begbie is concerned with the truth of a matter, and with a just outcome. He has established himself among the miners in British Columbia, especially the Americans, and among our own Indians, as a fair and reasonable man."

Blacklock was to be Meg's defence counsel, retained by Bruce Campbell. Of the same age and a friend to Alan Munro, Blacklock was not a barrister, but a solicitor with a small but flourishing practice in the city who had proven his reliability and competence in a number of assignments for Campbell's bank and Munro's personal and HBC business dealings. He had grown up and been educated at Lancaster, England's north-west county town of Lancashire, had spent two years in San Francisco in the offices of a prominent industrialist, who also had interests in Victoria, and had arrived in Victoria a year before Meg landed. As a solicitor he would not normally act in the role of defence counsel, or any manner of counsel, in an English court of law. The fact that he was so doing was due to a ruling made by Judge Begbie shortly after he had arrived in the colonies six years earlier and realized that there was just one person in Victoria qualified to act as a Barrister in a court of English law, and that there was no one else in either of the two colonies qualified to act either as a barrister, attorney, or solicitor. Begbie issued an order that declared 'all Barristers of this Court may appear and practise as Attorneys and Solicitors, and all Attorneys and Solicitors may practise and plead as Barristers.'

Blacklock was pleased to have been offered the responsibility for Meg's case. Meg, on being socially introduced to him at an earlier time by Alan Munro, had thought the young man a bit…affected, was the word. His long, wavy black hair was tied at the back with a simple piece of dark blue ribbon. He wore a green velvet coat with broad lapels, brown corduroy trousers, and pointed and polished brown calf-leather ankle boots.

"Bit of a dandy, don't we think?" Louis Campbell had ventured to Meg.

He had since proven that appearances and costume are no measure of character or ability, and Meg was feeling comfortable with him as her advocate.

They sat on couches in the Campbell's parlour, while Blacklock pressed for details of the stabbing. English law did not permit Meg to testify in her own defence. Her unsworn statement to her lawyer, they hoped, would provide him with all he needed to do his job at her trial, which was to begin two hours from now at the courthouse in the legislative assembly buildings.

It had been four days since the incident with Sweeney, four days in which Meg had abided wholly by the bail conditions imposed by Pemberton.

Judge Begbie had arrived by steamer from Victoria the previous evening.

"We will let the judge see that you have met all the requirements," Blacklock said. "First impressions are important."

Bit of a dandy, don't we think? Meg smiled privately.

They heard whispering and giggling from the Campbell children outside the door, the sound of their mother shushing them, then a polite knocking on the door before Louisa Campbell entered.

She indicated behind her. "The police," she said.

Constable James Watson stood at the house's rear door. The rain that had started as a light fall an hour earlier and now poured in earnest, dripped from the rim of his helmet and from the cape which hung from his shoulders and protected his tunic. Drops bounced of the glossy toes of his polished black boots.

"Mr. Pemberton decided that an escort would be proper," Watson said.

"Yes," Meg replied. "But we have some time yet. Would you like a cup of tea? It's just mashed."

A flustered Watson stuttered, "I..." before Meg ushered him inside.

"No need to get any wetter than you are," she said. "Come into the kitchen."

She gestured him to the open room to the left. "My mother always made a visitor a cup of tea. Said it was good manners and the least we should do, for anybody."

Nancy appeared then. She scowled at Watson. "What the...what's he doing in here?"

Meg took her arm and ushered here away. "Tea pot please, Nancy," she said. "And cups."

Nancy said "Humph!" but went off as asked.

Thank goodness for Nancy, Meg thought. The girl had taken charge of M and N's since Meg had been charged and given bail conditions. Fortunately the Campbell's niece Helen, a girl three years older than Meg, had arrived as promised and had happily joined in the house-keeping and child-care duties.

Nancy and Martha had run the fish shop well. Also, Rhys Llewellyn had been showing up each evening to keep an eye on them and insisting on walking Nancy home when they closed. Nancy kept him a choice piece of cod and pile of chips, which he ate from a page of *The Colonist* as they walked.

Meg thought that they made a fine pair and was keenly aware that the marine had been paying her young friend attention for some time, since the spring day that they had enjoyed a half-day off with a walk along Johnson Street and down to the waterfront. They were wearing their new straight-skirted cotton frocks, Meg's dark blue with a faint floral design, Nancy's in a plain light green. Louisa Campbell had helped them select the material and make the dresses, using the new paper patterns that had recently found their way from America.

Louisa had also asked their advice on colours for her own use, and had noted that she was not even considering the use of a crinoline or any kind of hoops with her new dresses. She cited Florence Nightingale as the inspiration for women to begin discarding the restrictive items.

"She did all of us a great favour when she rejected those things. It has taken a while for the rest of us to see the sense in it, but I believe the new style is here to stay."

"I've 'eard of 'er," Nancy said. "The lady with the lamp. The soldiers' nurse. My granddad met 'er. I remember 'e told me about her before 'e died. 'E was in that war, the Crime – whatsit thing and was wounded and she helped 'im. Fancy that, 'er doin' frocks an' stuff an' all. Bloomin' 'eck."

"Yes, fancy that," Louisa Campbell had laughed at Nancy's response.

As Meg and Nancy had neared the water front, a young marine in uniform offered a grin, a casual salute and said, "Afternoon, girls."

He winked at Nancy. "You look lovely today, darlin'."

Nancy blushed. "Cheeky sod," she said, but looked pleased when Meg said quietly, "He's right, you do."

The marine said, "I remember you getting off the *Tynemouth*. You looked a bit different that day."

"Aye, well, that was then," Nancy said. "Everything was different then, wasn't it? Now it's different again. So there." And she blushed even deeper.

The Marine laughed, as did Meg.

"I'm Rhys Llewellyn," he said.

Meg introduced them.

"I remember you, too," Meg said. "You kept us back from trying to help Martha when that Sweeney fellow was belting her."

"The squaw? 'Martha'? That's her name?" As if surprised that she had one. "You know her?"

Nancy glared at him.

"Yes, we bloody well do," she said. "She's our friend. So there."

***

Watson sipped his tea and seemed glad for it, though only after he had glanced several times from the cup to a baleful Nancy before raising it to his mouth.

As the party prepared to leave – Meg, Blacklock, Nancy, Bruce Campbell, and Alan Munro who had joined them to offer his support – Nancy handed Watson a black silk umbrella.

"Open it outside, not in here, that's bad luck, and make sure you keep 'er dry," she instructed, nodding to Meg.

Watson took the umbrella without a murmur and held it over Meg as they started out. For other protection over her frock, Meg wore a waist-length tunic of soft, tanned deer hide, created by Martha. It was fringed and decorated with a variety of dye-coloured native images. "They are for good future," Martha said. Any rain drops that touched the tunic bounced or ran off the surface without leaving a mark.

The group's progress took them over water-filled ruts that became small streams and mud puddles, causing Bruce Campbell to mutter once, "Damned roads – forgive me – must do something."

He seemed nervous, Meg thought. Not the best sign.

***

Judge Begbie, having agreed it was unnecessary to involve the grand jury, had wasted no time in swearing in the Petit jury of twelve men selected from the City's list of property owners. Now, clad in scarlet robe and full-bottomed wig, he stared down from the bench at Meg in the prisoner's box. His face registered a mix of curiosity and surprise. He had, he told himself, expected a somewhat rougher-looking figure for the first ever criminal trial – and that a violent one – of a woman in either of the two Crown colonies. *This one could have been a school teacher,* he thought. *And a most attractive one at that.* He nodded at Meg, to acknowledge her presence.

Meg saw a ruggedly good-looking man in his early forties, and a pair of keen, intelligent eyes weighing her. She watched the judge smoothing his full, well-trimmed beard and mustache as he examined her. She wondered what he saw, how much he knew of the events that had put her there. Mr. Blacklock had said that the judge would not have had the time nor, probably, the inclination to listen to any details before they came before him.

"His arena is the courtroom, Meg, his interest only in the evidence that is presented."

The judge's eyes now roamed the courtroom. The public seating was filled, people nudged others to move along the benches and make more room. A conspicuous musk rose from the blending of body heat and damp woolens.

Meg's supporting group smiled up encouragingly at her as she stood, tense, in the box. She saw that Martha had been invited to join them in the seating, to the obvious disapproval of some others. She also saw that Nancy had gone to sit beside Rhys Llewellyn, who was out of uniform. She caught Nancy's eye. Nancy grinned, gave her the thumbs up sign – *spare the gladiator! She and the Campbell children recently had been reading about the Romans: Bloody 'ell. Meg, I mean, Lions!* – then turned and spoke to Rhys, who looked up at Meg and repeated the sign. Alan Munro caught her eye and nodded encouragement, which buoyed her spirit.

Amor de Cosmos and reporters from the other newspapers sat at a table reserved for them behind the bar, which stretched across the courtroom in front of and below the judge's bench. Attorney General George Hunter Carey and Michael Blacklock sat at separate tables, prosecution and defence. Chief Justice David Cameron had instructed that Carey conduct the prosecution and it was he who now addressed the court.

"The defendant is charged with assault and intent to harm with a deadly weapon."

"And how does she plead?"

The judge looked across the courtroom to the prisoner box.

Meg glanced down at her defence counsel for a second before she responded clearly, "Not guilty."

The judge nodded to Carey. "Carry on," he said.

Meg was surprised at the high pitched tone of Begbie's voice. It seemed at odds with the rest of his decidedly masculine stature.

"Thank you, Your Lordship," Carey said. He began, "Eye witnesses will prove that on the night of Friday, October second past, the accused without regard for life or limb, leaped upon this innocent—"

"Thank you, Mr. Carey," Begbie interjected. "The jury and I will decide the question of innocence or otherwise, and of any leaping or such, after we have heard from the witnesses. Carry on."

"Your Lordship," Carey said and inclined his head with a wry smile in recognition of the judge and his known penchant for interjecting and correcting at will or, indeed, whim.

Carey then called Constable James Watson as his first witness and the officer who had laid the charge.

"You saw the attack from the first moment, constable."

"Is that a question, Mr. Carey?" From the bench.

De Cosmos chuckled audibly and made a note. The reporters on either side of him also scribbled.

"Something from the *Colonist* representative?" Begbie stared down at the press table.

"That would not be appropriate, Your Lordship," De Cosmos replied, with a smile.

"And it would be prudent of us to remember that," the judge said, his own smile a decidedly thin one.

The newspaperman nodded and returned to his notes. It was only recently, following Begbie twice overturning juries' verdicts in the Cariboo region and imposing those of his own, that De Cosmos had written: "If judges are to upset juries' verdict, then we may as well do away with our whole system of courts and hand it to the dictator judge."

The fact that Begbie's decisions had been widely approved of and indeed applauded in the particular jurisdiction had not been mentioned in *The Colonist*.

Carey rephrased, "Did you see what happened at the time concerned?"

"I did, sir. The victim had just—"

"*Alleged* victim," Blacklock interjected.

Alan Munro from his seat, whispered loudly, "Indeed!"

Begbie eyed him briefly, then said, "Carry on."

Watson continued. "The alleged victim approached the shop's counter—"

"Objection."

"Mr. Blacklock?"

"'Approached' hardly fits the action, Your Lordship. The man was a raging lunatic and threatening—"

"Are you attempting to give evidence, Mr. Blacklock?"

"Of course not, Your Lordship. I apologize. Carry on, Constable."

Watson continued, sarcasm rampant, "He 'approached' the counter. He was calling the Indian woman's name, 'Martha. Martha!'"

"Did you think he was threatening her?" the prosecutor asked.

"It did not seem so," Watson said. "He was on the wrong side of the counter for one thing. I saw no evidence of a threat." Watson had looked over to the press table as he answered and he smiled as the three men there bent over their note books.

"But I doubt that he seemed to be proposing marriage," Blacklock said quietly.

Stifled laughter followed and Begbie's lips twitched.

Watson continued. "He got to the counter and suddenly she," he pointed to Meg, "grabbed the knife and stabbed it right through his hand. You should have seen the blood!" This appeal to the public benches, and the reporters. "I was sure she would be going for the throat next." He drew his hand across his own throat, in case anyone might not have understood. He looked pleased with his account, and checked that the reporters again were taking notes.

"If she had taken that next step—"

"Thank you, Constable. Never mind the speculation." Begbie said.

Watson looked disappointed and seemed about to say more, but the prosecutor Carey said, "I have nothing further, M'Lord."

"Mr. Blacklock?" Begbie said.

"Nothing for the constable, Your Lordship."

He had told Meg, "The less we let Watson say, the better."

He turned to Meg in the prisoner box.

"Miss Tyson. You are pleading not guilty to the charge."

"Yes."

"But you did use the knife?"

"Yes, but—"

"Simple answers, Miss, please," Begbie said. "'Yes' or 'No' will suffice."

Meg flushed. There was much she could explain. She nodded her head, unsure whether she was supposed to respond to the judge.

Blacklock continued. "The charge is 'with intent to harm'. Was it your intent to harm Mr. Sweeney?"

"No."

"Then what was your intent?"

"To stop him hurting Martha. I have seen him hurt her before—"

"Objection, your Honour." Carey rose. "There is no evidence that Mr. Sweeney had any intention of hurting the Indian. Calling a name does not imply any specific intent."

Begbie nodded. "That is true, Mr. Carey." Then he said, "By the way, where is the alleged victim?" He looked around the packed courtroom. "Mr. Sweeney?" There was no response. "Anywhere?"

Silence. Everyone suddenly also looked about them, seeming to wonder the same thing: where was the wounded Sweeney? And then they were looking at Carey the prosecutor, and at Constable Watson.

"Constable?" Begbie said.

Watson too looked about the room, as if surprised that Sweeney had not answered the call and appeared.

"Well?" The judge said. "Where is he?"

"I told him to be here."

"When did you tell him that?"

Watson looked uncomfortable. "I sent him a message."

"A message?"

Watson nodded affirmation. "Yes, Your Lordship."

Begbie managed to seem bemused.

"And did he reply to this message?"

Watson shook his head. "Not yet."

Begbie stared at the prosecutor. "Mr. Carey?"

Carey got to his feet. "Your Lordship, I was under the firm impression that the vic—the alleged victim would be present for this hearing."

"And you were under this impression because…?"

"Because Constable Watson assured me that would be the case."

"Did you speak to Mr. Sweeney yourself, Mr. Carey?"

"No, Your Lordship, I never had the opportunity."

There was an extended silence before Begbie said, "*Never* had the opportunity? Are you saying that you have not spoken to Sweeney – the alleged victim on whom your prosecution case rests – about this matter that you have brought before my court? Never?"

"Yes, Your Honour. I mean, yes that is correct, I have not spoken to him." He glared at Watson. "I had every faith in the constable."

"The one who sent the message," Begbie said dryly. He went on, "Constable, you have testified to the alleged attack by the accused, that you arrested her and took her to gaol. Where was Mr. Sweeney at this point?"

Watson shuffled his feet. "I told him to get his terrible wound bandaged and that I would see him later. I told him to see Doctor Helmcken, who would save his hand from—"

"Did he see the good doctor?"

Watson stared about him, as if an answer might be somewhere at hand.

Begbie sighed.

"Very well, did you see him later? Sweeney, that is."

"Eventually, Your Lordship."

"After you had advised the accused of the charge against her and taken her to gaol."

"Yes."

"After you locked her up, you saw Sweeney?"

"I looked for him."

"Did you find him?"

"Not right away."

"When, then?"

"The next day."

Begbie scowled.

"And what was his condition when you found him? What was the state of the knife wound that you had sent him to have treated? The 'terrible' wound you described."

"The hand was bandaged, Your Lordship." Watson nodded his head several times to affirm this.

Begbie studied the constable. A thin smile hovered, and left.

"And who had bandaged it? Had he gone to the doctor?"

Watson looked past the judge, at the wall behind the bench.

"Sweeney had bandaged it himself."

"Bandaged, with what?"

"His handkerchief."

Begbie ignored the spatter of courtroom laughter.

"Then it was not such a 'terrible' wound?"

The answer came not from Watson, but from the figure that had just entered the main door.

Sweeney said loudly, "No, it was not. I've had worse scratches in the claims."

Watson spun round. He stared at Sweeney. "He screamed like a f—like a girl! His blood was all over the counter!"

Begbie glared.

Watson subsided.

Sweeney pointed to Meg. "And that lass meant me no harm. She has seen me before with Martha and feared for her. Though she had no need to, not that night." He added, "Nor any more at all. Not ever."

Meg looked over at Martha. The Indian girl stared at the new entrant to the proceedings.

"Never," Sweeney re-affirmed.

The courtroom was rapt. Those who knew Sweeney, which included many on the public benches, had never seen this version of the man. It was clear that he had taken pains to be presentable. His hair and beard, usually an unkempt and united bush with no visible dividing line, had been carefully trimmed and apparently pomaded, given its new slickness. He wore what obviously was a new tweed suit, complete with waistcoat, a royal-blue cravat at the neck of a white cotton shirt. He held a soft green felt hat in his hand.

Meg examined Sweeney. She realized that he was a much younger man than she had thought, the twice that she had seen him – the first time the day they disembarked and he was dragging Martha, the second time when he invaded her fish shop. The transformed character she saw now could not have been more than in his early or mid-twenties, and was less bulky than his earlier dress had made him appear. Not slim, perhaps, but – normal came to mind. Sweeney seemed normal. *Christ Almighty!*

Carey was on his feet. "Objection!"

"To what, Mr. Carey?" Begbie with eyebrows climbing. "I gather that this is the missing alleged victim?"

Carey grimaced. "It seems so, Your Lordship."

"The one we have been anxiously waiting to hear from?"

"Yes, Your Lordship. Seamus Sweeney."

"Then…?"

"I withdraw the objection."

"I should think so."

Begbie stared stonily at Watson in the witness box. "Is there anything you wish to add to your testimony, constable?"

Watson looked at Carey, whose attention now seemed to be fixed on a distant spot. Watson then seemed to decide that the hole he had placed himself in was sufficiently deep and that this would be a good moment to stop digging.

"Nothing, Your Lordship."

"Then you may step down. And you, sir," he gestured across the courtroom to Sweeney. "You may take his place."

***

"I met a man."

Sweeney had been sworn in, stating fervently while clutching the Bible that what he had to say would be the truth, the whole truth and nothing but the truth, so help him God. "And his son, Jesus Christ of Nazareth, our Saviour. And the Holy Spirit," he added.

Begbie blinked, frowned in the direction of where a laugh had been swallowed.

After a pause the judge, a devout Anglican, said, "That is commendable, Mr. Sweeny, if not entirely necessary. Now perhaps you would like to explain this situation from your point of view – unless either of these two gentlemen has a question?" He nodded the query to Carey and Blacklock. Each indicated he had none – Carey sulkily, because he recognized that his case seemed suddenly to be on thin and rapidly melting ice, Blacklock happily, for understanding the same.

Sweeney had begun with a flourish of self-denunciation.

"I was not a good man, Your 'ighness. I was a *terrible—*"

"Mr. Sweeney," Begbie stopped him. "There is no need to elevate me so. 'Lordship' is more than adequate."

Sweeney took a moment, said, "Right you are, then."

Begbie sighed. "Carry on."

"I was a terrible drinker, and I treated Martha—" he looked about until he saw her, "'er over yonder. I was bad with 'er. I beat 'er, and she never deserved it." He placed his right hand with his hat – the left one was wrapped in a flimsy, discoloured square of cotton – over where he judged his heart to be, and declared, "I am so sorry, my dove. And I am a changed man. From now on—"

Begbie sighed. "Address the court, Mr. Sweeney, if you would. There will be time for that later." A smile hovered. "Should the lady wish to hear it."

He waited for a ripple of laughter to ebb. "Now, please carry on with your explanation, which seems to have something of a Damascene conversion about it if I am not mistaken? But I must advise you that I have had many similar claims to sudden enlightenment laid before me, and very few of them convincing."

Sweeney's brow furrowed, and stayed that way.

Begbie sighed. "Very well. You met a man. Carry on."

Sweeney relaxed. "I did. And 'e changed me. The Captain."

"Captain?"

"That's what some called 'im. 'Is real name is Daniel O'Thunder. 'e is like something out of a story book."

The judge looked up. "O Thunder? The former prize ring fighter?"

"You know 'im?" Sweeney's face lit up. He smiled. A show of incisors, some aslant, others away.

"I have heard stories of him. Somewhat eccentric. I heard that he placed a notice in a newspaper in London in which he offered to fight the Devil – the actual Devil, that is."

"*The Sporting Life*," Sweeney affirmed. "I 'ave seen that very page." He added, "'e is still waiting for a reply. And still looking for 'im. The Devil, that is."

Begbie smiled. Those in the public seating chuckled. Carey grunted and scowled. Blacklock seemed at ease.

Sweeney added, "We 'ave much in common, me and the Captain. We are both from the auld sod, I milled in the ring an' all, and I think 'e saw that in me."

Meg looked and saw it too, the same marks and lumps she remembered seeing on the faces of the booth fighters at Workington and Whitehaven fairs when her brother Matthew went to work on them.

"You fought under the London Prize Ring Rules?" the judge asked.

Sweeney grinned. "When t' other lad did, aye. But not everybody stuck wid them all the time."

Begbie smiled and nodded his understanding. Meg did the same in the prisoner's box.

Carey groaned, "For heaven's sake!"

Begbie said, "Be still, Mr. Carey, we will unearth something perhaps."

Carey looked away.

To Sweeney, Begbie said, "I am not unfamiliar with the boxing ring and the noble art."

Sweeney raised a polite eyebrow.

"I sparred frequently at several of the London boxing academies. When I was at Lincoln's Inn. Much younger, of course..." The judge drifted for a moment.

Sweeney said, "I know them well."

"And the Fives Court?"

"Aye. Little St. Martin's Street. I fought there twice mesel'. One bare knuckles, one wid mufflers. Won 'em both, first twelve rounds and the second 'un twenty-four." He touched his lump of a nose. "Good purses, an' big side bets among the Fancy. I never got a chance at the top ones, things 'appened, I 'ad to move around a lot, but I know if I 'ad been given a shot...I could've contended..."

"Well, well!" Begbie seemed pleased, as if he might have just found an old acquaintance.

Carey groaned loudly and shifted in his chair.

Begbie frowned at Carey.

Blacklock contained a smile.

De Cosmos scribbled happily. His two colleagues followed suit.

Meg exchanged puzzled looks with Martha.

Begbie returned to questioning Sweeney.

"He changed you, you say. O'Thunder."

"Aye. Up in the goldfields. I woke up in the lodging house, Nell Rooney's place, and 'e was looking at me. 'e told me wot I had done the night before."

"And that was?"

"I 'ad 'it a woman. Being drunk."

"No change, then," resignedly from Carey.

A glare from Begbie.

Carey shrugged.

Sweeney shot a swift look across at Martha. "I 'ad not bedded the woman. It was not like that. I told Daniel that I 'ad done this afore, to Martha. Too many times." He looked across at Martha, bowed his head, apparently a penitent.

Martha frowned and narrowed her eyes, apparently a skeptic.

"'e said he saw a piece of the devil in me. 'E took me in 'is arms and said 'e would squeeze it out, that sinners could be forgiven and that 'e was forgivin' me. This was a man, it was said, 'ad raised another man from the dead – after 'e 'ad kilt him first, with his fists. A man of power. 'E hugged me, very tight. 'E asked me if I was seeing the light, and squeezed 'arder. If you 'ad ever been squeezed by O'Thunder you would see all kinds of light. I said yes. 'E said that I should leave the fields right then and get back to see Martha. Tell her she is my real love and I will never do her 'arm. Never. Not ever. And that I will stay from the bottle, the source of the devil in me."

He pointed a finger at Watson. "I wanted no part of making that lass a criminal."

Carey snapped, "Good God, man, she stuck your hand to a wooden counter with a fish knife!"

"She mistook me intentions. From what she knew of me afore. And anyway, it didn't 'urt."

Watson, livid, yelled, "You screamed like a big girl!"

Begbie pointed a warning finger at the constable.

Blacklock interjected quickly, "And the officer took it up himself to charge Miss Tyson with a crime – a very serious crime. Regardless of there being no 'victim' complaining."

Judge Begbie sighed. He nodded to Carey and Blacklock.

"Gentlemen, please come to the bench."

With the two of them before him, he said, "Is there any point in continuing with this? The onus of proof lies with you, the prosecution, Mr. Carey, but now you have no complainant. I will give the constable the benefit of the doubt and say he believed that he was doing his duty, although he seems, given his preening before the members of the fourth estate" – a disdainful glance towards De Cosmos and company – "to have been more concerned with putting Miss Tyson in gaol and scoring some kind of personal points than tending to what he thought was a wounded victim. And Sweeny clearly is not going to testify against her."

He looked at each in turn and asked the court's conventional final question, "Does anything further need to be done?"

Carey, grudgingly answered, "Apparently not, Your Lordship. Although—"

"Thank you, Mr. Carey."

Blacklock said, "I agree, Your Lordship."

Begbie thanked and dismissed the jury. He told Meg that she was free to go, that her business with the court was ended.

"And the best of fortune with your business venture," he said.

He added, as he rose to leave the bench, "I believe you are the right kind of woman for this new country."

***

The rain had eased when they stepped outside into a mild early autumn day. Just a slight mizzle persisted. To Meg the colours around her seemed unusually bright. Late wild roses, delicate pinks and whites, bloomed on nearby hedges, and the dainty blue of forget-me-nots embroidered a low grassy bank. People going to and from the legislative buildings said "good morning" and "how do you do?" Masts and funnels of cargo ships in the inner harbour punctuated the skyline. Just like any other day.

Meg, and those with her, looked up at the distinctive shrill whistling call of the Bald Eagle as a pair of the majestic birds floated on an air current high above them. Meg, as always, marveled at such a subtle, delicate sound coming from birds of their size. Martha tipped her head at the birds and nodded at Meg. She had taught Meg that the eagle was the main spirit bird of the Indians; that when the eagle appeared, it meant that they were being watched and cared for. Meg smiled.

Sweeney hovered a few yards away. He clutched his felt hat with both hands against his chest, looking like some form of supplicant. Martha walked over to him and they began talking. Martha's forefinger rose, pointed and lowered, repeatedly, and with each emphasis Sweeney nodded eagerly. Meg could barely stem a laugh of pleasure at the sight. What a difference in the Indian girl since Meg had first seen her! A newfound confidence. A growing-up.

And what a difference in Sweeney, who now looked over Martha's shoulder at Meg and offered a tentative, broken smile. Martha turned at the same moment and beckoned Meg over.

Meg joined them.

"Sweeney say—" Martha looked at the miner, waited.

Still clutching his hat, Sweeny nodded vigorously at Meg. "I apologize ter y'," he said. "I apologize very much indeed. I must 'ave scared y' somethin' awful."

Meg said nothing for a moment. Then, "How is your hand?"

Sweeney seized what he deemed a chance of amnesty. He unwrapped the square of cotton.

"It's fine, it's nowt, really."

Meg grimaced at the sight of the scab that had begun to grow over the knife wound, though the actual cut seemed not quite as wide as she had feared, and there was a healthy pinkness around the edges, which she knew suggested healing.

"Let us forget it," Sweeney said. "If you would. Please."

Behind him, Martha nodded at Meg.

Meg studied Sweeny. She remembered her mother saying, "Always look for t' best in folks, lass. Give them t' benefit of t' doot when you can."

Most folks, anyway.

Meg looked at Martha, who waited. Meg looked back to Sweeney.

She said, "Aye. All right, then."

Martha beamed. Before Meg could move, Sweeney reached out, bowed his head and took her hand and kissed it. He stepped back and said, "Right we are then. That's grand."

Chapter 15

At the Campbell house, a letter had arrived from Sarah.

Morthwaite, July 25, 1863
My dearest Meg.
By the time you receive this, you will be past a year in your new home.

Morthwaite has been shaken in the past week. Richard Benson and his oldest son Harold died within a day of each other when cholera descended on the mansion. Two of the house maids and one groom also succumbed to the frightening disease. It has been rumoured that the disease was contracted by Harold Benson while returning from a trip to the West Indies where he was selling the family properties left over from their days in the slave trade. The running of Coater Pit is now in the hands of the remaining brothers, James (who now assumes the title of Lord Benson and all of the estate) and 'Sandy', and there have been problems. Last week there was an attempt to cut back the miners' and the screen lasses' wages, and the Bensons were taken by surprise at the strength of resistance shown by the workforce. You will not be surprised to learn that the leader of the resistance was a Tyson. You may be surprised that it was not your father. No, it was your brother Matthew, he of the 'handy' fists! – though no fighting was involved. Unless a brief strike can be called a fight, because that is what occurred. The mine manager, Carrick, greeted a back-shift, which included Matthew and your father, at the pit head with the news that Bensons were having to cut wages. As you know there had often been talk of that happening before you left.

As it was described to me, Matthew did not waste a second before saying, 'Aye, well if Bensons are cutting wages, we are stopping work. Right now. In fact we're on strike.'

I understand that he took the other men by surprise as much as he did the manager. Apparently Carrick blustered and shouted and said they had better 'get into that bloody cage and doon and in-bye' or they would have 'mair trouble than you can handle.' He said that Sandy Benson, who had personally given the orders, was due there any minute and he had better not find them idle or on a ridiculous strike. He said this is not Yorkshire with their trouble-making unions.

Matthew said it might not be Yorkshire, but it was a union, because they had just decided to form one. 'Isn't that right, lads?' he called back to the others.

And they responded instantly by sitting down at the pit top! Then the screen lasses came out – all your old workmates – and joined them. They were scared, but Matthew gave them the courage to stay the course.

When Sandy Benson showed up, looking down from his new dapple-grey stallion, and began yelling that he would dismiss anyone who did not get to work that minute, Matthew actually laughed at him and told him the mine was shut and would stay shut until the threat of wage cuts was withdrawn. And then he said the next time the miners talked to any Benson it would be about demanding a wage increase, based on the production figures of the last several weeks – so it might be wise for Sandy to stay away from the pit! No one knows how Matthew learned what the figures were, but I suspect he simply made an accurate guess based on what he saw of the movement of coal to the railway. And of course we know that he would be more than happy to cause any kind of discomfort to that particular man. Whatever the answer, Benson turned his horse and left without another word. The pit has been working full shifts ever since, and there has been no cut in wages!

I thought it unusual that Sandy Benson had appeared in the ownership role, but it appears that James has been deferring to Sandy and spending days at a time away from the home, some say at Whitehaven or thereabouts, and that Lady Benson is most unhappy with the situation.

And we now learn – Benson staff are such great gossips! – that it was Sandy himself who had ordered the wage cuts, without any consultation with his brother and that Lady Benson was furious when she heard of it. Voices were raised and there was a grand row in one of the Benson's drawing rooms, which ended with Sandy storming out and cursing at any staff he passed on his way, even striking one of the maids. What a coward. They say that his behaviour is daily becoming more unpredictable.

If James continues with his neglect of the pit operations, then that would fall to Sandy, with Carrick the manager his underling. I *cannot see anything good coming from such a situation. We know what he is like with any kind of power at his disposal.*

Your three letters since you left us have been intriguing. I laughed aloud at your mention in the last one of plans to open a fried fish and potatoes restaurant. The laughter was of pleasure at such an ambitious step after such a relatively short time. I am so pleased that the Campbells support you in this endeavour and am equally pleased that your friend Nancy remains part of your plans. I think the pair of you have proven to have more than enough strength and gumption to succeed in whatever you choose to pursue.

I am fascinated by your friendship with the Indian Martha and I hope you continue to tell me more about her.

You mention Mr. Alan Munro several times. Is he of special interest? I am sure that you will advise me when and if there is a suitable moment!

In other matters, I have visited my mother and sisters in the south and my young brother Francis, presently in Yorkshire. All are well and Francis is spending his summer as Assistant Curate at the grand Beverley Minister near Hull in Yorkshire, before he returns to Oxford to pursue his goal of ordination as an Anglican priest. He also now has a bee in his bonnet concerning our family history and talked about little else. I am sure he will soon move on to other interests.

I trust this finds you well and thriving, as I am certain you will be.

I have enclosed a note from your mother.
With love – and congratulations!
Sarah

Liz's note was brief. She said not to worry about the 'strike' situation.

'I cannot help but think that our Matthew is taking a risk in doing what he did. I'm not sure how much good will come from it in the long run, but I have to admire that he was standing up for himself and the rest of the men and lads and lasses, and I am pleased with the way the others backed him up. I hope that he is not going to have any more confrontations with that evil Sandy Benson, that if any dealings over this union business have to be done, it would be better with the new Lord B himself. Although your dad says they're all the b----- same and t' world would be a better spot without them. Aye, but that won't happen. I had a laugh

130

when Sarah told me about the fish shop, but I think it's a grand idea! I would certainly like to meet your Indian lass Martha, but then we can all dream, eh?

All love from your mam, dad, Matthew and Thomas (who has decided he should be now called Tommy, like his dad, so think on!)'

Meg smiled at the image of Matthew in a rebel's role. She hoped his actions would bring him no harm, and took comfort from the knowledge that he had Tommy senior and junior alongside him. She folded the letters carefully and placed them in a drawer.

Chapter 16

Beverley Minster, Beverley, Yorkshire

Francis Teasdale nodded politely as Mrs. Farthington once more prattled on about how close she was to discovering the final links that would prove her family had arisen and were descended from some of the bluest bloods in the nation. Now she was to search Beverley Minster's parish records for proof. Francis had pointed to the records drawer in the vestry and left her to it.

The woman's repeated appearances and talk of her (apparently) grand antecedents had resurrected Francis's curiosity about his own family line. He knew that his late father, Samuel, had been born near Beverley and he wished to know more. At the end of the university year he had written to ask if he might serve, voluntarily, *unpaid*, as an assistant curate at the Minster for the summer before returning to Oxford for the new term. He was confident that the volunteer element had played a large part in the invitation that came by return post.

Francis returned to his search for a record of his late grandmother Annie's marriage to Jeremiah Teasdale. From birthdates given him in letters from his sister Sarah, now a teacher in that pit village in West Cumberland, he had worked back and had found the record of the christening of his father on October 9 1795, but there was no trace of his grandparents' wedding. There should have been banns read on three consecutive Sundays preceding any wedding, and that would have been recorded, but Francis had found nothing.

But there had to be a record of the marriage somewhere. He knew from Sarah that the record of his *parent's* marriage – of Hilda Parker of Ambleside in Cumberland to Samuel Teasdale – was in the church at Ambleside. Samuel had grown up here in Beverley and had attended the town's grammar school, celebrated as the oldest state school in England. He had studied at Oxford and, following his graduation and subsequent ordination into the priesthood, had taken the position at Ambleside and met and married Hilda. Francis had no memory of his father who had died, having drowned when Francis was only two.

Francis frowned at the notion of a gap in his family's history. Sarah had known no more about their grandparents than Francis did, and had been brusque with him when he questioned her, saying it was all in the past and he might have better things to do with his time than dwell on such matters. He thought that odd coming from Sarah, whom he knew to be a student of history and likely now also a teacher of it in her village schoolroom. She had not dismissed his queries completely, having explained how she had met their fragile grandmother Annie twice, at Ambleside, and had suggested that he should seek out a Miss Agnes Blunt who had been Annie's companion when she last visited Ambleside, for his father Samuel's funeral. According to Sarah, who had paid a courtesy call some time ago, the woman had been living in Hull, just twelve miles from Beverley.

Mrs. Farthington left, with a face on her that suggested she might have discovered something not to her liking, given the way she had slammed down an aged tome – perhaps not so blue-blood after all, Francis thought. He re-read Sarah's latest letter. As usual, she remarked on the progress of Meg Tyson, the pit girl who had emigrated to the colony of Vancouver Island and found work as a domestic servant. Now Meg had gone into business for herself, opening a fried fish shop, and had taken on an Indian girl as a helper and whom she described as a good friend. An Indian friend? Whatever next?

The next morning, with a weak sun barely breaking through a ceiling of low cloud, Francis caught the twice-a-day coach to Hull. Sarah had written directions to the old lady's cottage, which it turned out was just a short walk from one of the coach's regular stops.

The woman who answered his knock on the door was short, straight-backed and slim, and wore a pair of silver wire-rimmed spectacles. Her white hair was tied back in a neat bun. She wore a hoopless ankle-length dress of black cotton and over it a spotless white pinafore. Her expression was serious and quizzical, but kindly enough. Her cheeks bore the slightest hint of rouge, and Francis was aware of a faint scent of...rosewater, he decided, though not sure how he knew that. Memories from home perhaps, his sisters.

"Miss Blunt?"

"Aye." She dusted flour from her hands, which went some way to explain the white pinny.

"I'm Francis Teasdale."

A second of uncertainty, then a sudden smile, certainly of porcelain, given the whiteness, but nonetheless sincere.

"The babby? The little babby?"

"As was," Francis laughed.

She stared for several seconds, seeming to search.

Then, collecting herself, "Come in, lad! Come thy sel' in. By gum but isn't this summat," as she led the way through a narrow hallway and into a small sitting room with flowered wall paper and heavy, dark furniture. "Your sister said you might arrive on me step. That Sarah. An' here you are! An' me not recognizing you right off! Well, I'll be – just look at you!" Which she did, again, standing back and admiring, and continuing, "And you now going into t' church, just like your father. Well, I never. You were just a tich when I saw y', just a babby. Y' look like a proper young gentleman now. Come and sit down."

Francis did as instructed.

"I'll pour us some tea. And I just baked scones. I must have sensed a visitor, eh? Just sit yoursel' there and I'll be back in two shakes of a lamb's tail."

She was good to her word and the scones, still warm, with clotted cream and some kind of wild berry jam, lived up to the aroma that had met him at the door.

Miss. Blunt nodded frequently and said, "Ah," as Francis explained his mission, and the puzzle he had met in failing to find the record of his grandparents' marriage.

"Well, you see, that was afore my time. My mother would have been the one to help you with that. She would have known all the details like enough. She told me little bits, not much..." She frowned, trying to remember, then went silent.

Francis quietly sighed his disappointment,

"You see, my mother, Harriet Blunt – I'm Agnes, by the way – was Annie's companion in the early days. My mother was a young widow, my father having been killed as a soldier in India..." her thoughts drifted.

Francis waited patiently.

"Just little bits," Agnes repeated as she found her way back. "Annie was just sixteen when she had the babby, after they came back from Scotland... Of course!" Her eyes sparkled. "They were married in Scotland! Your grandparents were. I remember she told me that much, my mother, that is."

She sat back in her chair, delighted with her recollection

Francis said, "Scotland?"

"Aye. Yon Gretna spot."

She went on at pace before Francis could get a word out.

"And then it weren't long after that Jeremiah's heart failed him and she was left alone with the babby – your father, like. Luckily they had money that he left, Jeremiah, I mean, from his business – he was a carter, you know, had all kinds of wagons and things, built it up from nowt his sel' – and that let your father go to Beverley school and then Oxford, and enough left over to see her through. By then my mother had died and Annie had me stay on as her maid and her companion. We got on very well, I can say that. And I went with her to the funeral when your father died. She made such a fuss of you! And that's the last time I saw you." She chuckled, "And look at you now!"

A carter. A businessman, then. And obviously a fairly successful one.

"Did my grandfather's family come from around here? Are there still other relatives I could meet, other Teasdales, do you know?"

Agnes considered the question, then shook her head. "No, not that I know of. Annie never mentioned anybody like that. I don't know where Jeremiah was before he started his business here. She never said."

"And Annie – her family? What was her name before they married? Are any of her relatives nearby?"

Agnes shook her head and her glasses caught the reflection off the afternoon sun through the window in the wall at one side of the fireplace.

"She never talked about her own family either, and it wasn't my business to ask. I have no idea."

Getting nowhere, Francis thought.

He stared at a framed print on the far wall, above the fireplace. Richard Ansdell's '*A stag at Bay*'. A Scottish stag, maybe.

"Was Jeremiah perhaps Scottish?" he asked.

Agnes laughed and slapped a hand on her knee. "No, not a bit! Nivver talked owt like them lot do! He spoke quite proper. More proper than Annie did, in fact."

Francis could think of only one reason why his grandparents would have travelled to the Scottish border community to marry: The matter of consent.

As a priest-to-be he was fully aware of the history of the 1754 Marriage Act occasioned by Lord Hardwicke in an effort to make 'irregular' marriages – that is any not conducted in church – illegal. After the Act, couples – other than Jews or Quakers – had to be twenty-one to marry without the consent of their parents, publication of banns was required, and the ceremony had to take place in church with the blessing of a Church of England priest.

Scotland refused to adopt the act and it remained under Scottish law that a couple over the age of sixteen simply had to declare their intentions to be wed before two witnesses and their marriage was law. The ceremony could be conducted by almost anyone, for a small fee.

This loophole produced a veritable rush of English couples who would otherwise have been hampered, to the Scottish border. Francis recalled that it was only relatively recently, in 1856, that Lord Brougham's 'cooling off' Act had been passed which required one of the couple to dwell in the Scottish parish where they wished to marry, for twenty-one days. Francis thought surely that would discourage only the least determined.

The village of Gretna Green was the first community across the Scottish border from the English city of Carlisle and had become famous for marriages of eloping couples from the south. Either or both Francis's grandmother Annie and grandfather Jeremiah must have been too young to be married in England, and unable to get consent. So they would have eloped. Francis smiled at thought of true romance, a marriage between two young lovers, thwarting those who would deny Jeremiah Teasdale and Annie…Annie who?

Francis imagined Annie and Jeremiah fleeing across the Scottish border and finding temporary lodgings, while they waited the required three weeks. He wondered who might have objected to the lovers' wish to marry.

"Have another scone, lad," Agnes Blunt said. "And more tea afore you leave."

Chapter 17

The winter of 1863-64 had seen M and N's fish and chip shop prosper, in no small way because of the court case and the publicity it created. De Cosmos wrote an entertaining report of the event in which he congratulated Meg for her demeanour throughout 'what must have been a harrowing and surely undeserved experience,' lauded Sweeney for 'the (newfound) stance of a true gentleman, who had surprised all who had known him in earlier days,' and congratulated Judge Begbie on a 'level-headed and wise disposition of the case.' He concluded, 'Both Miss Tyson and Mr. Sweeney (he recently) have shown themselves to be assets to our fair city.'

Meg, Sweeney, and Martha had become fashionable. They were invited to Christmas and New Year celebrations around the city. Meg accompanied Alan Munro to homes where he was welcomed as a first-footer on New Year's Eve, a dark-haired man delivering a piece of coal, a symbol of prosperity and good fortune for the following year, as was the custom in both his Scottish homeland and Meg's own village. Sweeny and Martha, in a fleeting burst of social acceptance, were seen in homes where a few months earlier neither of them would have made it onto the door-step, let alone across it.

Martha had blossomed. Her growing command of English impressed all who met her, though Meg had to caution her against some of the selections she acquired from Nancy's occasional lapses.

By the spring of that year M and N's was earning them an income beyond anything Meg could have hoped. She had extended the opening hours to include a mid-day operation and the shop was always full with dock workers, ships' crews, and the like. Only on Sunday were they closed. Nancy was spending more time at the shop and less at the Campbells, where the child-care had fallen more to the Campbell's niece, Helen.

When Meg remarked on the degree of welcome, Alan Munro said, "It's called the power of the press. The De Cosmos blessing in this case."

***

On a warm Sunday afternoon in late May of 1864 Meg and Alan Munro sipped tea and chatted with Sweeny and Martha at a cedar table in the open grassy space behind Sweeny's home. The previous week had seen the May 21st annual celebration of the Queen's birthday with a crowd of several thousand watching horse racing and festivities at Beacon Hill. Sweeney's house sat on five acres at the far south end of Fort Street. The four corners of the property were marked by four flowering cherry trees, today resplendent in pink. Who had planted the trees and when, Sweeney knew not. His property bordered on forest where maple and Gary Oak trees grew beside white-flowering dogwood and two tall cottonwood trees whose fluffy seed carriers were floating and settling all around. Skunk cabbage abounded further back by a stream that ran deep in the spring.

"Lots of animal life back there," Sweeney said. "Deer and…" he recalled the moment the previous day when Martha had shushed him in mid-sentence and pointed to a movement which became the tawny shape of a cougar, almost the colour of the tall dry grass.

"I moved my 'ed and it was gone. Like a bloomin' ghost. One minute there, next, whoosh! Away. In 'er world" – nodding at Martha – "if you see one a' them it means somebody from the other side, their spirit world, 'as a message for you or for somebody you know." He chuckled. "'aven't got anythin' so far. Anybody else?" He chuckled as he looked at each in turn.

Meg felt the skin on her neck prickle and she shivered, despite the day's heat.

'Other world' stories had always given her a creepy feeling. *No doubt*, she thought, *caused by the miners' stories of the Tommy Knockers – supposedly ghosts of colliers who had been trapped behind cave-ins and hammered on the rocks hoping to be rescued.* The ghosts of the missing were said to be heard, still knocking in old mine shafts. The legend had been brought to Morthwaite and other Cumbrian pits by in-comers from Cornwall and Wales.

"Aye, and they should have left them back theer," Lizzie Tyson had said. "My man and my lad are both Tommy. We don't need that rubbish bringing us bad luck. And nae body believes it anyway. Nowt but damned superstition."

Her husband had laughed. "Knock on wood," he said with a grin, and rapped his knuckles on the front room table.

"That's not funny, you daft bugger."

Meg smiled at the memory. She looked off into the bush where Sweeny said he had seen the big cat. Just the tall grass, rustling in a light breeze.

Alan Munro was talking with Sweeny. "I have to take a trip up to Nanaimo in the summer. Things I have to take care of." He glanced at Meg, and smiled.

In recent months Alan had developed a surprisingly increasing need to visit the Campbell home late in the afternoon, ostensibly seeking guidance on business or political matters from the flame-haired Bruce who, when he happened to be at home on such occasions offered wise noddings of the head while waiting for Meg to enter and announce that she must walk into the city on one or another errand and for Alan to co-incidentally remark that he too must be on his way, and thank you for the advice.

As they saw increasingly more of each other in time away from their work, Meg had learned of Alan's interest and hopes for an involvement in an industry that was beginning to pay well for those who had committed to its beginnings. A significant trade had developed between the Nanaimo coal mines and buyers in San Francisco, as well as with the ships of the Royal Navy's Pacific fleet and trade ships now powered by steam.

He had said, "There would be further advancement for me with Hudson's Bay of course, eventually, but when opportunities could be waiting…"

A man's reach should exceed his grasp.

Meg had been at first amused and then pleased by the friendship she had witnessed growing between the two men of such differing backgrounds and experience: the Scottish-educated and comparatively refined Munro, a lad from a small-farm family on Ayrshire's coast, who had hungered to see more of life and the world, and like so many Scots before him, ten years ago at the age of fifteen had been accepted as an apprentice trader with the Hudson's Bay Company, who had made his way through company ranks and achieved status and respect in the community – and Sweeney, a rough and tumble former brawler and drunkard, but who had done all he could to redeem himself in the eyes of those who now mattered to him, especially Martha, and by that extension, Meg.

Now Munro continued, "Would you like to come with me? Just a short trip."

Sweeney looked up, eager, and started to respond.

But Munro had aimed the question at Meg.

Meg laughed. "What, to see a coal mine?"

Munro acknowledged the dry humour with a smile.

'Oooh, Alan, is it?'

'Shut up, Nance.'

Meg considered. There was the shop, but there was an always-willing Nancy for that, and Rhys always at her side.

And there was more to his question than just a boat trip, she was certain.

She nodded. "Aye, all right."

Meg had made sure as their relationship progressed from hand-holding to close embraces and gentle kisses laden with promise that he knew everything about her history and family. Everything except the Sandy Benson episode that had propelled her to where she was now, and which was her concern alone and had no place in her new life, or in Alan's.

For his part, Alan Munro had accepted Meg for what he saw: A young woman of remarkable physical attractiveness, of quick mind and, especially, with a personal strength and a determination to make the most of the new life she had taken on.

A strength she was going to need and which would be tested.

"If Martha agrees," Munro continued, "she could accompany us, as a chaperone."

Martha said, "Shap…?"

Sweeney explained, and announced, "And I'll come with Martha."

Martha beamed. Meg heard her say quietly to Sweeny, "…My people." Sweeney patted her shoulder and placed an arm around her. "…My dove." So far Sweeny had been true to his promises.

Munro was pleased with Meg's agreement to accompany him and, Meg noticed, especially so was Martha.

Chapter 18

On a day in late July they left Victoria at dawn on the stern-wheel paddle steamer *Glencoe*. The ship had been at one time part of the Hudson's Bay Company's Marine Division, now it was newly owned and captained by Donald MacDonald, a short broad man with a clean shaven face, and a former company trader. The Captain was dressed smartly in the manner of an officer of the Royal Navy (the shaven face complying with the service's requirement) with dark blue belted knee-length coat, with a parade of brass buttons and a full-dress cocked hat. Meg thought the image seemed a touch extravagant for a coastal steamer, but chose not to share the thought. Instead, she politely pretended interest as MacDonald showed them around and boasted that the twenty-year-old ship was, "London-built, of twenty-eight tons, fifty-five feet in length, fourteen-foot beam, a deck of Quebec yellow pine, with a draught of seven feet, an easy fit for Nanaimo's deep harbour, as you will discover."

The *Glencoe* had a crew of five, who handled the freight – the deck was stacked with crates of everything from books and dried fruit to fine wines and hardware bound for Nanaimo stores and businesses – and shovelled the coal to keep the boilers providing power to the stern paddle wheel.

"Donald bought the ship from a Douglas Campbell," Alan Munro told them. "A bankruptcy sale. Campbell was a waster who lost everything else through drink and the cards, so Donald was especially pleased over that – the man being a Campbell, I mean. And the first thing Donald did was to change the name of the vessel from *The Argyll*."

At Meg's query, Alan recited briefly the details of the Glencoe massacre of MacDonalds by Campbells of the Earl of Argyll's regiment.

"Almost two hundred years ago, but 'We dinna forget,' any MacDonald will tell you, 'And we dinna forgive.'"

Meg frowned. "But the captain came to a Campbell – *our* Mr. Campbell – for the bank loan, for the mortgage on the ship."

Alan laughed. "Aye. Because Bruce offered him the money at a full point less than anyone else in the city. Donald is a Scotsman foremost, after all. He forgave Bruce his heritage, for the once."

Sweeney said, "I thought it was bad luck to change the name of a ship. Puts a curse on it."

Donald MacDonald had heard them. "Not as long as you get rid of every piece of the old name – everything with the old name on it. And I certainly did that. And guid riddance tae it, and tae him." He spat over the side rail for emphasis.

The sun rose and a misty haze surrendered to an off-shore breeze as they cut through a quiet sea off Gordon Head. Streamers of smoke eddied from the single skinny-seeming stack and were whisked east. As they passed the point, the captain suddenly called out from the side of the high wheelhouse, "Ahead, off the starboard!"

No more than twenty yards from the ship, four orcas split the ocean's surface, the great black triangles of their dorsal fins rising followed by their massive forms, sleek black backs and white undersides, clearing the surface as they breached, seeming to suspend in the air, then crashed back into the sea.

Meg gasped. She had had glimpses of orcas before, in the water of Juan de Fuca Strait off Clover Point and Beacon Hill, and earlier near the Falkland Islands from the deck of the *Tynemouth*, but she had never been this close to the magnificent creatures the Indians called blackfish and killer whales. Behind the four, three more of the pod repeated the performance, even closer to the ship and Meg laughed and raised a hand to knock away the flying spume their antics created.

Alan had moved close to Meg as the great mammals performed, almost, it seemed, especially for them. Meg grabbed his arm and held on in her excitement and delight. As the ship rolled with the slight swell, they came closer together. Each time they did, Alan was stirringly aware of Meg's body warmth through the light wool jacket she wore over her dress, and of her firm, full breasts against his arm.

The whales finally moved away from the ship and soon disappeared from sight.

"My goodness!" Meg breathed. "What a sight!"

"They must have known you were watching," Alan said.

Meg laughed at the thought. "A command performance," she said. She had not increased the distance between them.

He touched her hand against his arm, closed his hand on hers. "We should spend more time like this, Meg. More time together."

"I would like that," she said. In recent weeks Meg had felt the growth of a genuine companionship between them, an increasingly warm intimacy, and more. What came next was both partly expected and fully welcomed.

"You are in my thoughts all the while."

"That is good to know."

"I am very much in love with you."

Meg's heart turned over. "And I feel the same."

"Then, if I ask…will you be my wife?"

"Yes, I will. Gladly."

They sealed the commitment with a long kiss on the lips, to the delight of the watching Martha and Sweeny.

"We will let people know the minute we get back," Alan said. "You can chose the date for the wedding. As soon as you wish."

'Oooh, Alan is it?' And now it would be, *'I bloody knew it!'*

He pulled her to him. "But, the sooner, the better." She felt his hardness against her

"Yes," she breathed. And held him there.

The mood was heady for the rest of the trip north. Passing the mouth of a narrow river, they watched three black bears paw the swirling current for a mid-day feed of salmon. Further along on a jagged rocky shore, two grey wolves posed side by side, one slightly taller than the other, then as if at a signal they turned and loped away through tall grass and into the undergrowth. Life mates, Meg decided.

Alan told them stories of the coast as they travelled. He had a diary kept by his uncle, Malcolm Blair, who also had been employed by the HBC in earlier years when the company had attempted to mine for coal at Fort Rupert, near the northern end of Vancouver's Island.

He read from the diary: "When we first arrived, we were met by the sight of sixteen heads mounted on poles on the shore."

Meg's eyebrows rose.

"Jasus!" Sweeney said. "And they stayed? Christ, I'd been out a' there right quick!"

"Apparently the heads belonged to enemies. The whites were welcomed, for the trade goods they offered – in fact the first white woman to land was offered any two of the heads as a gift." He laughed. "There is no indication that she accepted."

The *Glencoe* steamed into Nanaimo harbour in the early evening, dropped anchor and tied up at the end of a square wharf jutting out into the deep bay. On one side of the wharf a steamer waited to take on coal which would be shovelled into chutes from the wharf. On the other side, a collection of smaller craft and canoes sat tied up to the timbers. Off to the right, to the north, a gang of men, some of them Indian, worked on an unfinished single track of rails that curved along the half-moon of the bay and would end at the chutes on the wharf.

To the south, pilings were in place for an additional wharf which it seemed would dwarf the present structure. Alan estimated that the new wharf would measure at least four hundred feet out into the deep water and have a front of two hundred feet. How many ships at one time, using both sides of the new wharf, could be in place and loading coal? How much money was there to be made by those who had both the coal and the ability to put it aboard the ships? The man who was building the rail tracks – and waiting the delivery of a locomotive from England to run coal wagons on them – knew the answers to those questions. The man that Alan Munro was here to meet.

Alan knew that already more than a hundred tons of coal a day was being produced in the mines of the Vancouver Coal Mining and Land Company to serve a seemingly insatiable market in San Francisco, as well as ships of the Royal Navy and others who had gone to steam power.

He studied the whole scene, especially the wharf under construction, and the beach behind it. "And there is the key," he murmured.

Meg examined the town. Just to the north two Indian long-houses sat high back on the shore, the last two remaining of the village which had been moved further south – it was said to remove and cleanse the remnants of a smallpox outbreak, but which move also conveniently served the waterfront access needs of the coal company. The two squat, flat-fronted houses were made from thick, hand-hewn cedar planks fitted together and painted with broad swatches of red, white and black. The roofs were of cedar bark and shakes, weighted down by stones. Before each building stood a massive cedar pole into which was carved totems of beaver, bear, frog and eagle. She knew that, as with the Victoria Songhees tribe, several families, each with its own defined area, would live in each house.

Directly facing her on the inlet shore were a square stone chimney belching smoke and nearby a low log building, the structures of the original HBC Number One Shaft coal mine. There was no headframe such as the one at Coater pit which dropped colliers in its cage to the seams deep below ground, but there was enough in the buildings to produce a sharp image of Morthwaite, and a pang of homesickness that was never wholly absent.

Commanding the forefront higher up and back from the bay was the octagonal-shaped white-washed bastion, constructed ten years previously as a protection against possible attack but also serving as a gaol when necessary.

One of Alan's stories en-route had included the tale of the Royal Navy captain convicted of fraud and sentenced to be held in the Nanaimo bastion until his return to England for trial. The gaoler had allowed the captain out each day with the provision he would return by a certain time. The captain habitually began to be late for the curfew – "Until finally he was warned that if it happened again, he would not be allowed back into gaol that night!"

Behind the bastion and to the sides were houses built for the coal miners – two rows of simple white-washed wood-framed huts with cedar shake roofs.

A group of Indians stood in the shallows and on the beach, mostly women and children, some of the little ones naked, watching the *Glencoe*. A child aged about five picked out Meg and waved. Meg waved back and the child squealed, delighted.

Beside Meg, Martha called out to the child, a girl. The little one laughed and called back in the same language. Several of the adults turned and joined in the exchange, a hum of excitement in their voices as they pointed to Martha. These were the Snuneymuxw people for whom Nanaimo was now named. Earlier and briefly, it had been Colville, for a company director.

A young man left the group and climbed up and onto the wharf. He approached the steamer, his smile broadening as Martha moved toward the ship's rail. He and Martha spoke a few words and in no time he was over the ship's rail onto the deck and the pair were hugging each other.

Sweeney grunted and stepped forward.

The Indians on shore began calling, waving their arms about, and chanting, a joyous sound.

Alan Munro placed a hand on Sweeney's arm. "It's all right, Seamus. I believe it is a family matter – a celebration, from what I know of their language."

"*Family* matter? How can it be—"

In the next second, a sound arose from the women among the shore Indians that had Meg, Sweeney, and Munro suddenly utterly still.

The women were humming the tune to the old Scottish folk song, *Annie Laurie.*

Meg immediately thought back to the day she had first met Martha when she had delivered salmon to the Campbell home. She had left humming a tune that Meg had known was vaguely familiar. This was it.

And now Martha astonished them as she turned toward the shore and broke into song with the first two lines, and then, soulfully:

...Gied me her promise true, which ne'er forgot shall be,
And for bonnie Annie Laurie I would lay me doon and dee.

"Bloody 'ell," Sweeney said. "Just needs a piper."

Munro snorted.

"Oh, I've 'eard her wid the tune now and then," Sweeney said. "But I thought it was summat she just picked up, wid that many Scotch around, 'acos they're everywhere, aren't they?" He grinned and nodded at Alan. "But how in God's name does she know it that well?"

He pointed. "An' look at that lot now."

The Indians were crowding closer to the *Glencoe*, wading through the shallows, climbing on to the wharf, calling to Martha.

"What are they saying?" Meg said. "Can you understand them?"

"Something about '...our girl...come back home...' That's all I can make out just now," Alan said. He left Meg and Sweeney and walked along the deck to the ship's prow. The Indians, about thirty of them, now had gathered on the wharf. Munro picked out a man in the lead and began talking to him using Chinook, the pidgin language that had served Indians and whites through decades of trading along the coast. Martha joined them in the conversation. She seemed as excited as any of the crowd. Meg and Sweeney walked forward and joined them and listened as the story unfolded and Munro explained it.

"I have heard of the incident, the first part of all this," Munro said. "I did not know of the second part. The incident itself is quite famous. It happened ten years ago. There was a dispute between these Snuneymuxw and the Kwakiutl, a very aggressive lot from Cape Mudge, on an island further north. A few Kwakiutl had been hired by Hudson's Bay as labourers on homes for a new crew of miners. The Snuneymuxw objected, feeling the Kwakiutl were taking work and possibly future trade away from them. They told the Kwakiutl group to leave and when they refused, killed three of them. There was always going to be a retaliation. A few days later the Kwakiutl came in force, a hundred canoes of warriors, painted for all-out war. Women and children were ordered to go to the Bastion for safety and the Snuneymuxw went out to meet the enemy – but with far fewer canoes and men."

"Jasus." From Sweeney.

Meg said, "But what does Martha—"

Munro continued, "The Snuneymuxw chief, Wun-wun-shun, talked with his opposite number in the Kwakiutl and agreed that wrong had been done and that an equal number of Snuneymuxw should be sacrificed – I know it sounds barbaric, but that was their way. But – and this is the second part – at the same time, Wun wun-shun saw that some of the Kwakiutl were pointing to two young children on the beach, a girl and a boy, both about nine or ten. He knew what they were thinking: that, apart from what else was happening, the girl especially would make a valuable slave to take with them."

"Christ!" Meg said.

"It was common practice among the coast tribes," Munro said. "So, Wun-wun-shun spoke to one of his men and that man returned in his canoe to the beach. While that was happening, the Kwakiutl were waiting for the three Snuneymuxw volunteers to come forward to die. When none did, finally Chief Wun-wun-shun proposed that he himself would be the sacrifice and because of his status that should satisfy the Kwakiutl. The Kwakiutl accepted that. The chief stood up in his canoe and, after two bullets missed, he was shot in the head and killed. The Kwakiutl were satisfied, and left."

Meg said, "The girl on the beach. That was Martha?"

She looked at Martha, whose gaze was fixed on the Snuneymuxw on the wharf.

Munro said, "It was. And on the very same day she was on her way to Victoria. The chief did not trust the Kwakiutl not to return for the girl. He considered them *mesachie* – evil. His instructions had been that she should be placed in the care of Robert Carstairs,

147

a Scotsman who had lived here for several years and had been a teacher and lay-preacher. He was also a fine musician and had formed a choir that included many of the native girls and women – thus, *Annie Laurie*. Just the day before, he had announced that he was leaving that day for a new home and position in Victoria."

Meg said, "Why Martha, in particular?"

Munro turned to Martha and gestured, *you tell them*.

Martha said, "He was my grandfather, the great chief Wun-wun-shun."

Munro indicated the young man who had greeted and hugged Martha. "This is Martha's cousin, the boy who was with her on the beach. His name, his white name, is Matthew."

Meg had a momentary image of her own brother Matthew, with his familiar smile.

Martha now explained that Carstairs had been instructed to take her to her mother's sister, who had married into the Victoria Songhees people.

"I stay there until now," Martha said.

Meg looked into the crowd on the wharf. "Your parents? Your mother? Is she here?"

Martha shook her head. "Die when I was born."

Sweeney's right hand moved in the Catholic sign of the cross. "Your father?"

Martha shrugged. "Went away."

Martha concluded, "My grandfather…searching for the English…cared for me when they died. I was his girl."

"An' thank God for that," Sweeney said.

The visitors left the vessel and Martha took Meg and Sweeney into the crowd of Indians. The Snuneymuxw now appeared to be as interested in Meg as they were in Martha, as Martha explained in their language her connection with her white woman friend, and with Sweeney. By her actions, Martha was recounting for the group the story of Meg's knife attack on Sweeney – they looked disapprovingly at Sweeney as Martha's arms raised and stabbed down – and on Sweeney's subsequent penance and Meg's acquittal, they nodded approval and now smiled at him, which seemed to give him considerable gratification and relief.

While this was happening, Alan Munro signalled to Meg that it was time for him to go to the appointment he had arranged with Andrew Murdoch, the most powerful man in Nanaimo, and perhaps much further afield.

The Aberdeen-born Murdoch had originally worked for the Hudson's Bay Company as a collier, became a mine manager and then was hired by the Vancouver Land and Coal Mining Company when the HBC sold the mining rights two years previously. He also earlier had been granted a free-miner's licence, and had managed to interest investors to help form another private company, which was prospering and expanding its operations and now owned Nanaimo's three most productive pits. As designated Managing Partner of the company Murdoch had an iron grip on and total individual control of his business, and an increasing control and ownership of land surrounding the city of Nanaimo. Especially that land along the waterfront.

It was the latter situation that Alan Munro had come to address.

Earlier in the year Alan had arrived to spend a few days with Joseph Penny, a friend from their apprentice days who had left the company and settled in Nanaimo where he saw a future in the retail business and had opened a small general store. The Kilmarnock-born Joseph had not changed a great deal in the four years since they had last seen each other. He was still the same burly, high-spirited fellow, with a thatch of black curly hair and heavy beard, a ready smile, and a taste for a bottle of good whisky, one of which he brought with him on a day that was to be spent renewing the friendship, with Alan possibly taking a deer, and filling a creel with fat trout from a creek some way back in the bush. Joseph neglected to carry either rifle or rod. Instead he spent the time, between sips, in a flow of reminiscing, recounting some of the better-forgotten experiences of their younger years with the company, evenings spent with whisky and young – and some not so young, but willing – Indian women, who would be disappointed on discovering that neither of the two young Scots was interested in acquiring a "country wife," a situation encouraged by the Hudson's Bay Company among its employees as such a marriage would strengthen trade ties with the women's families and their tribes. Alan and Joseph were encouraged to move on and eventually found themselves at the westernmost edge of the company's empire.

"Enough for now," Alan said, as Joseph glanced at what was left in the bottle and began another, "Do you remember…"

Alan's attention had been taken by a fallen section of the creek bank. Behind the fallen sod was a black layer, a stratum, of what he realized, as he dug into it with his skinning knife, was solid coal. He dug further, clearing away a thatch of thick grass and alder sapling roots, and saw that the coal was a seam that appeared to reach from just under the surface and climb upwards on the bank to a height of at least eight or nine feet. He and Joseph followed the seam west along the creek, a rising hope and growing excitement gripping Alan as he began to realize what he was seeing: a discovery that, unless someone had laid prior claim to it, could well be the opening door to a new future.

He stared back down their trail, estimating the distance they had covered since starting out, which due to Joseph's unhurried approach to the day, was not great. Alan estimated that they were something less than a mile from Nanaimo and its harbour.

Alan asked Joseph to say nothing to anyone in Nanaimo of the discovery. Joseph Penny declined to join Alan in any venture concerning the coal. "I'm happy with the shop," he'd said. "But good luck, my friend."

Alan drew a rough map of the site, giving estimated distances and directions based on the city and harbour of Nanaimo. He returned with the map to Victoria and took the first step under the mining legislation, which permitted him as an individual to apply for a two-year prospecting licence on any given five-hundred-acre portion of Vancouver Island. He found to his great relief that no other application had been made for the area containing the coal seam he had found. He had studied the terms of a license closely: after the two years, a formal grant of the land could be acquired by payment of five dollars per acre – plus proof of a minimum of ten thousand dollars spent to develop the seam. Alan Munro had money. He was frugal by nature and his rise to the position of chief trader in Victoria gave him annually a share of the HBC profits. This had gone straight into a bank account that he maintained for just such an opportunity as he now saw. But he would need some assistance should his envisioned coal mine become possible, and it was this potential support that he had proposed in the company of Bruce Campbell and a few of Campbell's friends, and which had been committed, provisionally, 'Should your discovery prove to be…' and so on, including conditions for the recovery of any such investment, plus interest and/or future dividends… Lawyers and bankers language. Alan Munro would remain the principal in any company to be formed.

He also would have to prove, when the time came, that he would have (or be able to employ) the expertise and have funds enough to support the project until it became profitable and thus self-supporting.

And critically – that he had access to tidewater.

After several weeks of waiting, his prospecting license finally had been granted and that had provided the impetus for today's journey. He had something less than two years to test and prove the value of his discovery, and to meet all the conditions.

Much would depend on Murdoch, whose log-built house and office Alan approached under a brassy sunset now almost complete behind Mt. Benson, its final hard light sifting through the branches of the stands of cedar and fir, leaving the surrounding trails in gloomy shadow.

While no particular hour had been set for their meeting – 'At your convenience on your day of arrival' had been the note dispatched two weeks earlier to Victoria – Andrew Murdoch drew his pocket watch from its place and frowned at it as he stood aside to allow Alan entry to his office, which took up much of the ground floor of his house. Murdoch himself was a man of average height and build, carefully dressed in a three-piece suit with wide lapels, a white shirt and a loose dark blue neck cravat. He wore steel-rimmed spectacles which managed to lend a particularly serious, almost grim, look. His face whiskers were carefully trimmed, as was his thin fair hair. Alan had learned enough about the man's history to know that Murdoch had to be at least fifty, but he wore the years well.

The room held an imposing desk which Alan guessed was of mahogany and had a brass-studded fine green leather surface, a grander piece of furniture than any Alan had seen in Victoria. Two elaborately framed oil paintings hung on each of three walls. The scene was lighted by an ornate oil lamp suspended from a ceiling of closely fitted boards of fine-sawed clear fir. Behind the desk was a chair of oak with padded leather arm and back rests. Facing the desk, on the fir plank floor, was a plain wooden rail-back chair, which Murdoch indicated Alan should take.

Murdoch took his place in the bigger chair and settled an unsmiling gaze on his visitor. His ice-blue eyes behind the glasses gave no hint as to what lay behind the look.

Alan Munro had often considered what of a man's person was suggested by his chosen surroundings. Controlling, was the word that Murdoch's demeanour and the setting suggested.

Murdoch wasted no time.

"You asked to see me."

"And I appreciate your time. I'm looking for advice, and some assistance. I have recently—"

Murdoch interrupted and waved the words away. "You have recently acquired a prospecting licence on a particular piece of land less than a mile from here to the west where you believe you have discovered a coal seam that you think you can develop as an independent miner and..." he shrugged, "I'm fully aware of all of that, Mr. Munro."

Alan added arrogant, and calculating.

"I'm aware of most events concerning coal in this area." Murdoch smiled. "I've been at it a long time. Including the fact that the borders of the area of your so-called claim are touching the borders of land already claimed by me, well before you made your appearance."

Alan considered. Then, "Touching," he said. "So, separate from. In other words, our claims are side-by-side."

Murdoch nodded. "They are, and I would imagine will remain so."

Whatever that was meant to convey, Alan was not sure.

He said, "I intend to develop a mine there, Mr. Murdoch."

A thin smile from Murdoch. "Intentions are one thing."

"I know about the requirements, and I believe I can meet them."

"With one exception, perhaps."

Alan cocked his head, inviting the explanation though knowing well now what was to come.

"Access to tide water, Mr. Munro. You might mine all the coal you are able, but having it sit on site with no way of getting it to the ships would be a great waste of your investment – as those backing you, Mr. Campbell and friends, would be certain to point out."

Add, informed.

"But you have water access from your neighboring land."

"Indeed I do. And to get to the water you would have to cross that land – my land."

"And as men of business, we could come to some arrangement—"

Murdoch shook his head. "We could, but not of the kind that I am certain you are considering – which would be you offering me a fee for shared use of my access."

They were silent for several seconds, while Alan digested the words, 'not of the kind you are considering.'

"Then what other kind?"

"*I* would pay *you* – for your claim. I would purchase the claim from you. Take it off your hands. Save you a lot of trouble, and money."

There was no doubt that Murdoch had examined and evaluated the coal on Alan's claim.

"That was not my intent on coming here, Mr. Murdoch."

"Again, intentions. And we know what Dr. Johnson had to say about them."

"That Hell is paved with them, yes. Although it is debated whether he was the first to say it. I went to school, Mr. Murdoch."

"The Glasgow Academy, from the time you were twelve until at fifteen you joined the company as an apprentice. You have done well since, then, Mr. Munro – perhaps it would be best if you stayed with your career, with the things you know. You have my position. I suggest you go away and consider it. I will make a fair offer when you are ready."

He stood. "Good evening."

The meeting was over.

***

MacDonald was preparing the *Glencoe* for the return trip. Ashore, what seemed to be the whole Snuneymuxw tribe waited to wave them off.

They had spent the night in the recently built Victoria Hotel, where two rooms had been booked for the night, one each for the men and women. Sufficient to provide the proprieties for Meg and Alan, though each in their mind and heart would have been please enough to dispense with them.

"I don't think that went too well," Sweeney had said as he watched Alan Munro return from his meeting with Murdoch, and Alan had confirmed his guess.

"A difficult man," he said. "I will explain later."

They watched as MacDonald's crew prepared to raise the anchor, and that was when the wave struck. What sailors would call a rogue wave, it swept in from the strait, around the north shoreline of Newcastle Island, silent, swelling, and fast.

The *Glencoe* rose with it, as did one small canoe in the centre of the harbour. The wave lifted the canoe and its two tiny occupants – Snuneymuxw boys aged six or seven who had been trying to spear a seal the way their adult counterparts did, the spear-holder up front, the paddler behind, ready with a gaff – and slammed it up against the Glencoe's hull and close to the paddle wheel blades, which had just begun a hesitant initial turning in preparation for leaving the harbour.

A cry went up from the beach and one of fear from the two boys as their canoe flipped and rolled, ejecting them into the water and under the ship's stern and the moving steel paddles.

For Meg it was as though the world stopped. One second Alan was beside her, next to Martha and Sweeney. The next, he had doffed his light coat, removed his boots, and had slipped over the rail into the deep water and was swimming, surging through the water with strong over-arm strokes, towards the canoe and the wheel's paddles which now had stopped turning as Donald MacDonald cut the power.

One small head of thick black hair broke the surface next to the overturned canoe, which had remained afloat. Alan grabbed the child, righted the canoe with his other hand, and plunked the spluttering and frightened boy into it. "Stay there!" he yelled, the force of the words easily understood by the boy, who gripped the sides of the sturdy little craft.

Men from the shore group were wading, then swimming toward the stern where Alan had dived below the surface in search of the second boy.

"Alan!" Meg stared down into the water. "Alan!"

A movement below the water: The second boy popped up, gasping, and was grabbed by Matthew, Martha's cousin, the first of the shore group to reach the scene. Mathew lifted the boy into the canoe alongside his young friend and others caught the craft and pushed it to shore. Matthew looked around for Alan, kept turning in the now light swell of the wave that had spent its energy and left the harbour suddenly, and eerily, calm.

Meg had stopped breathing. *Couldn't* breathe.

Sweeny had dropped his jacket and boots and was on the rail at the stern and climbing down on to the paddle wheel, grabbing the blades and lowering himself. He kept hold on the lowest blade and ducked under the water.

"Not swim," Meg heard Martha say beside her. She grabbed and held Martha's hand.

Sweeny pulled himself up, gasping, spitting water. He glanced their way before lowering himself again, this time letting go of the one blade and searching for the next lower one under the surface. He stayed down so long that Martha cried out and clung to Meg.

By now other men from the Indian group were at the spot and were diving and searching. Meg had no idea of how long it had been since Alan had gone under the water, but fear dominated her senses.

After what seemed an age, there was movement near the wheel. Sweeney broke the surface. Meg gasped, at first with relief. But Sweeney had an arm around Alan Munro's still form, clasping him close, and was weeping. He looked up through his tears at the two women, and shook his head.

Dear God, no!

Donald MacDonald reached down to help Sweeney lift his friend's body onto the *Glencoe's* deck.

Chapter 19

Victoria, August 10, 1864

Meg sat in Michael Blacklock's office, facing the young lawyer across his desk. She had dark lines under her eyes and a face grey with the exhaustion of grief. Bruce Campbell was next to her in another chair. Meg contained her emotions as Blacklock concluded:

"He had me prepare his will."

"He said nothing to me."

"He would have thought it premature."

His death was premature!

Meg was no stranger to sudden death. Like most in a pit village, she had witnessed the burned and broken bodies being carried home from yet another explosion and fire, or roof collapse, had attended the front room where the bodies had been washed and laid out prior to burial, had seen the grief of the bereaved – and had come to understand that life, and the pits, and the deaths, would go on. But this…

She had pictured the return journey from Nanaimo over and again. No bright sun, as they had enjoyed on the trip up, but scudding, shredded clouds darkening the day. No orcas rising from the grey-green ocean, which had lain flat and sullen, as if cowering, ashamed of its own part in the event.

She had tended to Alan as he lay on the deck. She cradled his head and kissed his lips, now so cold. With Sweeney helping, she put back on Alan's coat and his boots. She dried and combed his hair. She commandeered a roll of soft linen, rejecting the canvas sailcloth at first offered by the captain, and folded it around Alan. She sat by him and held his hand, willing back a warmth that returned only in her imagination. She walked beside him as Sweeney and the Captain carried his body onto the inner harbour wharf. The news spread as if borne on the breeze, and people gathered. In no time Nancy was there with Rhys, and the Campbells, and Amor de Cosmos. Nancy enfolded Meg in her arms.

Alan Munro's death was reported in *The Colonist*: 'The loss of an upstanding and valued young man who contributed so much to our fair city.' The words contained by a heavy black printed border. His funeral had been attended by more than a hundred people and a blue-uniformed honour party of Victoria's police force, a sign of the respect he had earned in the city. Men and women had offered their condolences to Meg as if indeed she had been the widow. Nancy Lowther had held her and wept. Martha and Sweeney were at her side.

Blacklock gave her a moment, then, "It's straightforward, Meg. The will leaves everything to you."

A window behind Blacklock allowed the afternoon sun into the room and onto Meg's face. She felt the warmth. Little enough, against the numbing chill she had known for the past two weeks. Her eyes filled, but she had shed all her tears, other than those in private.

"Apart from the house and the money in the bank, which will become yours, there is this." He touched the thin sheaf of documents by his hand.

"The claim," he said. "*The Thistle*."

'That's what we'll call it, Meg. The mine. Our mine. The Thistle.'

She had laughed at the time, a joyous laugh.

"You have time to decide," Blacklock said. "But not unlimited time. The claim has conditions—"

"Perhaps later." Bruce Campbell help up a staying hand. "When Meg is—"

"No." Meg straightened her back. "There is no point in leaving things undecided. I wish to know all there is."

Blacklock nodded. "In that case I have this offer, a letter, from Andrew Murdoch to purchase the rights to the claim. It's a substantial offer. "

"The man wasted no time," Bruce Campbell said.

"He has wasted *his* time," Meg said. She stood. "I am going to open the mine. I am going to open *The Thistle*. It was Alan's goal. It was his dream."

Bruce Campbell said, "You must be careful, Meg. Now you have a thriving, successful business in the fish and chip shop, you have no debts, you have a fine house with no mortgage. You have good friends around you…"

Meg shook her head. "I'm decided."

157

Michael Blacklock said, "Then I shall do all I can to help. But I hope you know what you're taking on. The risks involved."

Meg recalled the initial trepidation she had felt on deciding to rent the shed that had become the thriving M and Ns. It was a minor thing compared with this. But…

"No doubt I shall find out," she said.

**

A letter from Sarah awaited Meg. It would be weeks, months, before Sarah and Meg's mam Lizzie received the ones from Meg concerning Alan's death.

Morthwaite, Cumberland.
May 15 1864
My dear Meg,
I will waste no time in saying, there have been deaths in an explosion at Coater Pit – though no harm to any Tyson – and a remarkable visit to my house from the lady of the manor.
It started yesterday morning…

Sarah had gone to answer the sound of a light but firm tapping at her front door.

Sarah had seen this woman only at a distance before this, the closest perhaps at the village fête when she had accompanied her late husband Lord Richard Benson on his annual appearance among his work force, usually in a carriage with four horses driven by a liveried man-servant.

Now on the rough road behind her was a nondescript single-occupant pony and trap, the off-white Cumberland fell-pony between the shafts seemingly content to wait un-tethered until needed, its reins hanging loose.

The woman said, "I am Jane Benson. I am here to ask for your assistance."

People, colliers and their wives and children appeared at their doors as word raced up and down the cobbled street, in and out of front rooms and back kitchens. Elsie Briggs, who lived two doors away, tripped over her frock as she fell into a curtsey from a distance, her exaggerated homage raising laughter, and advice: "Git a bit lower, lass. On thy knees, Elsie, git on thy knees!"

"My assistance?"

"I believe that you have the respect of the people in this village. That they would listen to you – that is, that they might listen to *me*, if you ask it of them."

Sarah studied her, a woman likely in her fifties, with worries clear on her face.

"You had better come in."

'Lady' Jane Benson was not what Sarah might have expected, had she given the matter any thought. The name, Jane, first she thought had the ring of plainness to it. One might have expected perhaps a Hortense, or Charlotte Virginia…if one made assumptions, which Sarah had long learned not to do.

The clothes, too. Jane Benson wore a waist-length black jacket over a simple dark-blue frock with tiny white flowers embroidered on the bosom. An unpretentious black hat sat atop long once-blonde now white hair which had been tied back with a single black ribbon, much like the style worn by many of the colliers' wives and daughters, for convenience as much as anything. The overall impression was that of a woman not set out to impress, by appearance at least. She could have been the wife of a well-to-do farmer, down to the practical sturdy brown shoes that showed under the hem of her frock.

In turn, Jane Benson observed a tall slim woman somewhere in her thirties with once-red hair that now accommodated broad strokes of iron-grey, a woman not inclined to defer, but being gracious in what had to appear to her an unusual moment. Her glance passed quickly over the port-wine-coloured scar covering most of the left side of the teacher's face.

"I wish to do something for the families of the two men who died," Jane Benson said, having politely declined Sarah's offer to be seated.

The explosion of fire-damp that Tommy Tyson had warned could happen, had done so two days earlier on the lowest of the three working levels of Coater Pit, when a spark from a hewer's pick had ignited a pocket of the gas.

"Two men and one boy," Sarah corrected her. "John Carruthers died when he tried to save his brother Robert who was killed under the rock fall that followed the first explosion. John died in the second blast. Adam Smallwood died because as many a child would, he thought he could rescue a pity pony. Adam was twelve." This was the minimum age for children allowed to work underground. "He is – was – the family's main wage earner."

"Sandy did not mention that."

Sarah contained her response, a moment not lost on Jane Benson, who added, "I am truly sorry."

She is genuine in that, Sarah thought. Which is why she is here to say whatever she plans to. Or at least, that is one reason.

"Of course we are all aware of your own losses last year," Sarah said, referring to the two Benson family deaths from cholera.

"And the affect they are still having on this village," Jane Benson said. "And on the future."

Especially your own welfare, Sarah thought, but she judged that the woman was simply being forthright. Coater Pit had been closed since the explosion. No coal was moving, no wages were being paid – and no funds were flowing into the Benson treasury. With only twelve government mines inspectors to serve the whole of Great Britain, a visit from one of them to Morthwaite was not expected to happen very soon, if at all. Miners – led by Matthew Tyson – were refusing to go down the pit until new ventilation fans were installed.

"I am given to understand that my son, Alexander, could have – indeed, does have – some responsibility for the accident. I had a long discussion with Mr. Carrick, our manager."

"If you mean by responsibility his ignoring of repeated warnings about conditions down the pit, then yes, he does bear responsibility. As I understand it, the miners had repeatedly asked for better ventilation, for new or bigger fans to remove the gases, expressly in the area where the explosion occurred, but their warnings were ignored."

Jane Benson calmly accepted the reproach from the village schoolteacher, further persuading Sarah of the woman's authenticity, and her needs.

"I have instructed Carrick to take charge and correct the situation. I will admit to you that there is a problem with Alexander. I am not a stranger to his shortcomings."

Sarah read a wealth of acknowledgement in the statement. But what was the woman prepared, or indeed able, to do about it?

Meg was sure that Jane Benson herself could survive for a time, but for how long? She had a large estate to maintain, staff to pay, and two sons – one seemingly unstable and his remaining older brother, heir to the estate and nominally in charge of the business, a known waster and philanderer – to support.

Sarah was judging the situation – and Jane Benson – accurately. Before her was a practical woman who was a far fit from the popular image of the so-called upper classes. Jane Benson had never been a debutante, never been 'presented.' She had been raised as Jane Whitaker, the daughter of a prosperous owner of a group of grocery shops near Birmingham. Her parents had ensured that Jane and her brother Silas had a sound education, and that Jane was carefully introduced into a world of business families with young and eligible men, such as Richard Benson. Jane was blessed with her parents' shrewdness and had seen the potential in the young man whose family was then emerging from the recently abolished slave trade, a practice she had found odious – but not sufficiently so as to reject a suitor whose wealth from the trade had flowed into the coal mines and purchased entry to the title and comforts she had so far enjoyed, and which she intended to continue enjoying. She maintained a close connection with her brother Silas who had gone on to study medicine and had become highly regarded as a physician and surgeon in his London practice in fashionable Harley Street, where doctors rubbed shoulders with politicians and an assortment of professionals, and from whom now occasionally she sought advice.

At present she was acutely aware of obstacles facing her, particularly in the persons of her two remaining sons, neither of whom by their current behavior she would trust beyond the mansion grounds with anything that might pose a threat to the family fortune and her own future. As Lady Benson she had established and carefully cultivated a network of loyal (for which read, well-rewarded) informants either from or closely connected to her estate staff – housemaids, footmen, grooms, gardeners. Thus she was aware of her now elder son James' infatuation and liaisons with Jinny Soames, the very young wife of a farmer more than twice her age from Cleator Moor. James was spending increasingly more time away from home and from the responsibilities settled on him with the deaths of his father and older brother the previous year. And then there was Sandy, whose behaviour appeared to grow more irrational, especially in his dealings with the colliers, where he seemed to believe that bullying and browbeating were the means of increasing production and who attributed any problems, at the mine or elsewhere, to anyone but himself – poorly maintained equipment and lazy and incompetent colliers caused production problems – and threats that ranged from wage cuts to evictions from homes were his solutions. The mine manager Carrick told her that "Mister Sandy listens t' naebody but 'is sel'." Jane Benson knew that Sandy was badly underestimating the colliers, a breed of men whose toughness and pride were not to be dismissed – and by doing so was putting much at risk.

"I need the mine to re-open, and to remain open," she said. "I will pay compensation to the families involved in the explosion. I will guarantee that the safety requirements are met, that the colliers will be paid for the time the mine has been closed through no fault of theirs, and that there will be no further threats of cuts in wages – so long as production is maintained and the market remains open to us."

Sarah said, "That is – that *sounds* – encouraging."

Jane Benson ignored Sarah's qualifier, understanding its origin in Benson-pit history. "Then you will arrange for me to speak to the villagers?"

Sarah wondered suddenly if old, long established barriers were being lifted – even though prompted by the woman's self-interest.

"I will do what I'm able to—"

Sarah was interrupted by a man's voice from the rear of the house.

"Sarah? Hello. I'm back. Ready for that tea that you promised."

Francis Teasdale entered the room from the rear door and through the back kitchen. He stopped when he saw Jane Benson. "Oh, excuse me, I did not realize we had company."

I am not sure what went through Jane Benson's mind, Meg, but she looked much surprised at the presence of a man in my home when Francis entered and she stared at him, and kept staring until I introduced him as my younger brother and explained that he was here for a short visit and due to return to his studies in the priesthood at Oxford. For a few moments she remained very quiet as she examined him before she prepared to leave. I had the oddest thought – that she was recognizing him from a previous meeting, which could not be so – but then more likely that she was perhaps measuring the young upstanding man that Francis has become against her two sons whom everyone knows seem to provide her with nothing but worries.

"Then you will become the Reverend Teasdale," Jane Benson said.

"That is my plan, yes."

"'Teasdale.' That is not an uncommon name in this area, I believe?"

"Possibly. But my father, Samuel Teasdale, was not from Cumberland. He was from Beverley in Yorkshire. As a priest he took the living at Ambleside, until his death when I was an infant."

Sarah watched Jane Benson for any signs that the story of her father's scandalous end, more than two decades ago, had made any imprint this far north-west and in this society, but there was nothing.

"We are in fact a transplanted Yorkshire family," Francis said. "My grandfather Jeremiah was in business in the Hull region. A very successful business."

Sarah smiled at Francis's way of letting the Lady know that they were from solid trading background and unashamed of it. Then she reached out as if to steady Jane Benson who as she prepared to leave had seemed to stumble on the worn carpet covering the flagstone floor, but as quickly collected herself.

"Jeremiah Teasdale," Jane Benson said.

"Indeed," Francis said.

With that, she left. And here is the good news. I was able to arrange what she requested. Two days later, she returned and spoke to more than fifty colliers, all packed into the Welfare. Your brother Matthew was introduced as their representative and it was to Matthew in that position that she made the promises she had outlined to me. She was frank about what she described as 'Alexander's mistakes.' When she was asked – by Matthew of course! – why the older son James was not being seen and not taking charge of the pit, she said, rather quickly, that he had not been well lately and she hoped that to change soon. When the meeting dispersed it was with the clear understanding by all parties that the future of Coater Pit rested with her commitments to the community. As she left, she said, 'I am grateful to you, Sarah.' No 'Miss Teasdale.' Almost as if to a friend – and certainly as an accepted equal. I am happy to be in that role so long as it serves the purpose it has done.

With love, and trusting that this finds you continuing well and prosperous.

Sarah.

Meg pictured the bodies of the two men and one boy she had known being carried home from the pit…

Her mood lifted somewhat as she imagined Matthew's act of taking a stand against Sandy Benson (for the second time!) and the intriguing visit by Lady Jane Benson to Sarah.

Meg folded the letter and placed it in a drawer with the earlier ones.

She now had to plan for her return to Nanaimo and her meeting with Dan Cunningham.

Chapter 20

Jane Benson watched the coffin bearing her son James' remains being lowered into the ground at Distington's Church of the Holy Spirit.

James had taken his pleasure once too often with Jinny Soames, the young wife of Abel Soames, at their farm at Cleator Moor, on a night that Abel had said he would be in Whitehaven until the morning. Abel had lied, and had returned in the early hours to confirm what he had suspected. He had fastened shut both doors to the house and set paraffin-soaked straw fires all around the building. Jinny Soames' and James Benson's mostly incinerated bodies were found a day later. A gold signet ring with the β stamp of his family's mark and the presence of his bay gelding would establish James as the unfortunate visitor. Abel's drunken and tearful confession months later would see him hanging and twisting and voiding his bowels on Gallows Hill at Harraby, near Carlisle.

Across from Jane Benson at the grave stood Sandy, now, under the rules of Primogeniture, the new Lord Benson, and in whose hands her future and that of the family estate rested. His face was gaunt and a dark drop seeped from under the ever-present patch over his left eye. He reached up and angrily flicked the mess away. Jane Benson wondered frequently what had really happened on the day that he had staggered home wounded. Certainly not the story he had spun, she was sure. She had heard hints that it had something to do with a screen lass who had since gone from the village, but none of her informants knew any details. Sandy took a small bottle from his coat pocket, drank from it, and glared defiantly at her. Laudanum, she knew, which he said he needed to still the pain in his eye. It seemed to settle him. He glanced down into his brother's grave, and smiled. In the past few days Jane had come to fear that smile.

She had been in the long hall, examining a line of framed portraits of the Benson family: One of the original patriarch Jonathon, the trader, another a likeness of her late husband Richard

165

painted a year before his death a year ago, a very young one of their eldest son Harold, who had died from the cholera outbreak along with his father. Two others were of Richard's father Jacob, and his grandfather Arthur, who as a young man in the last decades of the previous century had established the family's place in the slave trade – and caused a rift later in the family by doing so. The situation was never talked of, was treated as if it had never happened, but she knew it had involved another of Arthur's sons now long gone who had joined the politician William Wilberforce in his campaign against slavery, and been disowned by Arthur.

Sandy appeared beside her. He laughed. "What are you gazing at that old lot for, mother? They are the past. The future is what matters. We are the future. *I* am the future."

And may God help us with that, she thought.

She wondered where Sandy's evil streak…yes, that's what it was, evil…had come from. His father Richard had had none of that in him. While he could be a hard taskmaster with his mine workers – who were hard people themselves – and gave little that he did not have to, he was essentially a decent man, owning none of the low qualities that seemed to inhabit his youngest son. The mansion staff were afraid of Sandy. The previous day she had seen him in a hallway yelling at a new housemaid and raising his hand ready to strike her. It was only the sudden appearance from the library into the hallway of Jane's brother Silas, Sandy's uncle, here for the funeral after a hurried telegraph message from his sister that stopped him. Sandy had muttered something under his breath and stalked off towards the stables.

"I am so grateful for your being here," she told Silas. "I never know what he is going to do next."

Silas was a tall, slim man approaching sixty, with a carefully trimmed short black beard and moustache, wearing an expensive and fashionable fine Italian wool three piece suit, a navy blue necktie adorned with tiny red flowers, and shined black leather shoes. He watched Sandy's angry departure.

"Does he usually treat people that way?"

"I hear more than I see myself. I heard of a fourteen-year-old screen lass from one of the Whitehaven pits, daughter of a widow who is also a screen lass, who claimed she had borne a daughter by him. Sandy's words, I was told, were, 'You had better drown the bastard and if you ever come near me again I will have you seen to, you and your mother.'"

"Did you ask Sandy about it?"

"I would not have dared. I would have feared his response."

"Do you think someone could have invented the story? Perhaps someone trying to smear Sandy, or this family?"

"Not for one second. Not for a moment."

He looked the way Sandy had gone. "His behaviour is a concern, Jane. Is he drinking very much?"

"He empties a bottle of brandy daily and he is never without the laudanum."

He said, "If it would suit you, I would like to stay a while."

She touched her brother's arm. "Nothing would please me more, Silas. Thank you."

Chapter 21

On an October afternoon that had transformed from a promising late-summer day to a blustery one with sudden flurries of rain, Meg, with Michael Blacklock beside her, walked off the paddle-wheeler *Glencoe* onto the Nanaimo dock and from there to a road now beginning to change from dust to mud, and which was studded haphazardly with giant stumps of felled cedar and fir trees.

Nancy Lowther had protested vigorously when Meg announced her plans to return to Nanaimo aboard the *Glencoe*.

"Bloody 'ell, Meg, on *that* thing? I mean…"

"The *Glencoe* didn't kill Alan, Nance, nor did Donald MacDonald. Alan's bravery and his concern for those kiddies killed him and he would be the last to put any blame on the ship or its captain. Mr. MacDonald will get us there and back."

She had stepped aboard under the appreciative welcome of the Scottish captain and neither had needed to mention the events of that earlier trip.

She looked up as Dan Cunningham stepped forward from a group of four men in work clothes whom she immediately knew to be coal miners. They were on their haunches next to a stone wall that was part of a small enclosure, where half a dozen hens strutted and clucked. Three of the men smoked clay pipes as they talked quietly among themselves. Meg thought it could have been any corner at Morthwaite, where colliers off shift squatted just like this and smoked and talked for hours on end, rising occasionally to stretch themselves before returning to the down position.

"Hello, lass."

"Hello, Dan. So, here we are." Anticipation, and optimism. She waited.

Meg had met Dan three weeks earlier in Victoria, when he had walked up to the counter in M and N's and said, "Hoo do lass, hoos tha gaan on?"

Meg's mood had lifted and she had laughed, delighted at the words, the cadence, the accent. It could have been her father or any of her Morthwaite neighbors speaking.

Martha at the chip pan had smiled at her friend's sudden change in spirit, and thought: *Hoo-do-lass, hoos-tha-gaan-on? Bloody 'ell!*

Meg said, "Where are *you* from?"

"Lowca," he said, and laughed at Meg's broad smile. Lowca was another pit village, less than two miles below and to the west of Morthwaite, on the Solway coast.

"My grandfather, my dad's father, worked at Lowca at one time."

"Matt Tyson. A hewer, like me. Aye. I remember him. Older than me. Lungs got 'im, I think?"

"Yes."

"Like a lot. Anyway, I'm Dan Cunningham."

"And obviously you know my name."

"Oh, aye, we've heard about you, young Meg Tyson. Y've done well doon here. Fish shop and a' that. We get t' *Colonist,* few days late in Nanaimo, but we keep up wid things. Good f' you, lass." And quietly, "And so sorry for y' loss. We had met Alan, wid Joseph Penny, and he was a grand lad."

Meg nodded her thanks.

After a moment she said, "This is for cheering me up." She piled chips and a piece of battered cod onto a page of *The Colonist* and handed it to him. Dan smiled and said, "Well, that's grand. Thank you, lass."

Meg had returned to M and N's in the weeks since the reading of Alan's will. She had needed something to distract her from the thoughts racing through her mind: the fretting, the questions, the doubts…was she doing the right thing in insisting on pursuing Alan's plans for the *Thistle*? Could she do it, could she see it through?

…and so should a woman's, Meg.

Easy to say, Sarah. And some reaching, indeed. There was roughly nineteen months left on the two-year prospecting licence granted to Alan, and now in her hands. At the end of the two years she could acquire the land by first paying five dollars per acre – $2,500. With her own money and that left by Alan, that payment would be easy enough. Then she must prove she had $10,000 available to develop the seam. That too would be manageable. Just.

Beyond that the conditions dictated that she would have to prove that she had – or be able to employ – the expertise and have funds enough to support the project until it became profitable and thus self-supporting.

And – that she had access to tidewater.

Uppermost in her mind was the promise of future funding that Alan Munro had sought – and acquired the conditional promise of – from Bruce Campbell and a handful of other potential investors. Meg had wondered where those promises would stand now. How conditional had they been?

She did not wonder for long.

The question was answered the morning that Bruce Campbell showed up at the small two-story wooden house that had been Alan's and now was Meg's.

"I'm sorry, Meg, but none of the other guarantors is prepared to carry on with the arrangement."

"*Agreement*," Meg said. "It was an *agreement*."

"It was, between them – us – and Alan. But now that—"

Sharply: "Now that Alan is dead and the prospecting licence is mine."

"And with all that that entails, my dear."

"You mean because I'm a woman. Not capable of—"

"It's not just that, Meg."

Not just *that! Christ Almighty!*

"It *is* that, though. But look at what I've done since I arrived here. I've built a successful business out of nothing—"

"A *small* business, Meg. This is different, a move into an industry of which you have a very limited knowledge."

Meg laughed. *Only generations of my family labouring and dying in pits to make money for the likes of the Bensons!*

Campbell acknowledge the unspoken rebuke with a nod… "And none of the kind of experience needed here… And you're challenging a powerful and possibly dangerous man in Murdoch. I'm afraid—"

Meg interrupted, "I'm not out to challenge anyone – except perhaps myself. Alan went to great lengths – met all the regulations and requirements – to make a start on what he dreamed of doing, and he left it to me to continue. He was going to open the *Thistle*, and that's what I'm going to do. I had hoped it would be with the support that Alan had asked for – and thought he had been promised. Mistakenly, clearly."

Campbell shrugged and spread his hands. "I'm sorry, Meg."

"And your own part in it? Has that gone, too?"

"Meg, it was a collective commitment at the time. None of us alone could have taken it on. With the others stepping out…it's just business."

At least she knew exactly where she stood.

And she had Dan Cunningham.

At that first meeting she had wondered what had brought Dan to Victoria and was puzzled at his response:

"Lookin' for a job."

Meg looked puzzled. "But you're a hewer…" (and there are no pits here)

"And a good 'un, an' all. Had my lad Harry alongside me as me marra. We shifted a lot a' coal for that bloody man."

"Murdoch?"

"Aye."

"What happened?"

"It was a month ago. He sent a shift doon into t' old Number Two pit, into t' lower road. A few old timers said even though there was lots a' good coal theer and easy to bring oot, it 'adn't been worked for years because there was watter in t' old road behind it and a weak wall between them. I ast him if he knew aboot that, but he shrugged it off, said he'd nivver heard owt like that, and there was likely nowt to it. He'd just won a big contract with yan a' them San Francisco buyers and that was a' that mattered. He needed to get that coal, and quick. He finally sent a shift of fower doon and telt them t' start blastin' an' strippin'…there must a' been an inrush frae t'other side as soon as they fired t' first shot. T' shaft filled up in nae time. I'll give Murdoch a laal bit a' credit, as an old pit man: He led a rescue team in because he knew there was some other old roads doon theer, but I think it was mair for show than owt else. He knew there was nowt they could dyer. They did hear some knockin', but that was desperate men who knew they were done for. There was rock falls between them and t' team that nowt would 'ave got through. Any blastin' woulda brought mair rock doon an' killed them anyway. While they were knockin', t' watter was risin' fast behind them, and they soon stopped, and that was them finished. They're still doon theer. An' their wives and kiddies wonderin' what next."

"Was there an inquiry?"

"That's what they ca'd it. A quick'un. They asked him if he knew about t' old waterlogged road behind where they blasted. Said he didn't, that as an experienced collier himself he wouldn't knowingly send his men into danger. And that was that. He was absolved of any blame."

"Didn't you speak up?"

"I tried, but I couldn't swear that I knew for sure what I'd been telt was fact, and t' other old timers, they weren't sure either and wanted nae trouble wid him. He would have had them out of their hooses in nae time. He owns maist a' them and they rent frae 'im. I'm lucky in that respect, there was a chance t' buy, a bit back, and I took it.

"Reet efter that, I was gone. Me and Harry. Not enough work to keep us on, he said, though t' truth was that I knew ower much. Next day he hired three fellers frae t' Midlands who just got here and he knows nowt aboot – but ah think 'e might find out, frae what I hear." He shook his head. "So noo we've got a hoose, and nowt else."

Meg said, "There are other mines there, aren't there? Not owned by Murdoch? I remember seeing head-frames where trees had been cleared, when I was there with Alan."

Dan Cunningham laughed. "Aye. But if he doesn't own t' other pits, he owns them as does. His two sons are wed to their daughters and it was him they went to for their start-up money. They wouldn't give us a second look. And if you're on t' outs wid Murdoch, neether will anybody else. And noo I'm findin' there's nowt down here for me, either."

"So, what will you do now? "

With a wry smile, Dan Cunningham said, "Mebbe get back on t' boat and try Morthut (pronouncing it in the diminished way that a west-Cumbrian would) and them Bensons. What do you think?"

Meg examined him. A seasoned collier, all right. No more than average height, wiry, with strong wrists and hands below his grey rough-wool shirt sleeves. And, she knew, as honest as honest could be. A man she knew she could trust.

It took her no time to respond. She said, "Go back to Nanaimo. Go to where Alan found the coal, and when I come up there – I'll let you know which day – give me your opinion: what the coal looks like, how much there might be of it – everything it tells you. Then we can decide what to do next."

She added, "You'll be *The Thistle's* first employee. "

Dan laughed, then he protested when Meg said she would pay him for his first job. "Let's say, twenty dollars. I'm sure that any surveyor would ask that."

"No, no, lass. That's not needed. I'll be happy to tek a look—"

Meg waved him down. "I'm hiring you, Dan. I was told by my teacher that knowledge is power, and I'm going to be paying you for what you know and how I can use it. And my family always maintained that a good day's work was worth a fair day's pay."

"Well, likely your teacher was a smart feller—"

"A woman, Dan, my teacher was a woman – Sarah Teasdale."

"Teasdale?" He seemed to consider that for a moment. Then, with a grin, "Well, sorry, a' course, there's plenty a' clever lasses these days."

"Yes, so that's that, Dan, you've now got a job to do."

Dan had not argued further, and now three weeks later he was offering his opinion:

"Your Alan was reet, lass. In my years in these coast pits, an' that's mair than ten, I've nivver seen owt to beat it. Top quality bituminous coal that'll match owt that you or me grew up wid and that's at least as good as any that Murdoch's diggin' an' sellin', an' as for t' depth of t' seam, well…nae limit that I can imagine. Looks like it could gaa on for ivver!"

Meg felt a surge, a rush of hope, a certainty that Alan Munro had been right – right in assessing his find, and right in willing Meg to carry on with the work.

"We'll go there tomorrow," Meg said. "You're staying on the payroll. How does 'mine manager' sound? And your lad Harry as deputy, depending on how we get along?"

Dan smiled his acceptance. "But I think we might be gittin' a head a' oorsells. Don't know how we're ganna move it to t' shore frae where it is. There's Murdoch to t' south, Indians to t' north. We'll need labour…"

"Don't fret about that, Dan. We'll talk about it later."

"Aye, well, that'll be at oor hoose, then. I know you're stoppin' at t' Victoria Hotel toneet, but you'll hev yer tea at oors." He nodded to include Blacklock, about whom he had reserved any opinion on seeing the young man's appearance, which remained more suited for a city office than a visit to the coal town and included the blue hair ribbon and the well-shined dress boots. "Both a' y'. I've telt oor Rachel you'll be theer."

Dan's home was one of a row of similar log-built houses, most of them white-washed and well-kept with fenced-in gardens where produce waited to be picked – beans, potatoes, squash. A whippet and a beagle together at one of the houses solemnly watched their progress, the beagle uttering a brief and unconvincing challenge.

At the next they saw a rabbit hutch with three nibbling residents visible behind a wire-net front.

Rachel Cunningham could have stepped out of any of the houses that Meg knew at Morthwaite. A small woman, with graying hair showing some remaining wisps of black, wearing a long white pinny over a worn but freshly ironed grey frock, with her sleeves rolled up and a dish cloth in one hand, she smiled and said, "It's grand to see you, lass, and you mister. A' course I've heard all about you. And fancy, you frae Morthut. Funny old world, isn't it? Come and sit yersells doon. I've got t' kettle on for a cup a' tea, and there's a tatie pot in t' oven."

They were in the biggest of the house's three rooms, the two at the rear separated from this one by a heavy wool curtain. A rock-built chimney was set into the back wall and an iron box stove stood to one side. Two wooden cupboards sat against the side walls, one painted blue, the other plain wood, but oiled to a shine. Neatly fashioned shelves above the cupboards held decorated plates and cups. On one shelf at the rear of the room sat two soft work caps and beside each a Kilmarnock lamp for underground work, with its two spouts for taking in and burning its fish-oil fuel. The centre of the room was taken up by a cedar-plank table. Two simple benches did for seating, though a caring hand had crowned the benches with sewn cushions. Meg thought that Rachel had gone to lengths to make the little house as much as possible a Cumberland collier's home-from-home.

Rachel talked rapidly as she busied herself setting out cups, glancing ever so often at Meg and smiling quickly when Meg caught her doing so. Clearly Rachel Cunningham was putting on a show for her guests, making the best of what had to be a worrying time for her – uncertainty of the next step in a life that had had its shares of ups and downs, a decade or so ago on the promise of a better life in this distant spot uprooted from a homeland where everybody knew everybody, where days were predictable, where people knew their place, and now still trying to make sense of what had happened to her husband's and son's jobs and pay packets, and wondering how they were going to survive.

Meg read the other woman's thoughts: *I wish we'd stopped at Lowca. I wish Dan hadn't listened to the recruiter feller years ago that put us on the boat and ended up now wid nae wages where there would a' been two...an' who's this slip of a lass anyway? Used to be a screen lass? Well, we* all *used t' be bloody screen lasses...! I wish...aye, an' if wishes were horses...*

Meg would have liked to say something that might calm Rachel's worries but, and despite all her hopes and optimism, too many unknowns lay ahead.

A young man entered the house, stopped and examined the visitors. He was dressed like Dan in well-worn but clean trousers and wool shirt, and had straight chestnut hair that reached just above his collar. Meg guessed that Harry Cunningham was three or four years her senior. He was a youthful copy of his father, and like many an offspring from generations of colliers, was smaller than average in height, appearing slight, but wiry and strong from his pit job.

"How do?" Harry nodded to Meg while giving her a frank examination and seemingly being pleased with what he saw. "You'll be t' famous screen lass, then."

Meg laughed. Harry had the same teasing, open tone that she recalled from her brothers. A host of images flooded her thoughts, and tears pricked and subsided.

Harry offered a welcoming a hand to Michael Blacklock while looking him up and down and smiling.

"That's grand, then," Dan said. He reached into a cupboard and brought out a jug of home-brewed beer. He poured three mugs full. Michael Blacklock happily accepted his, took a swig, raised it to the gathering and declared it to be very tasty indeed. Meg settled for a cup of tea with Rachel.

The lamb chops in the traditional tatie pot turned out to be rabbit legs, but the rest was all that was needed to return her in her mind to Lizzie Tyson's table. She spooned thick chunks of crisped black pudding onto her plate.

"Frae oor own pig," Dan said. "Butchered 'er a fortnight back. Rachel med sausage and took some a' that and a few chops aroond to t' neighbours – they bring scraps to feed t' pig, so it's fair play." He watched Michael, who was poking with his knife at the black sausage pieces, turning them over as though in an inspection. "Pigs blood an' other stuff, oatmeal, an' fat, bit a' salt. Some ca' it blood sausage. Thoo nivver hed it afore, lad?"

Michael Blacklock, though himself a northern Englishman, was still struggling with Dan's Cumbrian speaking when Meg stepped in.

"Just like my mam's," she said as she sopped up gravy with a chunk of Rachel's bread, and Rachel said, "Git away wid y'!" but looked pleased.

Michael Blacklock speared a chunk of black pudding, chewed on it, nodded what seemed to be approval, and eventually cleaned his plate.

They talked about things here and back home. Dan on his second mug of beer was rambling a bit and talked about the Bensons who owned Coater Pit where Meg's family worked, and other pits along the West Cumberland coast and how he knew they had become wealthy in the slave trade before moving their money into coal mining.

"Reason I know a bit aboot them is my brother – Herbert, a good bit older than me – worked on yan a' their slavers, just a lad, a deck hand, an' was theer when that lad a' theirs 'ad the big row aboot 'ow the business was a disgrace and he wanted nowt to dyer wid it – or them! Went off to Yorkshire to join that Wilberforce feller as a protest. He was a rebel aw' reet! Took their kitchen lass wid 'im an' all. That'd been another issue wid them – said he loved 'er and was ganna marry 'er, and them shoutin' that nae servant lass could ivver be good enough for yan a' their lads, for their family name! 'Oh, no?' sez he, 'Well, we'll see aboot that!' and off they went. Nae idea where they finished up – but not wid any a' the Benson money, certainly! They'll be well deed an' gone noo, anyway. And—"

At this stage Rachel Cunningham placed the stopper back in the beer jug, and the jug back in the cupboard.

"Herbert tell me the lad's name, but I'm jiggered if I can remember it. Summat like…"

His wife said, "There's apple tart and custard for pudding."

Dan walked them back to the hotel where two rooms had been reserved. Meg had seen little of the place on her first visit, but now, under a reddish hunter's moon just rising, she noticed that Nanaimo had many of the signs of a thriving town. Lighted windows in shops along the main street attracted customers in this early evening, one advertising the latest fashions from Victoria, with Irish poplins and French laces, and two others dressmaking and millinery service. The Parkins store boasted of delivering groceries, and Alexander Mayer's Red House offered 'cheap goods' from Portland and San Francisco. A few doors along was the general store owned by Joseph Penny, whom Meg had taken a moment to visit. Butcher shops and bakeries, a hardware store and two laundries, a sign-painter – the handiwork a little less relaxed than Nancy's – and a store with fish, game, vegetables, and firearms and ammunition for sale.

Despite the signs of prosperity though, the place had little that was inviting. Two men cursed and brawled on a corner, and people passed them by. Mangy-looking dogs slunk in and out of the shadows and snarled as they passed. A girl of about eighteen whom Meg guessed to be of mixed Indian-white blood, stood unsteadily on an unfinished board sidewalk and offered her services to a passing group of miners, who taunted her and moved on. Further along, a white woman probably in her forties and wearing nothing but a once-white chemise, leaned in the doorway of a ramshackle house and feigned coyness while clearly also plying the oldest game. The streets, more like cart tracks, were rutted and in many places they strayed off line to accommodate stumps two or three feet tall left there long after the trees had been felled and hauled away.

All of it built on coal. 'Where there's muck, there's money.'

So be it.

Dan was waiting for them the next morning.

Meg was dressed for the bush in a pair of Alan's trousers, a thick wool shirt, a pair of Alan's boots that two pairs of socks had made comfortable, and a wool cap over her tucked-up hair. Michael Blacklock had retrieved similar clothing from his baggage, along with a sturdy pair of boots. The outfit brought an approving nod from Dan.

Meg noted that Dan and Harry carried weapons, each with a long-barrelled shotgun and Dan some kind of hand-gun tucked into his belt. Both wore knives in leather sheathes. "Just in case," Dan said, seeing both Meg's and Michael's eyes on the weapons.

"In case we get a deer," Harry explained. "Or if we meet a cougar, but they normally want nowt to do wid y'."

Michael Blacklock murmured, "Comforting."

"Or a bear," Harry said. "If that happens, don't run away. They're fast. But there's a sayin' that you don't 'ave to be faster than t' bear – you just 'ave to be faster than ivvrybody else." He laughed.

Michael Blacklock muttered, "Christ!"

Dan continued, "Anyway, if it 'appens just wave yer arms and shout at it. That usually does it. Or we'll shoot it if needs be." He added, "Won't tek us ower long," and pointed the way along a narrow trail ridged with tree roots and into the woods.

Meg's mood was light with anticipation. She smiled as a plump red-breasted robin lit on a branch near her face and watched her with its head cocked. The bird was twice the size of its English

177

relative. A fat bumble bee with grey hoops around its behind nosed into a lone purple blossom. Meg stared. It was a purple thistle!

Nancy: 'The Thistle? That's a daft name for a coal mine, isn't it?'

'He was Scottish, Nance. They might as well have it on their flag.'

'But thistles are nowt but sharp prickles.'

'There's a story that the prickles came in useful way back when some attackers were creeping up on Scottish soldiers who were sleeping. The enemy took their shoes off so the Scots wouldn't hear them – but they stepped on thistles, and everybody heard them!'

'Bloody 'ell!' Then, 'Fancy that.' And, 'Well, that's o'right, then.'

The trail petered out at the beginning of a shallow swamp bordered by stands of alder and maple trees and evergreens. At the base of one of the alders were several primroses, their creamy-yellow petals indifferent to season's change. The sight of her favourite flower kept Meg's spirits high. A sudden sharp breeze loosed a shower of autumn-gold maple leaves, sending them swirling to the forest floor. Fir cones crunched underfoot, and Meg brushed aside dark green salal shrubs as Dan led the way. They passed outcrops of moss-covered rock and stands of so-far untouched giant firs and fragrant cedars whose towering canopies seemed to rest against the sky. A juvenile arbutus tree protruded from a rock, its strange paper-like bark hanging from its slim trunk, which bent in several directions on its way upwards

Somewhere close by a cricket sounded its note. Other creatures large and small made noise all around as they walked, but none showed itself and in less than an hour Meg was looking at the seam of coal that was her legacy, and possibly her dilemma.

She touched the surface, rubbed it, pulled back her hand and examined the black mark left there… She was back at Coater Pit, machinery clanking and groaning in the pit yard, a heap of coal and slate on the screening table to be sorted, her hands reaching out, scarred and bruised… But not those hands today, not the hands that had made Charles Dickens frown, and others to wonder. Martha had seen to that. The week after she had delivered that first basket of salmon to the Campbells, and had seen the state of Meg's hands when she dropped the tea cloth, Martha had returned and brought with her a small cedar-wood box filled with a soft, aromatic ointment – Meg sensed honey, and her favourite primroses, maybe cinnamon – which, without a word, she took and spread over the backs of Meg's hands, kneading it gently into the scars. She had closed the box and handed it to Meg, saying "Every day, little." Martha had regularly replenished the mixture. Now, two years later, Meg's hands bore no evidence of her life on the pit top.

She felt a touch on her shoulder. Dan pointed across the creek, twenty yards away. Two men stood watching them.

"Murdoch," Dan said.

Arctic eyes behind steel-rimmed glasses. Grim.

"Yes."

"Don't know the other feller," Dan said.

"I do."

Meg stared across the creek at Bruce Campbell. Her thoughts flew, scattered like panicked sheep on a Lakeland fell.

Christ almighty!

The big Scotsman responded with a nod and an odd smile – what was it…embarrassed? Sheepish? Apologetic? but a smile which quickly became a quizzical frown with a trace of what might have been alarm as the attention of all was taken by a sound from the undergrowth behind Meg's party. Meg turned, dismissed Campbell from her thought and beamed as she recognized Martha's cousin, Matthew, of the Snuneymuxw. He was accompanied by two other young men of the tribe. The three had uncombed hair down past their shoulders and wore sleeveless tunics made of hair from dogs like the two white-coated wild-looking things alongside them.

On their way through the bush, Dan had listened to Meg's plans and the arrangements she had made and the particular involvement of Michael Blacklock, and Martha. He nodded his understanding when Meg described the role Martha had played on two visits back since Alan's death, the connection with her cousin Matthew and the Snuneymuxw, and the tribe's lasting gratitude to Alan Munro.

"Matthew, the new chief," Dan had said.

"Yes, since his father died, shortly after we were here."

Dan said, "You know there's nae love lost theer, don't y'? Wid Murdoch, a' mean."

"The burial site," Meg said.

"Aye. He buggered that up. Even when he was telt aboot it. Naebody can tell Murdoch owt."

Meg had learned the details from Martha.

Murdoch had marked a stand of ancient cedar trees for felling. The trees stood on an area measuring roughly one hundred yards square which was sacred to the Snuneymuxw, who before the introduction and imposition by the Europeans of their churches and graveyards, had placed their dead within its bounds. Evidence remained of these hallowed practices – burial carvings, scraps of blankets that had enfolded the dead, and bones where over the years the elements had wrought change.

Murdoch was advised of the location's history and of its significance to the Snuneymuxw. He responded that that section of land was believed to contain coal and the property law as far back as the mid-1840s dictated that Indians were forbidden to have any land that held coal. The Indians dispute this, claiming that only coal was to be ceded – and paid for – to the whites, not the land itself. Murdoch claimed that Governor Douglas some years ago had ordered that the natives were to be considered the rightful possessors of land only if it were cultivated, and he quoted, "All other land is to be considered as waste and applicable to the purposes of colonization."

"So Murdoch decided it was waste land," Martha had told Meg. "He had the trees chopped down and used them for walls and pit props in his mines. His men made a fire and burned all the pieces that were still on the ground. There has been no more talk of the coal that was said to be there."

Matthew and the two came to the group, and Meg exchanged a light hug with Matthew and nodded a greeting to his companions. Dan Cunningham greeted the three by name and shook hands. The Indians examined Michael Blacklock, and accepted him. Then they stared bleakly across the creek at the two men there.

Meg also looked back across the creek at Bruce Campbell.

The anger that she had suppressed, now rose. *Fucker,* she thought, and a second later realized she had thought it aloud.

Dan choked back a laugh, then let it out. Harry was already laughing, as was Michael Blacklock.

***

Andrew Murdoch frowned. What could they possibly find amusing? The woman – a screen lass, for God's sake! – had the rights to mine the coal she had just handled, but even if she got it out of the ground, she had no way of moving and selling it. And

Cunningham and his fucking son must be almost on their uppers by now. He was surprised that they were still around. It was too bad that they had not been paying him rent. They would have had no roof over them.

He studied the pair. The girl who had been set to marry the HBC trader Munro, and the slim young man Blacklock with long black beribboned hair – a fop, a bloody dandy by all appearance, whom Murdoch thought looked a sight more confident than he should under the circumstances, which he thought Blacklock probably did not fully understand: that he and the fish-shop girl were essentially supplicants. She had been bequeathed the prospecting rights by the dead Munro to the coal seam that bordered Murdoch's property. Blacklock was along as her solicitor, with nothing to offer but fine words and opinions for which, if his own experiences with solicitors were any measure, no doubt she was paying handsomely. Murdoch had expected them to propose the same arrangement that Munro had suggested: pay him a sum in order to move their coal through his land to the water – *his* water. And Murdoch would have given them the same response: No, but I will repeat my offer to buy the rights to the scam – which he believed, after examining it himself, to be one of the richest deposits with the most potential for mining and profit that he and his coal masters had seen within a dozen miles of Nanaimo. He was furious that it had sat within touching distance and undiscovered by himself or his own people.

So he had been surprised when they never even approached him, rather they went ahead with this…this act…whatever the hell it was pretending to be. She had lost her financing, Campbell and the others having wisely backed away. And she could not have been left enough by Munro to carry through all the commitments she faced. The clock was ticking on her licence agreement, she had little more than a year left to complete the requirements – this made no sense. He would make the girl another offer to buy the site outright when she came to her senses.

He turned to Bruce Campbell and was about to speak, when Campbell said, "Good Christ." Murdoch followed his gaze across the creek, where six more men of the Snuneymuxw had emerged from the trees. They carried an assortment of pick-axes, long-handled augers, and shovels. Behind them was a group of women of the tribe, carrying woven baskets of willow and cedar.

"What on earth do they expect to do with that lot?" Campbell said.

Murdoch grunted. "More than you might think." He reminisced: "When I first got here, Eighteen-fifty, the coal was at Fort Rupert, lot further north of here, maybe two hundred miles. It was still Hudson's Bay business then, with just a few of us miners before they got busy contracting more colliers from Scotland and England. That coal ran out and then they found Nanaimo's and moved the work south. And they hired Indians to work with us. They dug out fifty tons on the first day. It was a seam exactly like this one, a surface pit, one of the first big discoveries. Black Diamond, they called it."

He added, "But it was a hard business to move it. A ship wanting coal would anchor off-shore, about five miles up the coast from where they were working. They would transport the coal that five miles then take baskets of it out in canoes and dump it into tubs lowered from the ships. It took a month to load a ship."

Campbell said, "Not very economical, surely?"

"Except for the labour rates. The Indians were happy to receive a new shirt—" he laughed "—or an old one for that matter, for a day's work. And they soon found a way of bringing the ships to anchor closer to the diggings."

"How things have changed," Campbell said.

"Aye, back then I had nothing."

"And now you're—"

"Aye, I am. Now is a different story."

"Indeed. With your three pits, and them close to the water, the rails and the wharf for loading…"

"Which is something she doesn't have. Nor is likely to."

Campbell debated with himself for a moment, then said, "If this is as good a find – more black diamond – would it not be good business to propose some type of arrangement with her?"

"I do not want an arrangement, Mr. Campbell. I want that bloody coal. I *need* that bloody coal."

Campbell looked curiously at him, but let the matter sit.

The Snuneymuxw new arrivals stared at Murdoch and Campbell

Murdoch maintained a hostile front, but his restless eyes spoke of disquiet.

As well they might.

He was staring at what he was certain would be the richest coal discovery since mining had started on Vancouver Island, but which was out of his grasp, while two of his own pits were under threat – one from nature's relentless insistence on correcting man's follies, the other ironically from his own over-hasty planning, verging on panic.

Meg turned to Matthew. "Tell the people thank you. They will be paid a full shift for today and we will start tomorrow." Her last four words carried across the creek.

As did her next question, to Blacklock, "He is definitely on his way?"

"He assures me of it. Before the end of the year."

Two months, if all went well. Two months to determine the *Thistle's* future.

***

In the town, Bruce Campbell waited on the shallow verandah that fronted the hotel.

"Meg—"

"Mr. Campbell."

"Whatever you are thinking, Meg—"

"I'm sure I don't know what to think."

"You must be doubting me. You too, Michael."

Blacklock said nothing.

Meg snapped, "Because you let me down once, and now you appear at the side of the man you warned me against? That would be 'Just business,' surely."

On the way back she had thought of what else she might say to him: *You used to be kind. You were a friend to me and Nancy. You supported us. You were our* teacher*, for God's sake!* And: *Is this what fickle means?* She held onto the words, for now.

Campbell smiled at Meg, turning his earlier words back on him. "As a matter of fact, yes. I had no choice over meeting with Murdoch, and secondly—"

"We *always* have a choice. Everybody has a choice!"

This man whose house she had lived in, who had been her strongest supporter when she proposed her own business, whom at one time she would have trusted without reserve…and now this bloody smile! She stamped her foot.

"*Everybody* has a choice!"

Michael Blacklock bowed his head and barely contained a laugh.

Campbell raised open palms. "Bear with me a moment, Meg, please. And listen."

Blacklock touched her arm. She looked at him. He nodded toward Campbell. *Let him speak.*

Meg glared, but waited.

"I was sent to Nanaimo – I had no idea that you were arriving at the same time – to see about opening a branch of our bank. This town is on the rise. If we fail to open a branch, some other bank will – and there is too much money here in need of a home for us to take the chance of being second, which would mean last, and far too late."

Meg waited, but her stance had begun to soften with his explanation, her shoulders lowered slightly from their angry set. She hesitated, then she shrugged, an invitation – if he must – for him to continue.

Campbell said, "You know the influence that he has in this town, on the businesses and their owners. I had to put our case to him, persuade him that it was in both our interests for my bank to establish here, especially if he were to be given the opportunity to invest with us. I believe he has accepted that."

Still short on warmth, but with a wavering of the conviction that she had been betrayed, Meg said, "Congratulations."

Blacklock said. "Yes. Well done."

Meg continued, "You started to say, 'secondly'…"

Campbell smiled. "Secondly, this gave me the opportunity to see what you were up to at the *Thistle*. "

"And?"

"I would like to know more of your plans." He paused. "As a friend."

Campbell looked and sounded as open and honest as Meg had always known him to be. Even when his group had withdrawn their backing he had been nothing but straightforward, and concerned for her future. And she had jumped down his throat, anger overcoming any thought of understanding. Now, his explanation for being with Murdoch today seemed perfectly reasonable, and her moment of anger, like the passing of a brief storm that clears the air as it leaves, waned along with her misgivings. She felt now a qualm, a prickling of guilt for her assumptions that his presence had meant an alliance with Murdoch – and against her.

She regretted her rush to judgment. (Again!) She had been wrong, and if she had been that wrong so easily, what else might she have misjudged? About the future? About her plans – Alan's plans? Could she indeed carry them through? What about Dan, and Harry, who were placing their confidence in her?

On the other hand, she had recognized and would correct this error – and would look out for others. She put the doubts aside, remembering Sarah Teasdale's admonishment that just because she was born into a pit-village life '...*does not mean that you have to become a victim of it... You can control your own destiny. There are more things in life...*'

Where would she be now without Sarah? Could she ever repay her teacher for what she had given her – apart from the assistance that had resulted in her being in this spot a world away from danger – Confidence? Determination? Even perhaps the courage to admit error.

She told Campbell, "Of course. And...I am sorry."

"Ferrrgotten," the Scotsman said, lightheartedly exaggerating his Scottishness. And then with his familiar broad smile, "And now I feel much better."

The confrontation had turned into a conversation. Meg answered his questions and explained the arrangements that she, along with Michael Blacklock, had made for the immediate future, and with whom.

"Well," Campbell said. "That should be very interesting."

Chapter 22

Coater Pit, Morthwaite, Cumberland

Billy Gregson, a 12-year-old labourer, cried and cowered against the brick wall of the building used for storing various small tools – shovels, brooms, and the like. Sandy Benson stood over him about to deliver another blow with his riding crop. The boy's face was a mess of blood and snot, his nose and one front tooth broken from the hardened leather of the weapon wielded by Sandy, whose face was contorted with rage, with madness.

"You idiot! You fucking idiot. Do you not understand simple English?"

The boy whimpered, lifted a hand and spread the mess further across his features.

"Answer me, you fucking fool! I told you to get one shovel and one brush and clean up some of this mess." He gestured to a scattering of horse droppings and other detritus around the pit yard, and to a single shovel the boy had dropped. "Is that too fucking much to ask!" He raised the crop for another blow…

"You leave our Billy alone!"

A slight girl of about ten with short chopped brown hair had stepped in between Sandy and the boy. Ivy Gregson carried a paper-wrapped slice of bread and bit of cheese – her brother's bait, which he had left behind.

"Leave 'im alone!" She reached a hand down to her brother. "Get up, Billy."

Sandy turned his attention to the girl.

"You want the same, you little slut?"

He slashed her across the shoulder with the crop. The bread and cheese scattered into the mud. She screamed, grabbed at the end of the crop and pulled it as she fell. With the crop looped to his wrist, the sudden move of the girl's slight weight was enough to pull Sandy over. He landed heavily on top of her.

The girl lay, quivering, sobbing. Sandy Benson straddled her. His breath came in gusts. He grinned as he slid a hand beneath her flimsy patched cotton dress with its faded flower pattern, and placed it between her skinny, scabbed legs. He looked about him, saw only the sobbing Billy. "You old enough yet? I'll wager you might be." He lifted the dress above her thighs, where she was naked. "Yes, by Christ, I think you'll do."

The girl cried out, covered herself with her hands and tried to close her legs against his groping fingers.

Benson laughed. He grasped her hands and pulled them away. Ivy screamed.

"Stop it, sir!" A hand took Benson's collar and dragged him off the girl. He fell sideways into the pit-yard sludge, then looked up, astonished, at seeing the mine manager, Stanley Carrick, dressed in his usual dark suit with a white shirt and tie, who now released his grip on Sandy's coat. Carrick had watched the events from the window of his manager's shed, and finally had seen enough.

"That's it." Carrick's voice was hoarse and shaking. "Gaa yam, Mr. Benson, and we'll say nowt else aboot it. I'll look efter these two." He looked over at the far side of the yard where his son Jackson had appeared and was making towards Sandy Benson, apparently with some intent of his own. He had doffed the leather jerkin he wore in his work around the pithead. "Bastard," Jackson growled, as he approached. Carrick waved him to stay back. Jackson did so reluctantly, but never took his angry glare off Sandy Benson. Carrick stepped over to where Sandy had tethered his horse, loosed the reins and held them out to their owner.

Sandy gaped in disbelief.

"You..." he started. "You dare to put a hand on me?"

"You went ower far," Carrick said, his voice gaining strength in his conviction of what was right and what wasn't – Sandy Benson or no Sandy Benson. Especially with Sandy Benson, who was never hampered by consideration of the difference between right and wrong, and who lacked even the smallest humane quality owned by his late father, including a fundamental decency when dealing with his workers.

"Y' can't dee that to a laal lass like her. And look at Billy, a reet mess you've made of him. You went ower bloody far!" Carrick's own anger was mounting as he looked at Ivy, lying in the dreck like a damaged doll, hands desperately holding her skimpy frock tight against her bare and now muddied legs. He clenched his fists, a motion not unnoticed by Sandy Benson. Carrick had been a collier before catching Richard Benson's attention and being placed in charge. He was as tough and strong as any of those who worked for him.

"Tek yer 'oss and gaa yam, Mr. Benson."

Benson climbed to his feet, brushing various filth from his clothing. His face was contorted. He laughed, an ugly sound.

"You are finished, Carrick. Finished!" He took the reins and swung himself up into the saddle. "You are sacked, as of this minute. Do not come near this pit again." He pointed his crop at Jackson Carrick. "And the same goes for you. Both of you are fucking-well finished!"

He wrenched the horse's head into a turn, and jammed his heels into its flanks.

***

Alarm and disbelief shaped Jane Benson's features.

"Sacked? You sacked Carrick?"

"He attacked me."

Sandy elaborated on the lie. "Threw me to the ground. First he countermanded my instructions to a worker and then attacked me when I reminded him of his position." Sandy sniggered. "The one he no longer holds."

Jane Benson looked about her. They were in the main entrance hall to the Benson mansion near the open double front doors where Sandy had stormed in, shouting about Carrick and how he and everyone else would learn who was to be listened to and what would be in store for them if they failed, that he was Lord Benson now, and by Christ…

"But Carrick…he *runs* the mine, Sandy. He *knows* the mine…we cannot do without him…"

He shut her down with a raised hand.

He leaned into her, growled, "And my name is, 'Alexander,' from now forward." He waved his arms around, barely missing his mother with a wild swing. "I'm not a fucking child anymore and I will not be called by a childish name!" he yelled. "And *I* will say who runs the mine!"

Jane Benson stepped back at his cursing. Never, in this house…never that crudeness, a collier's word, a commoner's word…never in her home.

"So, 'Alexander' from now," he instructed. "And for others it will be 'M'Lord.'" He put his face close to hers, his gaunt, and more so daily, it seemed. Flesh sunken at the cheek bones, and

188

around the nose and eye areas. And a smell of…something…corruption of sorts…from his left eye, the damaged one. "Is that understood, mother?" and when she did not immediately respond: "*Is* it?"

"It was certainly loud enough," Silas Whitaker said from behind him.

Sandy Benson spun to face his uncle. "Good!" he barked. "So it should be quite clear!"

Silas examined his nephew. Shook his head, and sighed. "Sandy, you are not well."

Sandy put a hand to his damaged eye, mopped away a dark blot from under the patch.

"Christ! I do not need a fucking jumped up London doctor to tell me that! Of course I am not well!"

Silas made to speak, but Sandy ranted on. "I have not been well for two years, since that Tyson bitch attacked me and did this." He indicated his eye. "I should never have let her get away with it. It is all her bloody fault, the whore! She offered herself to me for a shilling and when I told her to leave she attacked me with a rock! Cunt!"

Jane Benson flinched. Her thoughts flew back to the day Sandy had returned home with blood oozing from his wound. Both she and Richard had known there was something suspect in Sandy's report on events – the badger, the horse throwing him – now, what was he saying? 'That Tyson bitch?'

Muttering, "A drink…" Sandy wheeled away from them and stormed to his living quarters. Before he reached his door he spun and pointed a finger at his mother and held the stance for a moment. It was nothing less than a warning, a threat. Then he was gone and they heard his door slammed shut.

"Silas?" A plea.

"Yes, there is a serious problem. I believe he is a danger, to himself and to others – especially, and more worryingly, to you."

"I am more afraid each day," Jane Benson admitted. "And I am lost for what to do."

"Let me think about it. First I need to talk to your manager, Carrick."

Two hours later he returned.

"He is out of control, Jane. He attacked a girl, a child, just a child. It seems he would have actually raped her, right there in the pit yard. And he had already beaten and bloodied her brother, who is barely older. Carrick and his son were close to it and stopped

189

him, and I believe their account of what happened. If he continues this way, he will cause some great harm."

"Then, what on earth must I do? He has the lawful power and authority. He is indeed the Earl, he is Lord Benson."

Silas took her arm, pointed her into a drawing room and to an arm chair, sat opposite in another, and proposed his solution.

"Good God, Silas."

"It is the only way that I could leave and know you were safe."

She twisted a lace handkerchief in her fingers, back and forth, and back. "That would be such an extreme measure, surely?"

"Hippocrates said, 'For extreme diseases, extreme methods of cure, as to restriction, are most suitable.' I believe he was much ahead of his time."

"Disease? Sandy does not have a disease…surely?"

"He has a mental illness, Jane. I believe it is caused by what appears to be an addiction, in his case to alcohol and laudanum. For the last few years I have been studying the science – some would call it an art – of psychiatry. The workings of the mind, and mental illness, which is what we are dealing with in Sandy. I believe he is unbalanced, by whatever cause. He is delusional, and dangerous. I believe what I propose is the only solution."

She sat, unsure, a woman normally certain of herself but now faced with a decision that would take her life, her future, into…what, exactly? (What was it her grocer father used to say? *Things happen, and other things follow, consequences, and we cannot always foretell what they will be, but decisions have to be made.'*)

And she recognized the truth in her brother's words.

"Carrick of course would continue running the mine," Silas said. "Things will be better in every way."

Finally she nodded. "If it has to be so."

"It must. Stay clear of him, avoid any arguments with him, take yourself away from the house as much as you can. Just let him carry on. I will attend to the rest."

Jane Benson took herself from the house almost immediately. '*…since that Tyson bitch attacked me.'* The phrase echoed in her mind. The Tyson family she now knew, having listened and made commitments to the son Matthew in his representation of the colliers. There was another son and the father, both working at the pit. And the mother, whom she had never seen. She knew of no daughter, but there was one woman she did know in the village.

Sarah Teasdale listened as Jane Benson described Sandy's outburst, and she laughed. She told Jane Meg's version, and explained it was she who had determined what Meg must do, for fear of her future if she remained in Morthwaite, and Jane Benson knew she was hearing the truth of that day.

"And this Meg now is, where, exactly?"

"In the city of Victoria, on our colony of Vancouver's Island, off the Pacific Coast of what is now called British Columbia. And prospering, I am very happy to say."

She told Jane Benson what she knew of Meg's life seven-thousand miles distant, about the successful business she had established.

Jane Benson smiled at that. Her own father had started his business with a single produce stall at an open air market in the town of Wednesbury, near Birmingham.

"So, obviously you communicate. Does she ever speak of returning?"

"I know she misses her family. They were close. But I doubt for one second that she misses being a screen lass at your pit."

A smile at the forthright teacher, and, "I'm sure." Then, "Should she indeed ever think of returning, in whatever capacity, I can assure you that she could do so free of worry."

Sarah thought, as if this woman – or anyone – for all her talk, could control Sandy Benson!

Which was the thought she related to her brother Francis when he arrived at her house later that evening, but Francis was more interested in what he had to relate concerning his discovery of the details of the marriage of their grandparents Jeremiah and Annie Teasdale. Taking a week away from his studies at Oxford, and with the words of Agnes Blunt in his mind, he had travelled to Gretna Green, the famous ultimate resort for young lovers intent on marrying.

"It is right there, in the Lang Collection!" Francis said.

She smiled at her brother's excitement.

"It is named after David and Simon Lang, a father and son who acted as so-called 'priests.' They performed a host of marriages in Gretna Green – including that of Jeremiah and Annie Teasdale – on September twenty-fifth in Seventeen-ninety-five!"

"Here." He offered a sheet of paper, a copy he had made of the marriage record.

'Jeremiah Teasdale.' The writing was clear, a bold, firm signature. Jeremiah was described as a Businessman of Beverley in the county of Yorkshire in England.

"And here, although... There was an X followed by, 'Her mark, Annie Teasdale.' Annie was a maid, also of Beverley."

"Not at all uncommon," Sarah said of the formally required sign of an illiterate. And dryly, "Especially for women. And still common enough."

Francis pointed to two scribbled witness names at the bottom of the sheet. "So, all that...all of it, was recorded quite clearly and signed by the witnesses." He paused, frowning. "However, I believe a mistake has been made in that record. Or in another one, because our father was born on October second that same year. According to the Gretna records, that would have been just a week after they were married. He was christened a week later at Beverley, where we know he was born. Something does not seem quite correct."

He stood, puzzled, studying the copy of the Gretna records.

"I'm sure that I made no error in copying..."

"I am sure that you did not, Francis."

"Then...?"

Sarah stood with arms folded, saying nothing, but waiting as one might for a curtain to be drawn back and allow light to enter the room, or a mind. Her brother could not be so naïve – could he?

She was about to assist, when "Oh," Francis finally said. "Oh."

"Indeed," Sarah said. "She was expectant, which is why they went to Gretna, but they were wed before he was born, albeit by just a week. Which is why you found our father's name properly recorded as christened – he was legitimate – and not declared a bastard."

"Ah."

"Or as 'merrily begotten,'" Sarah said, with a wry smile. "Which I am sure he was."

Francis smiled, but inwardly flinched as he recalled two parish birth records he had come across, notices from the previous century and entered by a vicar. They had read: 'Elizabeth, a bastard of Mary Bromley, a most forsworn abominable whore.' And a few years after that, 'Thomas Hinks, a bastard of Jane Mousel, a most egregious whore and adultress and begotten by Thomas Hinks, an unparalleled roué and adulterer.'

Francis had vowed that he would never burden any child with such weight of history when his turn came to keep the parish registers.

And he thought, *But what a difference a week could mean.*

***

Two weeks after he had met with Stanley Carrick and assured him that his position was secure – though he must wait a little while before returning to the pit – Silas Whitaker sat in the waiting room of the rented house in Whitehaven of Dr. Atticus Howard, a physician who had qualified at the same establishment as Silas, that being London's Guy's Hospital, though their paths had never crossed there and had certainly taken different directions. Howard had graduated two years after Silas. His career advancement, as Silas had ascertained through Stanley Carrick, who was proving to be of invaluable assistance in Silas's quest, had been less than laudable. The best that could be said of Howard's living-consulting quarters when Silas was admitted after a wait of fifteen minutes – though no other visitor was evident arriving or leaving while he sat, and Silas assumed that the wait was by design, though to what end he could only guess – was that they were seedy. The room smelled stale, heavy velvet curtains covered the windows, the little of which he could see were streaked with dust. A free-standing screen divided the room into sitting area and examination space, the legs of a flimsy table visible below the screen. On a shelf behind the screen was a row of bottles of various solutions, tinctures and the like, some of which bore labels and which Silas thought he recognized as common supposed curatives. At one end of the shelf sat a lopsided tin tray holding half a dozen of instruments, only one of which, the simplest, briefly held Silas's attention.

He examined Howard who was sprawled in a shabby red velvet-upholstered wing chair. The Whitehaven doctor's expression, initially a mixture of curiosity and suspicion, now had become an ingratiating though still wary smile, beneath which he wore a straying rust-coloured spade beard, and that topped by a full and overflowing moustache and side whiskers. The whole left Silas with the impression of a design intended to disguise, or conceal…he could not be sure of what.

"And to what do I owe the great pleasure of a visit from such an eminent practitioner?" Howard waited, while Silas continued to examine him and his surroundings. Howard stroked his beard, then shifted in his chair and dusted off the dandruff that his action had caused to fall and settle in speckles on his waistcoat.

Then, "Doctor?"

Silas explained, and watched the man's smile slip away.

"You ask a great deal," Howard sat up and straightened his rumpled coat, arranged an untidy cravat. "The Bensons are—"

"Are my family," Silas interrupted. "And I am going to protect them. My sister especially."

"Ah, the Lady Jane—"

"Whom we are not here to discuss." A finality and impatience in the tone.

After a moment, during which Howard assessed his position and concluded correctly that it was not strong, and shamelessly wheedling now, "Are we discussing a fee?"

Silas managed to restrain himself – the man was sickening. He said, "There can be. A nominal one. But your payment largely will be my silence concerning the abortion industry you run in this…this place." He looked toward the tray, and the slim pointed instrument that sat there. Nothing more than a stiff wire with a sharpened end, with which Howard would break the amniotic sac inside the womb, and do God only knew what other damage and set the scene for infection and possibly death, which undoubtedly had occurred at his hands.

"Hah! As if—"

"I am not on a moral mission, Doctor Howard. I am fully aware that you are not alone, that colleagues in London and elsewhere are not above 'helping' women in trouble, for a price, and perhaps one day there will be an alternative to this back-street butchery. But for now the practice is illegal, and a physician indulging it can lose his livelihood at the stroke of a pen."

"Your wealthy friends in Harley Street—"

"Are offenders, some of them, amid their fine furnishings and impeccable reputations. But they usually are protected by those of their even richer and powerful clients with the influence to do so, the luxury of which I am sure you do not enjoy. I repeat, I am not on a moral crusade. I will pay you one hundred pounds, and you will attend the hearing and testify as I have instructed. If you refuse…"

Silas had acquired his additional expert witness.

Silas went about the business of what he needed next, using information supplied to him by Carrick, who had lived his whole life in the area, and whose knowledge of his environs and its citizens at all levels ran broad and deep. He knew much about who had done what, with and to whom, and where and when. Using this knowledge, supplied enthusiastically by Carrick and confirmed in two instances, though grudgingly, by Dr. Atticus Howard, Silas sought out four men of standing in the West Cumberland region whose families had suffered from the attentions of Sandy Benson. He took this action deliberately and with no concern that some might have judged it to be scheming and manipulative – indeed with the certain knowledge and not a shred of guilt, that it was. His singular concern was for the well-being of his sister, to ensure which he would do whatever was required.

Of the four men he approached, two were mayors, one a town commissioner, the fourth a moderately wealthy wine merchant. One of the mayors and the commissioner each had a daughter who had caught the interest of Sandy Benson, consequently had visited Dr. Howard, and as a result would never provide their parents with grandchildren. The oldest son of the second mayor several years past had intervened in a scuffle between a seventeen-year-old drunk Sandy and a sobbing girl whom Sandy had pinned in the doorway of a dilapidated house on the fairground at Workington and had stripped her of most of her clothing. The boy had knocked Sandy to the ground, then accompanied the girl home. A week after the event, the mayor's son was attacked at night by three men and beaten so severely that both his speech and vision faculties were permanently impaired and his plans to attend university made null. There was little question – but no proof – about who had instigated the beating. The wine merchant had been invited into a card game with Sandy and 'a school of gentlemen friends,' who had blatantly cheated him out of more than a thousand guineas and threatened his life if he tried to expose them.

These four men were named as a jury to a board of inquiry ordered by the county sheriff following a writ of *De lunatic inquirendo* directed by Silas to the sheriff, requiring him to "Inquire by good and lawful men whether the party charged is a lunatic or not." The party being Alexander, Lord Benson, the Earl of Long Fell. The sheriff, Clarence Cartmell, a resident of Cockermouth, was a long-standing acquaintance of the Bensons, had attended the funerals of Richard and his two sons, and had a special affection for the Countess, Lady Jane.

The board, which at the sheriff's suggestion, convened in his own drawing room on Wednesday October 5th, away from the public eye – and prying newspaper correspondents – required witnesses, who arrived in the form of Lady Jane Benson, the Benson's trusted and reliable mine manager Stanley Carrick, one nervous groom and one smiling footman, and two young female staff from the Benson estate, for whom an opportunity to serve Sandy Benson his proper desserts was more than they could have dreamed of. All had been thoroughly prepared and rehearsed by Silas and all spoke to the erratic, fearful and increasingly violent behaviour of Alexander, Lord Benson. Medical opinions were offered by two graduates of the renowned St. Guy's Hospital in faraway London: Dr. Silas Whitaker and Dr. Atticus Howard. The board reached its decision before lunch. Dr. Whitaker was instructed to take whatever action the family deemed suitable.

In the late afternoon, at Fell View, Silas invited Sandy ("Alexander, my boy," shamelessly) to join him in a glass of brandy in Silas's drawing room, noting that he, Silas, was preparing to return to London and would prefer to leave on good terms. Sandy was more than happy to see his uncle on his way, and joined him.

The opium derivative that Silas had introduced to the brandy he poured for Sandy soon had the younger man drowsy, then asleep in his chair. Silas concluded his medical attention by placing a cloth soaked in chloroform, provided unquestioningly by Howard, and holding it for several minutes under Sandy's nose (unlike the villains in countless popular novels who invariably, and improbably, incapacitated their victims with a brief sniff of the chemical) until he was certain Sandy was unconscious and would remain so long enough for the next part of the plan to proceed. As an experienced anaesthetist, he was careful during the application to support Sandy's chin and be certain that his tongue did not slip back and obstruct his breathing. With the eager assistance of Stanley Carrick, Silas removed Sandy Benson to the coach he had waiting. Over the next twenty hours, with several stops to carefully administer further applications of chloroform, Silas delivered a drowsy Sandy into the care of the staff of The Garlands, an institution opened two years previously near Carlisle, some thirty miles north of the Benson home.

"A Benson in a lunatic asylum? Good God," Jane Benson had said when Silas had first made the proposal.

"It is not what you imagine," her brother had cautioned. "There is a new kind of care being practiced, a combination of medical and moral treatment, and the Garlands was built and is operating with that in mind." No alcohol would be permitted to the patients, a healthy diet, exercise in way of walks, daily prayers... "The care is shaped to the individual's needs and is designed toward recovery."

"You mean he could get better...and return?"

"That is not something for your concern at present, Jane. Not for some considerable time, I am certain."

Neither could have known how fully his prediction would be borne out.

For now Sandy was gone. Witnesses to his sentencing and departure were sworn to secrecy and indeed, when asked to, enjoyed distributing the story that he had been dispatched abroad on urgent family business matters. Morthwaite enjoyed a sense of relief.

Jane Benson felt numb as she sat in her own small drawing room. Numb, but relieved beyond measure. She could sleep at nights now. She could leave the house and return home without fear of facing another mad outburst, or the recounting by staff of another bout of physical abuse. Her future? She knew only of the short term: While under the law of *Primogeniture* there was now no male to inherit the title, Richard Benson's will had ensured that Jane would retain all the family property and wealth. The estate would continue to be run by her and her reliable servants, the mine by Carrick. She would have ample funds to be in comfort for as long as she lived. She had decided she would never re-marry. Beyond that? The estate when she was gone? Silas had two children and two grandsons...perhaps...she put the thought aside for the present.

Chapter 23

Meg was spending one or two days each week at Nanaimo. By mid-December Marcus Adams still had not arrived from San Francisco. Work continued at the *Thistle* and Meg was paying wages with still no certainty that she would have access to a market for her coal, which now almost filled the roughly three-acre site that the energetic Snuneymuxw crew had cleared as the piles spread and grew higher. It was obvious that they enjoyed the fact that what Meg was doing was a challenge to Murdoch, the desecrator of their sacred ground.

Michael Blacklock continued to assure Meg that Adams would carry through with his commitment to be there.

"He is the largest importer of coal from Nanaimo to San Francisco. He is shipping thousands of tons a year. He buys a huge amount of Murdoch's product, and that of the other three pits – that is, any coal that they don't sell to the navy or to Victoria. He ships it as far away as the Sandwich Islands – Hawaii now – and carries it using his own steamships. He can never get enough. You just need to be patient."

And while Adams had not appeared, a blast of arctic air had. Nanaimo suddenly was enduring freezing rain and snow, and icy temperatures that the city had not known for a decade. The first snow settled on tree limbs and froze there. More snow fell, settling and freezing on top of the first, and so it went, until the limbs surrendered and snapped with a noise like rifle shots in the woods. The citizens of Nanaimo were forced to melt ice and snow for water, as the town's main spring sat in sculpted, frozen splendour.

The *Glencoe* arrived from Victoria a week before Christmas and anchored for the night under a quarter moon. The next morning it was bound in a fully ice-locked harbour.

Meg ordered the work stopped at the *Thistle* until things improved. When Donald MacDonald, with assistance that included lighting cedar-bough bonfires on the ice, managed to break the Glencoe free, Meg went aboard for the return trip.

When she arrived in Victoria, Blacklock showed her a letter just arrived from Adams, in whose offices in San Francisco Blacklock had worked for two years before moving to Victoria.

The letter explained that the San Francisco industrialist had indeed left the California city on December 1st aboard the steamship *Brother Jonathon* of the California Steam Navigation Company (of which Adams owned a substantial share):

I had expected to arrive in Victoria on schedule on December 9 after four days tending to business matters in Portland. However, those matters became complicated, to the point where I was forced to return to SF and deal with some people at that end who have not been tending to their duties and consequently have caused me some embarrassment, not to mention a considerable loss.

"Those 'people' will be looking for new positions," Michael told Meg. "If indeed they stay out of gaol."

Meg had listened, though more out of courtesy than any sincere interest, to Michael's flattering description of Adam's business empire and his influence in both Victoria – where he owned or had interests in two hotels and three of the drinking establishments – and San Francisco. The fact that he also ran trade between the West and East coasts, using the Panama Isthmus railroad – 'And when the continental railway gets to San Francisco in a few years it will only make him more powerful.' – was interesting enough, but it was not solving her predicament with the *Thistle*. His arrival was supposed to do that, though she had no idea how. Nor, she was beginning to think, had Blacklock.

Meanwhile she had Nancy – and Nancy's dilemma – to consider.

Rhys Llewellyn had proposed to Nancy. (*'An' about bleedin' time,'* according to the bride to be.) Nancy had accepted (*'course I will, y' daft sod.'*), and had been proudly sporting a slim silver band with a modest gem set into it. *The way Nancy flourished her left hand*, Meg thought – but did not venture to say – *she might have been wearing the famous Hope Diamond.*

But the shine on everything had been dulled. No wedding date had been set, as they awaited the military trial that had the young Royal Marine charged with 'assault causing bodily harm' against a senior officer. Should he be convicted, he would face dismissal from the service, a return in chains to Great Britain, and certainly years in gaol.

"Far too long for anybody to wait, love," he had told Nancy.

The incident had occurred two days after Rhys had given her the ring.

Nancy had been showing it to the newest helping hand at M and N's – Dorcas, named for her of Biblical good works and one of Martha's many cousins, who had proven more than able to handle the work behind the counter, and even the roughest of the customers. The pair had been outside on the boardwalk when three 'blue' Marines from the artillery, complement of a ship visiting Esquimalt, stopped, just as Rhys, in his scarlet of the Marines Light Infantry arrived, the two broad white stripes on each arm announcing his recently acquired rank of corporal. The 'blues' were a sergeant and two ordinary marines. They had just finished a largely liquid lunch at the Brown Jug Saloon. The sergeant, a man named Hodgins, pointed at Rhys and laughed, "Lookee here, then, a fuckin' Lobster!" – the casual reference to the Royal Marines in scarlet, and most often used in a jocular fashion, but not in this case.

"Sergeant," Rhys said, formally, correctly.

"That's right, Corporal Lobster. That's wot you call me! Sergeant! Wi' respect! In't that right, boys?" This directed to the two blue marines privates, who grinned and nodded, though looking nervously at their superior, and at Rhys.

Rhys stayed quiet. He recognized the sergeant from the ship's previous visit. The man was famous for brawling and was tolerated by his senior officers because of his record as the Pacific Fleet's undefeated heavy-weight boxing champion.

The sergeant turned to the two young women. "Coupla little tarts here, eh?" He reached out to touch Nancy's breast, which won him in return from Nancy a sharp, "Fuck you!" and a hard slap in the face. He recoiled, glared furiously at his two marine companions, who had dared to laugh at Nancy's reaction.

"You cunt!" he snarled, and made to punch her, but a hand, a strong hand, was placed on his shoulder and he was spun about. Rhys said, "No. Try *me*."

The sergeant's eyes glinted. This was his element. He was enraged by Nancy's slap, and now he had been challenged to a fist fight. He squared up in prize-ring fashion, fists raised and weaving the air, and grinned at Rhys. "Mistake, Lobster," he laughed.

"You should leave, sergeant," Rhys said.

The sergeant threw a swift right fist, and looked puzzled when it found only air. He tried a savage uppercut, and then a wild left hook, with the same bewildering result. He was suddenly breathing heavily, from a mixture of exertion and frustration. He stared at Rhys, and rushed him with a flurry of punches, all of which were blocked.

The sergeant suddenly was wary. He stepped back and studied Rhys.

Rhys Llewellyn was a child of the streets of Cardiff's Tiger Bay, the city's notorious docklands. He had never known his father, a feckless drunk who disappeared shortly after the boy was born. His mother had kept the two of them fed and sheltered by working as a cleaning woman for inns in the district where the languages and cultures of more than forty nations had established a unique city on the edge of the Welsh port. Rhys roamed the streets and found his own work on the barges and ships that filled the Bute docks. He knew the red light districts and the gambling dens and those who frequented both. He learned to fight in a place where agility and the ability to retaliate with clenched fist were requisite to survival. He never sought battles, but nor did he run from them when they came his way. Early on he gained respect, and bullies and thugs learned to avoid him.

An ambition for more than loading and unloading cargo ships, and the sight of a group of six Royal Marines in a mix of scarlet and blue uniforms one day determined his future. He was just shy of his fourteenth birthday when he watched the marines with their easy swinging gait as they strode along the docks, noticed people step out of their way, not from fear, but respect, the young, tough dock labourers nodding their heads, some of the older ones offering crisp salutes, testimony no doubt to their own service years. And there was the interest from the ladies for these young military men, their welcoming and promising smiles and invitations.

To be accepted into the marines, Rhys learned that he must produce 'a certificate of birth or a declaration made by parents or guardians before a magistrate to prove he was of the proper age' – between fourteen and a half and sixteen.

Rhys's mother possessed no such certificate nor was she inclined to search for one. The certificate was acquired from an Italian businessman and sometime-forger for whom Rhys had done many a job on barges owned by the man. Antonio Piffaretti declined to take anything for the service. He wished Rhys well and said there would always be work for him if he were to return. The certificate gave Rhys's age as sixteen.

The recruiting sergeant who admitted him to the service for an initial term of ten years, while recognizing that the boy's cheeks were still some time away from meeting a razor, glanced at his sturdy, almost-six-foot frame, and approved his entry.

That ten year term was nearing its end and Rhys had been considering whether to sign on for a further term, with now a wife alongside him, and no doubt then, children. A life with a family, and a permanent posting in Esquimalt and Victoria.

That decision now was out of his hands. The sergeant had attacked again, with both fists flailing. Rhys hit him first in the mouth, splintering the man's front teeth, then in the ribs, cracking two of them and robbing the 'blue' of breath – and of any ambition to pursue the contest. The sergeant went to his knees on the rough boards.

Needing an explanation for his bruised face and damaged teeth, with his two marines lickspittles as coerced witnesses, Hodgins reported the affray as a sudden attack on himself by a 'red' marine corporal whom, he said, he had admonished for having an untidy uniform.

Major Samuel Stone, who first considered the charges and would decide whether they would proceed to a court martial, knew both combatants well. He knew that the sergeant was a bully and braggart who exploited his fighting fame and got away with behaviour that would not have been tolerated in others. The major, who had approved Rhys's two promotions in the past five years – from marine private to lance-corporal and more recently to full corporal – had listened to Rhys's version and had been convinced. He had barely held his tongue when Hodgins claimed that Nancy had "opened her frock to show her teats." A girl who had just become engaged to Corporal Llewellyn? He did not disguise his contempt for Hodgins, but the sergeant was also a great favourite of officers senior to the major, men who enjoyed having 'a character' among the non-commissioned ranks – a pet, in effect – especially one about whom they could brag and who invariably won them money on wagers against other ships' fighters when in port, and the major, a relatively young man of twenty-nine, with his own career to consider, was not keen on antagonizing any of them. Whichever story he chose to act on, his decision would leave a serious mark on one of their lives and careers – likely a lowering in rank and reputation for the sergeant, but much worse for Rhys. "Bloody Solomon," he muttered to himself as he sought a compromise which would satisfy the commander and other of the sergeant's admirers by allowing the fleet's chief thug to remain with his ship, his rank intact, and yet would not result in ruin for Cpl. Llewellyn. An hour later, he found one.

***

"San Juan? Where the hell is San Juan?" Meg asked when Nancy told her of Stone's decision, and what it meant. "Sounds like Mexico. Is it? Christ, Nance!"

"See, you don't know everything," Nancy laughed. "No, it's just down there," and she pointed vaguely to the south. "It's an island. Not very far."

Bruce Campbell explained the rest when Meg asked him.

"We – Great Britain – and the United Sates about five years ago, agreed to a joint occupation of San Juan Island while the water boundary between us was being debated – it still is! So, the Americans have a camp at the south end and we have ours, in the form of a garrison of Royal Marine Light Infantry – that's Rhys's mob, isn't it? at Roche Harbour at the north end. There was a bit of a kerfuffle early on, something to do with an American shooting a pig that belonged to the Hudson's Bay Company who had a farm on the island, but that was settled and I gather that all is very friendly. I've been there once, half a day's sail, and it is a beautiful place."

The major, in hunting for a compromise which would also keep himself safe, had offered Rhys a posting to the San Juan garrison, and Nancy had decided he would take it. "I've got you now, and I'm not going to lose you because of some arsehole in a blue suit."

Nancy expressed a concern to Meg. "What about you? You won't have me for company anymore."

"No, but that doesn't mean I won't have someone else for company."

"Oh, *really*. And who might that be? Has Michael?"

"No, he hasn't. And I did not mean anyone in particular."

Not anyone she chose to name at this point, anyway. Until she was more certain of herself. And the other person.

*"*Oh, *really*...well, if you say so…"

"Shut up, Nance!"

Nancy and Rhys left on a navy ship with a replacement company of marines on Wednesday, January eighteenth of the new year 1865, a week after they were married at Esquimalt by a Royal

Marines chaplain in an Anglican service. The finer spiritual details of the ceremony passed by both Nancy and Meg, neither of whom had become affiliated with any church in their time in the city. Meg had grown up with a father who dismissed the overtly devout as 'God-botherers, likely wid a guilty conscience about summat.' And her experiences with Rev. Richard William Scott and the domineering and self-righteous Mrs. Robb on board the *Tynemouth* had done little to dissuade her of that thought. In Nancy's case, when once asked by Louisa Campbell if she believed in God, she had replied, "Oh, no, A' don't think so. Not yet anyway."

Meg was Nancy's maid of honour. The bridesmaids were Martha and her cousin Dorcas in sweeping blue, straight hoopless frocks. Seamus Sweeny, comprehensively groomed, liberally pomaded, and impeccable in a hired morning-suit and top hat, was a peacock-proud best man. Present was the complete Campbell household, the twins Amelia and Ethan now as tall as Nancy, whom they hugged madly, and a scattering of regular customers of M and N's. Rounding out the attendants were Major Samuel Stone and four of Rhys's Marines comrades, the latter, who after forming a swords-raised guard of honour for the married couple, immediately stepped up to a refreshments-spread table, with particular focus on the heavily rum-infused bowl of punch.

The day before their departure Meg handed Nancy $500 which she said was a partial payment for Nancy's share of M and N's. "And there will be more to come, eventually."

Nancy gaped. "Bloody 'ell, Meg, I don't want that! I don't want owt. Nowt!" She shook her head, hair flying, eyes filling. "You know, sometimes good things 'appen to a body. Just sometimes. And that was you, for me."

She took Meg in a fierce hug. "I love you Meg Tyson. I allus will. An' if that sounds soft, well, let it!" Her tears were wet against Meg's face. Meg smiled through her own tears. "I know, lass, and it's all right. You're going to be all right." She laughed, "And you're going to take this money. Here." She handed they money to Rhys. "Take care of it. And of her."

Nancy said, "Oright, then…! But forget your talk about any more. I want you to give my share to Martha. She's earned it. Maybe y' can make it M and M's!"

The day following their departure, a letter arrived from Sarah, with a note from Lizzie Tyson.

Morthwaite. October 20, 1864.

My dear Meg,

We are deeply saddened to hear of Alan's tragic accident. But, two considerations: He died as a hero and the parents and other family of those two children will be forever grateful. And by now I hope the time will have dulled your pain. Stay strong.

Typical Sarah, Meg thought. No over-reaching sentimentality. Just uncluttered, sincere thoughts.

Now, the strangest thing: Alexander Benson has departed the scene. He has not been seen for three weeks and it is said that he has been sent abroad on family business. Which is strange as I understood that the Benson's had been done with their foreign affairs at the time of Richard and his elder sons' deaths. Even stranger, my new 'friend' Lady Jane Benson asked about you – and learned the truth about your leaving! – and said if you ever decided to return it would be in safety.

She ended the letter,

I will keep you informed, and look forward to hearing more of your business venture.

In Lizzie's note:

My tears are on this bit of paper, my darling. So are your dad's and the boys. We never know what life is going to bring, and we have to be strong enough to deal with it. All our best love and maybe one day we will see each other.

Meg cried softly for a few minutes. Then she wiped her eyes. She started thinking again of the difficulties she faced with the *Thistle*, difficulties concerning time, and money.

Marcus Adams finally landed in Victoria on Saturday the fourth of February, on board the *Brother Jonathan*, this time having by-passed Portland on the four-day, almost eight-hundred mile journey.

Meg studied the man of whom she had heard so much. His blonde hair, carefully tended, touched the collar of his knee-length winter coat of what seemed to be very fine grey wool. A matching and embroidered waistcoat over a cream silk shirt, and a neat maroon cravat. Black pants tapered down to sturdy but stylish laced black ankle boots, and the whole topped by a wide-brimmed hat with a dented crown that Michael Blacklock described as 'a cowboy hat.' Adams carried a cane topped with a silver knob inscribed with intertwined M and A.

"Busy, busy, all sorts of complications," was his brief explanation for his lengthy delay. Then, "When do I get to see this coal?" His accent was distinctly British upper-class.

They left the next morning aboard the *Glencoe,* Meg accompanied by Martha and Sweeney, who had insisted that his business interests in a new sawmill and some unnamed ventures could take care of themselves for now. Michael Blacklock had said he would accompany her, but Meg thanked him and declined his offer. "You have your own affairs to see to, Michael. You have spent far too much time on mine already." He seemed chagrinned at the rejection, but said nothing other than, "Bon Voyage, then."

At the *Glencoe,* Adams greeted Donald MacDonald like an old friend.

Of course, he knows him, Meg thought. *He knows everybody.* On his arrival he had listed the people in Victoria he had to see about business – all prominent merchants and the like – before they headed for Nanaimo, and had spent the day doing so.

In Nanaimo Adams wasted no time in changing into what he called his 'bush outfit,' which included a rifle with an intricately decorated stock and a bandolier of ammunition criss-crossing his chest. Harry Cunningham hid a smile, and winked at Meg. Adams was conducted through snow-thickened woods along hard-frozen icy trails to the mine, where the Snuneymuxw crew had resumed work a week earlier after a modest thaw had arrived.

He paced around the stacks of coal, brushing accumulated snow away and turning lumps of the black mineral in his hands.

"Excellent. Just like the coal they showed at the World's Fair in 'Sixty-two, six tons of the stuff. I was in London at the time. Steam power coming on, it did a lot for the industry here. In fact we've never looked back."

Meg said nothing, but she smiled at her memory of the Fair, and Nancy: *'It's still only bloody coal!'*

Adams walked the whole of the stacking area, and paced out the substantial length of the seam that remained visible above ground. He asked Harry Cunningham's opinion on the extent of coal remaining and laughed when Harry said, "How much would you like? It'll last a lifetime."

Harry had led them this day. "Me Dad's a bit down." And at Meg's concerned look added, "Chest. He says nowt to worry about. Mam's getting goose grease and that. He says he'll be back on t' job in a day or two. I'm managing 'til then."

He kept his attention on Meg.

"And doing fine," she said, looking around at the growing stacks. "Thank you, Harry. I'm glad we've got you." She smiled and held his gaze.

Had it not been so chilly still, Harry Cunningham would have been seen to blush.

Adams tossed a clump of coal back onto a pile, and rubbed his hands.

"We can do business, Miss Tyson," he said. "I will buy every ounce that you can produce – provided that your prospecting licence does not expire, and that you can meet the rest of the conditions, which means us getting it to my ships."

Us?

As if she needed reminding! The licence had barely a year to go. Finding the required $10,000 provenance was looking less than certain, given her outlay on *Thistle* labour so far. Her bank account stood at $6,000, enough to pay the $2,500 to acquire the land when the year was up, and while the profit from M and N's was steady, it was relatively modest and would not be sufficient to bridge the remaining gap to secure her position.

What would Alan have done, in the same situation?

She knew the answer: He would have borrowed money.

He had said, more than once, "Business and ventures are built on credit. Without it most of commerce would close down." And, "To make money you have to take risks."

Risks. The word, the thought, worried her. What would she be risking? She knew for a loan there would have to be collateral. She had a mortgage-free small house, but that with its memories would be too precious to lose in a gamble that might fail. She had M and N's, but the same reasoning prevailed.

And she had the *Thistle*.

'To make money, you have to take risks.'

She considered, and concluded that indeed what had she done *but* take risks in the past three years? She had risked embarking on an unknown future seven thousand miles from her home. She had risked putting everything she had into a new business, and had succeeded…

If she failed, her collateral – the *Thistle* if that were to be her choice – "would be hypothecated," Bruce Campbell said.

"It means simply that the bank would take it," he explained.

"But Meg, while the *Thistle* and its coal sales especially would be considered excellent collateral, I see no point in even considering the risk until you have found a way to get your coal to the water. If that doesn't happen in good time, you will lose the mine anyway."

Again, something of which she was depressingly aware.

All of this tumbled in her brain as Adams ended what he was saying, with "There is always a way, Meg," and he turned to begin the walk back.

As they ploughed through the bush, Meg was bothered by a thought. Harry Cunningham had been far too off-hand in attributing his father's absence to 'nowt to worry about.'

"I'm going to your house," she said. For now, that was her concern, and anyway, she could not have been aware of the problems facing Andrew Murdoch, and which had provoked from Adams the words that reminded her of Alan Munro's similar approach to life, 'There must be a way.'

At the Cunningham home Dan sat in a chair by the fire. His face lit up as she entered the small front room.

"Hello, Meg. What's thy fettle, lass?"

What's thy fettle? A collier's friendly greeting to any friend or neighbour at Morthwaite. Or, *What fettle, marra?* Like, *How do?* A simple general inquiry into the other's health and general well-being.

"I'm grand, Dan." Studying him, as he remained in his chair.

Rachel Cunningham smiled at Meg from where she sat darning a tear in a work shirt belonging to one or the other of her men. It was a tired smile. Rachel appeared weary. She got up from her chair. "I'll put t' kettle on." The English woman's solution to any disquiet: a cup of tea.

Looking at Dan, Meg thought he must have lost half a stone in the past month, from a frame that had had nothing to spare. And she had been too caught up with her own concerns to notice.

Dan coughed, a wheezing sound, placed a cloth to his mouth, inspected the cloth, grimaced, and folded it and placed it in his lap.

Matt Tyson. A hewer, like me. Aye. I remember him. Older than me. Lungs got 'im, I think?

This was more than coal dust on the lungs.

Dan caught a breath. "It's nowt much, lass. Just a laal cough. Be ower in a day or two." The words seemed to tax him.

Meg exchanged a look with Harry. Harry gave a slight shake of his head, which Meg took as a suggestion not to pursue the matter just now.

Rachel poured tea and put out a plate of shortbread biscuits.

Meg sipped, and nibbled.

"Delicious."

Rachel smiled. "Made them last week. They've kept well...even wid 'im around." She nodded at Harry, who raised his hands, a disclaimer, and laughed. A light moment, and Meg took advantage of it with a thought that had just jumped into her head

"Have you been to Victoria much, Rachel?"

Rachel blinked, surprised. "What...Victoria? *Your* Victoria?" Utter puzzlement, which brought laughter from the other three.

Rachel blushed. "Well, we came in through there when we got here, didn't we? 'Ow lang ago now, Dan?"

"A good ten year. Bit mair."

"Then I think it's time for a visit. For both of you, Rachel and Dan. It's my thank you." She said, "Not you Harry, you need to look after the *Thistle* "

She continued talking as she turned to Dan's wife. "Change as good as a rest, eh, Rachel? Donald MacDonald will have plenty room on the *Glencoe*. He'll be in tomorrow, and we'll go back with him day after that. There's an extra room in my house. It'll do you both good."

Dan laughed between coughing.

"Well, that telt ivvrybody, didn't it!"

Harry said, "And she's the boss. And I think it's a grand idea, Mam. So there. Pack your stuff."

Rachel had first looked alarmed. Why would she want to go that far? What for? What would she do? And stopping in this lass Meg's house? But it seemed like Dan was for it, and Harry certainly was. Maybe it would do Dan some good...

"Aye, well...mind, I've nowt much to pack!"

A noisy ocean settled down like a suddenly hushed grumpy child as they left the harbour. Rachel and Dan spent much of the journey on the Glencoe's deck, until the darkening afternoon chill sent them into the captain's cabin, where Donald MacDonald asking neither permission nor preference poured a whisky for Dan and a sweet sherry for Rachel.

"Nivver 'ad that before," she said. "Quite nice." Her cheeks acquired a slight blush and her eyes shone. She nodded as Meg offered her a second glass. "Don't mind if I do." Dan put an arm around her and chuckled and said, "Good lass."

They settled in at Meg's house and spent that first night in comfortable conversation, Dan and Rachel dwelling on 'back home' memories that had Rachel – and Meg – laughing and dabbing at their eyes. Martha delivered a basket of packages of fish and chips wrapped in pages of *The Colonist*, which Rachel found funny. She judged the meal as "Champion, that was, lass. Just champion." Dan was delighted at the way his wife seemed to have perked up. He sent a look of gratitude toward Meg, who acknowledged with a nod and a smile.

The next day Meg took them shopping. Anderson and Co. provided a pair of sturdy brown laced shoes for Dan, who finally had been persuaded that his clogs – even if they were his 'good' ones, with the non-iron-caulkered wooden sole and polished tops – and which he wore every day at home, maybe were not the best choice for Victoria. Andrew Robertson the tailor on Front Street measured him for a suit and said it would be ready for fitting in three days.

Meg waved off Rachel's protests at her spending money on them after Meg took them inside M'Cutchan and Callingham and insisted that Rachel choose from a selection "Direct from San Francisco and the latest fashion." Meg judged Rachel's eventual choice of a pink and blue patterned frock was perfect.

"But where will I wear it, lass?" Rachel fretted.

"You'll see," Meg replied.

She had dismissed any concerns about spending. She had enough money for now. Especially where these two were concerned.

Their next stop was at Vaughan's Photographic Studio in the Victoria Theatre on Government Street, where portraits were made, first of Dan and Rachel, then of Dan and Meg, one of Rachel and Meg, and finally one of all three together. Meg asked for them to be framed and said she would pick them up later.

Meg shook her head when it seemed that Dan was going to his pocket.

"My gift," she said.

Rachel stared at the finished photographs. She shook her head and, wonderingly, said, "It looks just like us!"

Later, Meg left them making (another!) cup of tea while she walked the muddy, rutted road to the legislature to seek out Dr.

John Helmcken, speaker of the assembly and the city's longest-established and certainly most competent physician.

Meg had learned that the birdcages, as the five buildings comprising the legislature were known, were so named because of their mix of architecture, of which someone had written in a 1859 issue of the *Victoria Gazette*, a year before they opened – 'resembles in its mixed style of architecture, the latest fashion of Chinese pagoda, Swiss-cottage and Italian Villa fancy birdcages.'

As she climbed the wooden steps up to the half-timbered front, she met Judge Begbie on one of his frequent visits to the city, smartly dressed in a frock coat over a three-piece suit, who held the front door open for her.

"Miss Tyson," Begbie said with an open smile. "A pleasure to see you. I trust things go well with you?" He had raised his stovepipe hat as he spoke.

"Good day, sir...your honour... *(Christ, was it Lordship?)*...quite well, thank you."

What else would I say? she thought. The man does not need a list of my problems

A clerk pointed her to Helmcken's room. She had met the short, slight, generally cheerful man several times and he always appeared to enjoy the occasion.

"Meg, welcome to this rowdy place, although it is quiet today. I believe Mr. De Cosmos is not in attendance." He laughed at his quip. In the slight pause that followed, Meg noticed that among the books on Helmcken's shelves, next to a part-full bottle of cognac, were two she recognized: Charles Dickens' *Great Expectations,* and Charles Darwin's *Origin of the Species.* The first had arrived in Victoria about the same time as Meg, a year after its publication in England, and later Meg had purchased a copy from Hebben's stationery. Pip's progress into adulthood had kept her enthralled. Darwin's controversial book was in the Victoria subscription library, if she ever felt inclined. She saw also on the shelf a portrait of Dr. Helmcken's wife, the eldest daughter of former Governor James Douglas. The governor had retired the previous year and had been knighted. Sir James, now.

Helmcken said, "What brings you here?"

She explained her concerns about Dan, his place in her life, and asked Helmcken if he would examine him.

"Of course, Meg. Willingly."

He asked her a few more questions about the change she had noticed in Dan, and they agreed on a time for her to bring him to Helmcken's house.

"Might as well have a checkup while we're here," she told Dan offhandedly. Dan confirmed her suspicion that he had never in his life visited a doctor, and asked if he would have to take his clothes off.

***

Marcus Adams sat across from Andrew Murdoch in Murdoch's home. Each man held a snifter of brandy.

Adams swirled his drink, as he spoke.

"We have a problem, Andrew. You are already short six-hundred tons and we're barely two months into the year." He tapped the thin sheaf of papers he had placed on the table between their armchairs. Murdoch had insisted they be comfortable for this meeting. He looked nervous now. He was squinting after having removed his steel-rimmed spectacles, which he was tapping on the table top. Without the glasses his face seemed softer, almost vulnerable, which indeed he was.

"And when you are short, then I am short," Adams continued. "When *you* are not meeting your contractual commitments," he tapped the papers again, "that can make things very awkward for *me*. You must have some idea of how far my commercial interests spread – and how my own contracts could be jeopardised if this continues – it's like a standing row of dominoes: knock the first one over and the rest fall in turn, until the whole lot crashes down. And you must appreciate that I cannot allow that to happen." He enunciated every word clearly, carefully, as if to a slow-thinking child, as if concerned that Murdoch might not understand his points. "And that I will take whatever steps I must to ensure that it doesn't."

Murdoch showed he was understanding. His normally unflappable state was deserting him by the second. He shifted uneasily in his chair as he sought to offer excuses, reasons, for his shortcomings. "I have had some drawbacks that have affected production. These will be corrected and I should be back on schedule…" he paused. "Shortly."

"Drawbacks? I should think so. You have one pit of your three that has once more been flooded – the same one that resulted in your sacking two of your most competent employees – the

Cunninghams, who are now working for your competition and, from what I see, are doing a fine job of work. That pit is giving you nothing at present and will continue giving nothing until it is pumped and drained dry – if indeed it ever is."

Adams' detailed knowledge of his troubles depressed but did not surprise Murdoch. The man had people everywhere and his touch on everything.

"Competition!" Murdoch waved a dismissive hand. "She cannot even—"

Adams interrupted him. "In another of your mines you have a work disruption caused by men you hired to replace the Cunninghams. Did you ever check their backgrounds before you took them on, those three from Staffordshire?"

"The agent…" Murdoch started.

"Knew nothing, either. Or was so damned anxious to get his commission that he didn't trouble to find out that they had been the worst of union trouble-makers back home. The most radical of their kind. The type who march around with burning torches and call for revolution and the end of the system we know." He placed his snifter down on the table by his side. "Christ, man, their own union 'brothers' chipped in to help get them here, so much havoc they were creating." He sat up and stretched forward, gazing into Murdoch's face. "And now you have them here, threatening more havoc, from what I hear."

***

That night, Meg took Dan and Rachel to the Victoria Theatre where two plays were being mounted, both farces – *Who Speaks First*, by Charles Dance, and *His Last Legs* by William Bayle Bernard. Rachel gazed around, amazed, inside the 600-seat building. "Where does ivvrybody come frae to fill it?" she said, and soon found out, as the seats beside and all around them became taken, and the theatre was filled with the chatter and laughter of an audience excited to be out for an evening's entertainment.

The seat prices had been reduced since the last major event, when the most celebrated acting couple in the English-speaking world, Charles and Ellen Kean, had appeared in December, when they had mounted nine days' performances of Shakespeare's tragedies, including *Hamlet* and *Macbeth*. Then the prices had been $25-$20 for boxes, $3 for orchestra seats, $2.50 for parquet seating and $1.50 for the pit.

Meg selected three seats with good views, at the side in the third row of the orchestra section, at $1.25 each.

Rachel and Dan, but especially Rachel, were transfixed as the play opened, the setting as described in the programme being the drawing room of a country house, where Mr. And Mrs. Militant sit at separate tables with their back to each other. They have entered into a contest about who would speak first, which has continued for a week.

After some comical opening internal monologue from his wife, Ernest Militant says "Who would have credited that my wife, or indeed any man's wife, could have held her tongue for a week? And yet she has. A wonderful fact in modern history."

Dan listened to this with a straight face, until Rachel elbowed him in the ribs, at which, along with the rest of the audience, they both broke into unrestrained laughter. Rachel laughed until she wept, and laughed and wept, but soon she was just quietly weeping. She leaned across and placed her head on Dan's shoulder. "Oh, my lad," she whispered. Dan put his arm around her and kissed her face. "It'll be all right, lass. You'll see."

John Helmcken had been forthright in giving his opinion that Dan was suffering from cancer of the lung, and likely other places. And Dan was…typically Dan, Meg thought, in responding to it.

"Aye, a' thowt it might come to that," he said. "Wid t'pain and that."

Rachel had stepped in and asked straight out, "'ow long do you think, doctor?"

Helmcken said, "One can never be precise, never certain, but I believe, a few months."

Meg stayed back to pay Helmcken for the visit but he said, "I'll send you a reckoning, Meg," which he had to be reminded of months later, and months later again, and again would forget.

He looked after the departing Cunninghams.

"What now for them, one wonders," he said.

"I'm taking them home," Meg said.

"Of course."

Assuming that Meg meant Nanaimo.

***

"The other pits will help me catch up," Murdoch said. Plaintive almost, and short on conviction.

Adams said, "They can't. It is all they can do to meet their own contracts with me."

"Jesus Christ! And people say *I* have a monopoly!"

Adams drew the papers to him. "Andrew, you have already forfeited on this contract. I could simply cancel it—"

Stubbornly, interrupting, "There are other buyers. The navy—"

"Not when you are limping along the way you are, and I have a guaranteed supply and can undercut your prices in a minute."

And would do, Murdoch knew. He started to find an angry response, but stopped. He frowned, said, "What guaranteed supply?"

"Ah, you *are* listening," Adams said. "Here's what is going to happen."

He explained, to Murdoch's increasing consternation, and ended, "You have no choice, Andrew."

Two days later in a meeting in Victoria, Adams was explaining to Meg what "Andrew and I have agreed to." He nodded at Murdoch who had also travelled south for this. Murdoch seemed to clench his jaw. The meeting also included Michael Blacklock and Bruce Campbell, the latter pair whom Meg had asked to attend. "I have no idea what is going on – other than that Marcus Adams says it will be something to my advantage – and I might need advice."

Adams said, "I am proposing that we form a joint stock company."

"Proposing," Murdoch muttered, and was ignored.

Adams continued: "There will be three stock holders, each with a certain number of shares. To simplify things: I will own forty per cent, Andrew here will own ten per cent, and you, Meg, will own fifty per cent."

Michael Blacklock, who had guessed correctly what was in the air, said quickly, "Meg will be the Managing Partner."

Adams smiled. "Indeed, with that many shares."

Bruce Campbell said, "Collateral from each? Provenance?"

"Cash from me and from Andrew, to bear the cost of full start-up at the *Thistle*. Total amounts to be agreed upon and to be deposited as good faith in your new bank, Bruce."

"And Meg?" Blacklock said.

"Her collateral? The *Thistle,* of course, its future production."

As he had explained to Murdoch in their acrimonious meeting, "That is our guaranteed supply. You know as well as I do the potential for that coal. It will be moved across your land—"

"For a fee," Murdoch snapped.

Adams had burst into laughter. "For Christ's sake, Andrew, will you never learn? Talk about hope trumping experience. *I* am telling *you* what the arrangement will be! It is only because you have that access that you are getting any consideration at all. I could build a way around you, with the co-operation of the Snuneymuxw and a few people I know in Victoria, including in the legislature – think of De Cosmos for just one, whom I've known since we were both in California – and leave you on your own, but that would take time and money and I would rather get on with things now. Consider yourself well done by." He waited a moment, smiled, and said, "The alternative is that I could break you."

After a silence, one of capitulation, Murdoch said, "Why are you falling over yourself to help this...pit girl...Tyson?"

"Because, Andrew, in the simplest of terms, her property is a good investment, and I like a good investment. Oh, I could wait her out, until her licence expired, but what then? Nothing but a tangle of government red tape and re-applications and God only knows what." He added, "And I like her – no, not in that way, for Christ's sake," at a look from Murdoch. "And I trust her. That mine is her *raison d'etre*, it is why she has persevered. Even a cold fish such as you must understand that. She will be a sound partner, for both of us. We will all profit."

But there was another reason Adam was helping the pit girl. To someone other than Murdoch, he might have explained:

'My name, my family name, actually is McAdam. We are related to the wealthy McAdam of road-building fame, and profited from that connection. We became wealthy, also. Too wealthy. My father and mother spent their lives doing nothing – riding to hounds, dressing up to visit people as idle as themselves, and talking nonsense.

I left home when I was twenty. I changed my name and I made my own way, and my fortune, through my own efforts, in America. Where I saw opportunities, I took them. I gambled on businesses, and succeeded.

A little more than two years ago I saw the name of Meg Tyson in an article in the Colonist, written by De Cosmos. I had known him from California. In fact due to my friendship with the governor I helped De Cosmos have his name changed, from William Smith.

It wasn't her name that caught my attention, rather it was the mention of her home village, Morthwaite. Given Miss Tyson's age, I was certain that she would have known – indeed probably had been taught by – a woman named Sarah Teasdale. A woman I had done a great disservice to and which caused her much suffering.

Adam's/McAdam's listener would have been quiet as his tale unfolded.

She was hired as a governess for me and my brother. I was fifteen Because of me, because of a lie I told, she was dismissed, without references. She eventually worked in the coal mines. From somewhere, she acquired an ugly burn scar on one side of her face, which would have made her unfit for any genteel employment.

I learned this after I recognized her in that village during some business dealings I had with a family, Bensons, when I was a commission-agent trading coal from mines to manufacturers. I did not re-introduce myself. I was a coward. I have always regretted what I did to her. I am hoping that by helping Miss Tyson, whom undoubtedly she knew well, and cared for, I may make some repair.

Perhaps you can understand.'

Meg, Blacklock, and Campbell had stepped away from the meeting briefly. Both her advisers recommended she accept the arrangement, without reservations. Meg had done so; they had returned to Adams and Murdoch, and Meg had rounded off the meeting: "Harry Cunningham will be the Thistle's manager." She ignored Murdoch's lifted face that clearly said, *What about his father?* "Any dealings when I am not here will be done through him. He will be in charge of all workers – and any of the Snuneymuxw who wish to continue working there will be allowed to do so and will be paid the going rate for any collier." She ignored a grunt from Murdoch. "In the meanwhile, you will all have to get along without me for some time. Possibly some months."

The 'Thistle Coal and Mining Company' was registered a week later at the Colony's administrative offices at the 'birdcage.' Michael Blacklock was named as Company Secretary, and the registration was witnessed by the Hon. Bruce Campbell along with Chief Justice Matthew Baillie Begbie, who chuckled, seemingly delighted, as he read the company's articles with Meg's name dominant.

Two days later Meg was back in Nanaimo, at the Cunningham house.

"You're what, lass?" Dan stared at Meg. He wore a half-smile, one of puzzlement.

"I'm taking you home, Dan. You and Rachel."

"Tekkin us yam?" As if the Cumbrian dialect version might make clearer for him what she seemed to be saying.

Meg laughed. "Aye, ah's tekkin y'yam. t' pair a' y'.

"Tekkin us…?" Rachel said. She looked around the tiny house. "But this is…"

"For a visit," Meg said. "Home. Yam. To Cumberland. To Lowca."

Rachel stared at her.

"Or I could just take Dan," Meg said. "There's a thought…"

Rachel stared at her a few seconds longer. Then her face split into smile of pure wonderment. "Well, mebbe you could," she said. "But yer not ganna!"

Harry Cunningham had enjoyed listening to the exchange. He had spoken with Meg about all recent events, including Helmcken's opinion, and knew well what was happening. Knew that he could be seeing the last of his parents – at least here in Nanaimo. He had said to Meg, "But *you'll* be coming back, won't you?"

"Yes, of course. And I'll be looking for a house here, in Nanaimo."

Harry smiled, a broad smile. "Mebbe I'll build one for you."

Meg nodded. "Mebbe you will."

Chapter 24

Their journey in late March from Victoria, by way of steamer to San Francisco, from there to and across the Panama isthmus railroad, and steamer to New York, took forty-five days. Without the isthmus connection it would have taken a hundred more. The Cunninghams travelled in considerable more comfort than when they had arrived in Victoria a dozen years earlier.

In San Francisco, at Adam's insistence, they stayed at his four-storey mansion on Bush Street. On the first evening, following dinner and a desert which was set afire – causing Dan to make a quick retreat, along with his chair – when they were finished eating, Rachel began to collect the plates and dishes, ready to wash them. A maid whisked them away without a word, while Meg placed a napkin over and partly in her mouth.

Meg had sent a telegraph-letter addressed to Sarah Teasdale. That message would arrive in New York hours later, would continue by mail packet to Liverpool, by telegraph to Whitehaven, and by delivery boy to Morthwaite, all in less than two weeks. She wondered why she hadn't thought of doing that earlier. But earlier, she would have had to consider the cost of such convenience, so-much a word for the telegraph. Such constraints no longer prevailed: 'You will be wealthy, Meg. Or, at least, very well off!' The words of Marcus Adams.

They arrived in New York on Thursday, April 20.th The city, with the rest of the country, was in mourning for the death five days earlier of President Abraham Lincoln, who had been shot at a performance of *Our American Cousin* at the Ford Theatre, Washington D.C. on Good Friday.

The city was gloomy while it waited for Lincoln's funeral train to pass through on its way to Illinois. Theatres and entertainment centres closed their doors – with the exception of Barnum's American Museum, the massive five-storey building at Broadway and Ann Street, where for 25-cents each they spent much of a day intrigued by its wax works, its aquarium – with a white whale – and the Freak Show, which included 23-year-old

General Tom Thumb, a dwarf only twenty-five inches tall, the Siamese twins Chang and Eng, and Zip The Pinhead, a black man with a tapered skull whom they were told had been captured in Africa, and was dressed in a furry suit. Rachel jumped back a foot and squealed when the man rushed at the bars of his cage and roared at them, as Phineas T. Barnum had instructed him to do.

Dan had studied Tom Thumb and proclaimed, too loudly, "Mind, we 'ad some short 'ns doon t' pit, but nowt like that. 'E would be useful in-bye wid a low roof!"

This earned just a withering look from the tiny General.

Meg had had no hesitation in booking two first-class cabins on the National Steam Navigation Company's *Louisiana* for the one-way trip to Liverpool at $105 each.

"Well, this is summat, lass," Dan said, on examining the cabin to be his and Rachel's, and next to Meg's.

"It's another world," Rachel said. "I still can't believe where we're at!"

They sailed on the Saturday and arrived in Liverpool ten days later.

Meg dispatched another telegram to Sarah.

They stayed the first night after disembarking in the Adelphi Hotel. By this time Rachel had exhausted her supply of exclamations at luxury she could never have imagined. She pretended that they were living some kind of dream, and that she might wake up any second back in Nanaimo. Two days later they stepped from the train onto the station at Whitehaven, and the dream became a firm reality when the uniformed station guard touched his cap and said, "Hello, lass, just comin' yam? Been far, 'ave y?" and without waiting for an answer went on checking and slamming shut carriage doors for the train's departure.

Rachel laughed and looked at Dan, took his hand and squeezed it

He smiled. "Aye, a' know."

Meg told them to wait with their few cases and left the station. She hired a man with a carriage that was more of a cart and seemed not in the best repair, but was the only one in sight, with two horses in the shafts. (A far cry from the Baroness and her monogrammed vehicle!) This would carry Dan and Rachel the two miles to Lowca, where Dan's brother, another hewer, and his wife were expecting them due to another earlier telegram from Meg.

Rachel looked at the carriage. "On'y time he went yam wid somebody drivin' was when they browt him back in a wheelbarra frae t' Pig and Whistle, 'e was that gone wid drink."

Dan coughed on a laugh.

"Mind, that was t' *last* time, an a'," Rachel added.

The Cunninghams loaded their sparse baggage onto the cart. Meg hugged both of them and they climbed onto the bench seat beside the driver.

"Remember, a' still want to meet that teacher of yours," Dan said. "What's 'er name. Aye, Teasdale, a' think."

Meg would leave her belongings for the same carter to pick up and deliver to number thirteen, Morthwaite. She would return the way she had left for London a little more than three years gone: on foot.

She met only a handful of others walking and a couple of farmers with horses and carts on her way. All said a brief and friendly rhetorical "How do, lass?" as they crossed paths. The tracks seemed narrower than she remembered. A hedgehog, looking puzzled, wobbled out from behind tufts of yellowed rye grass. Meg said, "Hiya," and was ignored. Daffodils sat upright, primping and posing in a slight breeze from the west, and primroses, reliable as always, showed off their stuff. The Friesians in Greggains' field lifted their heads. *Maybe trying to remember her*, she thought. She laughed quietly.

She stopped at the top end of Morthwaite. The four mile walk had taken her little more than an hour, excitement, anticipation – and a puzzling buzz of apprehension – quickening her pace.

From where she stood, everything before her seemed smaller than she remembered. The houses seemed closer together, squeezed in, as if leaning on each other. Half a mile past the bottom end of the village the headframe of Coater pit stood out against a bright sky. Smoke poured from the chimney stack. Faintly, the sound of rattling tub wheels on steel rails rose to greet her. While all was familiar, things somehow seemed to have changed, she thought. It would be a few days before she would realize that it was not Morthwaite that had changed.

She saw them on their doorsteps. Lizzie and Tommy at number thirteen, Sarah at her own door, neighbours and friends out front, watching. Then they were on the road, coming to her. Lizzie ran the last few yards and flung herself into Meg's arms. Tommy grabbed and hugged both of them. Sarah stood slightly back, smiling through tears of joy.

221

"T' kettles on, lass." Lizzie could barely form a word. "An' there's a tatie pot in t' oven."

Meg laughed, and laughed. What else would she have expected?

She hugged Sarah, who said simply, "Oh, Meg!"

She thanked neighbours as they shouted, "Welcome back, lass."

Inside number thirteen she asked where the boys were.

"Travellin'," Tommy said. "Three weeks now." He beamed. "Matt's tekken on some fights, and won 'em all so far. ''E's in Blackpool, and Tommy went wid him to be 'is corner man. Said his big brother needed lookin' after! They'll be back next week."

Meg went to her old bed that night. It felt familiar, yet strange.

Lady Jane Benson heard, of course, that the Tyson girl was back. She knew not for how long, but she was going to meet her, apologize to her, reassure her…

Especially reassure her…

Three Weeks Earlier. The Garlands, Near Carlisle, Cumberland

Sandy Benson, wandering, fuzzy-minded from whatever it was in the pills they had been making him swallow, found his way to the steam-wraithed laundry room in the Garlands basement. His visit coincided with the arrival of Ruth Hudson, a big-bosomed twenty-four-year-old laundress carrying an armful of bed sheets to be washed. Sandy was behind one of the washtubs and watched as Ruth bent over one ten feet away to dump the washing.

Whatever the treatment Sandy had received in his brief stay at the Garlands, it had done nothing to stay his appetite for the carnal, nor his belief that what was there, was there for his convenience and pleasure.

He stepped quietly across the flagstone floor, put his hands around her neck, and dragged her down backwards onto the floor. He straddled her, knees on her shoulders, and shoved his hands down the front of her frock. "Lovely titties!"

The fall had stunned Ruth, but her head cleared as Sandy advanced his interest and reached down and dragged her frock up to above her waist. Ruth shouted, tried to turn her head. Sandy giggled, leaned further forward, and laughed aloud as his hand found the top of her underpants and touched warm flesh. Just like that other one…that…bitch!

"…Fucking bitch!"

His voice was much louder than Ruth's cries for help, and was heard by Connor Byrne, a large immigrant Irishman from County Wicklow who was an attendant at the Garlands, and was affianced to Ruth Hudson. Sandy could not have chosen a worse intervener. Byrne banged the door open, took in the scene, stepped up to the sprawled Sandy, reached down and unhesitatingly placed his hands around Sandy's throat and squeezed, an act which soon discouraged Sandy from moving, let alone pursuing his intent on Ruth Hudson. Then Byrne – assisted by an enthusiastic Ruth, who muttered "y' mad shite," as she joined in – took a just-washed flannel sheet, formed it into a crude rope with a noose at one damp end, placed Sandy's head through the noose, tightened and knotted it, lifted him and hung him from a pulley-hook set high on the granite-block wall.

"Off y'go, y' fucken loonie," Byrne grunted. He then wrapped his arms around Sandy's legs and pulled downward. He waited until Sandy stopped struggling and had voided his bowels and bladder as life departed. Kelly and Ruth then also departed.

When Sandy was found, the authorities concluded that his disturbed mind had driven him to commit suicide. They knew nothing, and likely – in the interests of not complicating operations at their institution – were content to remain ignorant of the earlier events in the steaming laundry room.

They had advised the admitting physician, Dr. Silas Whitaker, who had travelled north and would tell his sister of the death of her last remaining son.

Three days following Meg's return, and after Jane Benson had sent a boy to Sarah Teasdale with a message, the countess ordered her pony and trap prepared and made the short trip to Sarah's house.

She arrived at the same time that Meg, with Dan and Rachel, got there. Meg had had second thoughts about chastising Dan for hiking the two-miles uphill through moor, gorse, and pastures from Lowca, 'in your state,' when she saw the delight on his face as she introduced the pair to Sarah. Jane Benson also was introduced.

Dan wrinkled his brow. "O, aye. Benson…Teasdale…I knew there was summat…" He laughed and shook his head. "It's funny, but it gits easier t' ferget than t' remember, sometimes, doesn't it?"

He waited, thinking, then, "That Benson lad that took off and went wid Wilberforce, ower t' slave business – they finally stopped that a' course. Government, a' mean. Put them oot a' business, Bensons and folks. Not that they've suffered much, wid their coal mines, eh?" He stopped, his brow furrowing.

Where is he going? Meg thought. Sarah caught her eye and with comically raised eyebrows was asking the same question. Meg wondered if Dan's illness had taken more from him than she realized.

"Dan—" Meg said, but Dan had resumed.

"Couldn't ivver remember 'is name, the Benson lad, but a' do now…wid the Teasdale name comin' up, like." He smiled at Sarah. "Must've been wid thinkin' about you, what wid Meg 'ere allus talking aboot y'. Y' did a grand job wid 'er, mind…!" He drifted again.

"Dan—"

"…see, the lass he took off wid…the servant lass…'*er* name was Teasdale. She was frae up in t' Borrowdale area, past Keswick theer…'er family 'ad sheep, on t' fells…common name up theer, Teasdale, a' believe…lot a' dales, y' know…"

Christ, Dan!

"…aye. Her name was Annabelle, our Herbert telt me. But their lad, the Benson lad that is, the yan that defied them…that's the word, isn't it…defied…aye…anyway, 'e ca'd 'er Annie. Annie Teasdale. That was it!"

Meg lowered her head, almost laughing. When would he stop?

Sarah Teasdale stared at Dan.

Dan persevered. "When he took-off – their lad, a' mean – the Benson's telt 'im 'e would nivver be part of their family again, would be disowned, that 'e would nivver use their name again…"

"Dan—" Meg tried.

Sarah Teasdale stared harder at Dan.

"An' the lad, the Benson lad, said that if the lass, Annabelle – 'e ca'd 'er Annie, like a' said – was good enough to be 'is wife – and by God she was! He said. By God, she was! An' they'd better know that! – If she was good enough to be 'is wife…then 'er name was good enough for 'im! So 'e took it – Teasdale. An' I remember 'is other name noo…Jeremy, wasn't it…? Or…no, summat like that…a Bible name, like…oh…oh, aye, that was it…Jeremiah…Jeremiah Benson…Jeremiah Teasdale." Dan smiled, a smile of triumph, and relief. "Theer, a' knew a'd remember."

Jane Benson gripped the back of one of Sarah's chairs. She said, "Good God," and sat down. Her mouth was working as she stared at Sarah Teasdale.

Sarah stared at Jane Benson, said, "Christy Almighty!"

Meg looked from Sarah to Jane Benson and back to Sarah, and said, "What?"

And again, "What?"

THE END